THE TIMES
OF
KERIM

Katy Hollway

The Times of Kerim
Copyright © 2015 Katy Hollway

SozoPrint
SozoPrint.com

ISBN 978-0-9929404-5-4

Contact or follow the author

www.KatyHollway.com
www.facebook.com/KatyHollwayAuthor
www.twitter.com/KatyHollway
www.pinterest.com/katyhollway/

Other titles by the author:
The Days of Eliora
The Compassion Prize

Other titles by Katy Hollway

Books in the Remnant Chronicles Series:

The Times of Kerim – Book 1

The Days of Eliora – Book 2

Books in the Compassion Series:

The Compassion Prize

Dedication

To my mother,
Who shared with me her beautiful colours and inspired me
to reveal mine.

1

Wickedness

Kerim crouched in the locked cage in the master's hut. She had been stripped bare and left alone for two days. Her body ached from the cramped conditions and the blood on her feet and fingers was still fresh.

The conversations she had heard from the villagers, played over in her mind. The small openings in the hut were covered with old, stiff animal hide which blocked the light but failed to keep out the cold and the voices. It seemed the entire village, except her own household and one other, were caught in the master's sticky web.

Knowing what would happen was worse than she could have imagined. She had to escape. Hour after hour she had kicked, pushed and picked at the bars. The burns on her hand were inseparable now from the other pains. Her body ached and trembled.

In the beginning the differences the master bought were subtle, but now the contrast to life in the village was startling. Recent life for Kerim had changed dramatically. Her herd had become small, so small that she had been forced to trade the wide, lush pasture for food. The few sheep remained in the pen close to her father's hut for their own safe keeping. Her father had also become increasingly tired and withdrawn, often refusing to eat the meagre meals she had prepared. Her brother now lived at the far side of the village near his master.

She had woken to the sound of her own screaming in the hours before dawn. Tears flowed down her dirty cheeks as she remembered how she had once rushed outside with a blanket wrapped round her. Now she was unsure if she cried out of grief or fear. Her only friend, Miriam, had been dragged by her hair down the track by the frenzied mob of villagers. The image was still very clear in her mind. There must have been twenty around her, declaring obscene things that should never be said about one she loved. Kerim's father had appeared at her side and grabbed her about her waist before she could run down the track after her friend.

'You can do nothing. They will kill you too. Please Kerim,' he had whispered urging her inside. 'Hide.'

She had never seen her father look so weak and fragile. But his grip, however, was strong, and would not let her go. And so she had seen her only friend disappear, the one who knew her best and who agreed that what was happening was utterly wrong. Guilt plagued her. She had done so little to save her friend and now her error was being repaid.

Her father had kept her hidden ever since. And when she asked what had become of Miriam, he would not say. But Kerim knew, she had overheard the gossip. It seemed that the villagers were now at ease with the events. She shuddered to think of where the sheep had gone. Had they all been ritually killed too? She retched at the thought of what happened to Miriam. The god of the mountain had taken those she loved. The whole village had taken some part in the evil the stranger had brought.

Kerim had not reacted well to her father's protection. She had been used to the cloud filled expanse of sky as her ceiling, and the wide open space. Each day, confined in her home bought further trouble. The walls of her hut had drained her of all energy and hope. The food had run low, but neither of them ate much. Kerim had been unable to imagine life outside the house; yet she had not anticipated the torment she was now subjected to.

What she first bitterly thought was her overprotective father, now gave her heart a sense of warmth. There had been no way of escaping his watchful eye. He gave her privacy only when she needed it. Kerim had used those moments to expel her frustration. She wept now with shame for the muttering against her father and her inner rage filled with angry words. There was now little light left in her world, compared to this present darkness.

Somehow she always knew it would come to this. The terrifying memories would soon flood her. She could not hold them back. As she closed her eyes she willed them to disappear. The noise reverberated in her mind as if it was really happening. She clutched at her ears to block out the sound. She heard the echoes of the chatter as the restless crowd formed in front of her father's hut. And suddenly, she was there again, hiding in her home.

Kerim's airways constricted as she focused on her brother. He and his hordes called to her father and burst through the blocked door. The wooden barrier burst off its hinges. Her father stood up, as the last line of defence. Outraged by his son's intrusion, he demanded that they leave. Kerim looked at her brother's vacant eyes. She no longer knew the man who stood before them. His warm smile was now replaced by a grimace; even his soft boyish features seemed hardened. There was an eager, hungry look in his eyes. She swallowed hard.

Any resemblance to the boy she had grown up with had vanished years ago. 'What are you doing?' Darius asked. 'She is your sister.'

'That means nothing,' he said with malice. 'Stand aside!'

Some others pushed their way inside. She could see the crowd forming outside.

'I will not. What you are doing is wrong. This is all wrong. Please turn from this evil that has consumed you.'

The broad body of her brother threw her frail father to the floor and cackling, he snatched at Kerim. She dodged his hand and grasped the hot pan from the grate over the fire. She flung it at her brother, but it dropped to the floor in front of his booted feet.

He laughed at her attempt and bent down to try the stew she had been cooking. With an evil grin he lunged forward. She stared wildly.

Her blistered hands stung now as they clung to her ears as if to double the pain. She pulled them away and hugged her body. She found no comfort. The images wouldn't stop.

Her brother grabbed her arm, and pulled her forcibly from the hut. She dug her heels into the ground, desperate to be left alone. Her traitor brother's fingers burrowed into her soft flesh. Her strength outmatched, he presented her to the waiting crowd who cheered.

Kerim continued to struggle, but her brother's grip was firm and vicious. He was leading her to the centre of the village.

There, perched on a large woollen rug decorated with gaudy, bright woven stripes, sat the master— a pale man adorned in a dark robe. He welcomed Kerim by flashing his row of pitted decaying teeth. Behind her, Darius appeared.

'You can't take her,' he shouted staggering up the lane. 'You can't take my daughter.'

'But we have.' The master grinned. He reached out to fondle her hair.

Kerim cried at his touch. 'Dad! Help me!'

'This is wrong, it is evil.'

The crowd mocked and started to move away to prepare for the festivities.

'Please, my daughter!' He ran after them shouting and pleading. 'How can you depart so far from the truth? Please!'

A woman turned from the back of the crowd and struck Darius in the face knocking him to the ground, blood gushed from his nose. Her strength was unnatural. She spit upon the man and waddled around him.

'Dad!' Kerim cried. 'Save yourself, get out of this place.'

The images disappeared.

She dare not look at her shameful wounds on her arms, inflicted by herself. She would not even be given the dignity to end it here by her own means. She had no tools, but her fingers, and what remained of her blunt nails. She had ripped off the surface layer of skin when she gnawed at her wrists.

It was then, when she was at her lowest that she prayed. Her words were silent. A cry from her broken heart.

You have been heard.

She pushed back the horrendous images of what might come. The festivities, the celebration, the sheer evil. She would not be sacrificed for evil. Would it be the knife or the flames that would finally end it all? She would not give up; she could not give up; she had to escape.

He suddenly appeared, silhouetted in the doorway. He strolled towards the cage with a white silk dress in his clawed hand and a bowl of stale bread and water in the other. The fabric as pale as his skin, draped loosely from his outstretched fingers. 'Put this on!' he demanded as he forced his hand through the bars. 'The time is nearly here.'

He brushed his long fingers against her thigh. She shuddered at the filthiness of his touch. Her heart burned with anger. She pulled away as much as the cage would allow, and spat on her leg scrubbing at the place he had touched. His eyes shifted from her body to her wrists. He laughed as he fingered his grotesque necklace, 'I see you have been busy.'

2

Grieved

Kerim's green eyes were heavy with exhaustion. Slowly they closed, even as she battled to stare at the landscape over which she had travelled—A landscape that was both thrilling and frightening. A landscape she thought she would never see again.

Mist swirled about the rocky ground and curled up her tattered dress which was damp from sweat and stained with sand and crushed plants. Burrs had snagged and branches had caught and torn the fine fabric.

Crawling behind a clump of bushes, hidden from the outside world, Kerim fell fast asleep, though her rest was fitful.

Hiding had been all she had done since her escape. It filled her waking and sleeping moments. Even now her bloodied fingers twitched and pulled at the nearby undergrowth.

It was a dreamlike memory. She had got out of the cage. Had someone feed her? Her intellect said no, but then how had the lock opened?

She travelled down the path and through the centre of the village all without being seen. How was that possible? Maybe this was her dream, her escape and freedom, but her aches told her it was true.

The villager knew who she was and yet this dream told her she walked calmly down the busy dirt path without anyone bidding her attention. Furthermore, she remembered her last meal, a meagre piece of stale bread and unclean water, but she was not hungry or faint.

She had accepted the fact that she blocked the events of the last few days from her memory. There was one thing that she knew for certain; she needed to find safety.

The screech of a distant animal startled her. Her drawn eyes flickered wide in fear, and she was on her feet. Chill ran through her veins, what little hope she had gained, she clung to. Her body, aching from trauma, and weary from real sleep, must react to her mind, it had to obey. But she had been set free, by some miracle, and now she was running. She ran on into the night and in a matter of seconds was gone.

I follow with a white streak of light, the exact path she made.

I will leave her momentarily to view her history and her destiny.

In a moment I arrive on the slopes of the mountain.

Gazing to the bottom of the valley, I can see the small specs of light flickering, marking the community of which Kerim was once a part.

I turn and watch as a tall, pale man steps from the shadows of a large tree pulling his sheepskin bag from his shoulder. He is the master. He rummages inside the satchel and pulls out a folded and dried palm leaf. His bony fingers open the packet and grasp a small handful of sweet smelling herbs.

'Carefully you imbecile!' he commands.

'Yes master.' A short man bows as he lays another flat stone atop a substantial pile.

'It must be ready by daybreak. And it needs to be perfect or you will ruin it.'

'How many more slabs master?'

'There are enough to keep you busy for another half an hour. Now stop jabbering and get on with it. It needs dedicating tonight.'

The night that had been lit gently through the clouded sky, and the fragrant fire alongside the tree, suddenly becomes heavy. The darkness itself is swallowed by a deeper realm of night. The servant peers about, looking for a shadow that has darkened the sky, but there is nothing. Instead, all he can see is the sleek form of his master standing still, as if captured in a trance. Then quite suddenly, the tall pale man begins to chant, scattering the herbs over the stone mound that has been built.

But I see them, numerous dark, scaly bodies, restless in the tree. The darkness is where they feel the most comfortable.

The largest creature climbs on the man's back and clings to his shoulders. It whispers the words of the chant and the man repeats. The words are unworldly and they summon the deeper darkness.

The squat man stands back and watches. He knows he has to wait until the chant is finished before the last stones will be laid, but he is not complaining, he is grateful for the rest. Building the mound has taken two days, and he has not been alone. It is only at these times, when his master is so consumed in his acts that he has felt the brief relief, but he is not alone, even now. Above him, plumes of smoke continue to rise into the night air. He watches the shrouded moonlight captured in the swirling forms. There is only a little rest for Ishmillimech.

I have seen enough of her history to know that she is safe for a while. But what of her future? Has my friend been as unhindered as myself?

I concentrate and watch the vision he sends from some distance away.

The buzz of noise spreads through the thick earthen walls and into the night. Raucous laughter ripples through the building. The joke is on an inhabitant and his family that lives on the outskirts on the hill above the village. This is the place of Kerim's destiny.

The meeting house is the place to be for the village community in the evenings and early hours.

The fire smokes in the centre of the round mud building. Men and women perch on benches or lounge on the floor. A large man has caught the attention of the smoke encased audience. His long black hair that is bunched in a ponytail runs half the length of his back. His presence is superior to the majority not only in his bulk, but also his stagger. His choice of subject of ridicule is a favourite among the crowd. He thrives in the cheers of agreement and swells in the appreciation of his jibes.

'The arrogance of that man is a joke!' he continues his speech, his black beard ruffling and small eyes twinkling. The smoke does not hide the acidic green atmosphere that he weaves with his words and actions. He takes a swig from his cup, as others agree. The brown liquid overflows, and runs through the bristles, dripping from his chin, and down his woven tunic. 'The fact that he wants me, Tarlin, leader of this hamlet, to convince any of you to take what he says seriously makes me laugh. I'd rather jump into this fire here, and perform a dance on the hot coals!' He makes to leap into the flames, but instead performs a little jig on the spot. A great howl of laughter flows into the air as he is joined by one of the many women he calls his wives. She is young, much younger than him, and her beauty staggers the watchful human. Her dark hair flows as she prances about her husband provocatively; her gaze fixes him in a sensual stare. The outbreak of dancing stirs others to bang out a rhythm. Other women get up and dance about him, as he hops from one foot to the other with a fake pained expression on his face. 'Oh it's hot! Oh it's hot!' he sings out. Others begin to get to their feet and take part; it does not take long for the whole of the room to join in. Some dance; some make music, while others mock at the expense of the fool that they will not listen to.

My friend stands guard over the watchful human who is hooded and sat by the entrance. He is hidden by the drying racks of vegetation, listening carefully and watching the events unfold. He gets to his feet and leaves the unpleasant atmosphere. He has seen enough. The fresh air of the outside fills his lungs with clean breath, the cool night acting as a strong decontaminator. Pulling the woollen jacket tighter around his shoulders, he lets the hood fall down, no one will see him but us, they are all inside enjoying the mockery of his family. He moves quietly through the large cluster of huts and pens that make up the village, that are lit with a few oil lamps or open fires. What he has seen has disturbed him. His colours swirl about him energetically.

'Thank you for showing me what she was like and saving me from her,' he offers as a prayer. I smile as he lifts his hand to his head and ruffles his hair. There is sorrow as the blue swirls of colour gently calm. 'Help me to be patient,' he sighs. 'Well, I guess that's the end of me trying to work it out. It's over to you now!'

He moves into the darkness of the outskirts and heads for the hilltop.

I can feel that my friend is at ease. I will see him soon.

3

Corrupt

Beyond the ever increasing steam that issues from the mountain top, and the ceaseless blanketed sky, the lights in the heavens have been joined by another. Its light is not a single dot against the blackness. It is moving across constellations leaving a tail gas and dust that appears to be light behind it. A mass, sent on its long journey when time began, soon to reach its destination.

The sky was getting lighter through the thick cloud. Somehow the steam from the mountain did not look quite so threatening in daylight. Ishmillimech had watched the whole ceremony from the shelter of the tree. He so wanted to return to his bed but had not been given permission.

The embers in the fire had all but gone out and the morning had bought some relief from fear of the night. He sat on the only dry patch of ground, as the dew was heavier than usual, with his knees tucked to his chest. He had never seen his master so out of control as he was last night.

This dedication had taken much longer than any other time, and it was the way in which the tall dark man had pounded the ground and flung himself into the wild dancing that had unsettled Ishmillimech the most. At each altar blessing, the dancing had been the most entertaining part of the whole ceremony for him to watch, but this time his stomach squirmed and his heart had beat too fast in fear.

'Get up man. We return to the village to prepare the sacrifice.'

'Yes master Bruja.' Ishmillimech replied carefully.

'What is it?' Bruja questioned.

'Are you not tired?'

'Quite the contrary, Ishmillimech. I feel invigorated. Energised and rejuvenated.' His thin lips spread, revealing his pointed blackened teeth. Bruja was tall and pale. He wore long black robes that dragged along the ground, soaking up the dew in his hem. From his neck dangled an ecliptic string of ornaments, teeth, and a hideous twisted claw. Ishmillimech had never seen such a sight.

Bruja's own fingers were unconsciously drawn to touch the claw, as he stepped out ahead of Ishmillimech with an air of arrogance. He stroked the claw affectionately, walking down the well trodden path. His confidence was unmistaken, unlike Ishmillimech who slipped and floundered falling several times.

Bruja caressed the claw with his long fingers. 'This is going to be the best one yet! There will be much to gain from this and much to receive. I have waited long for this moment. It is not every day that one of such importance is given. There will be rewards beyond that which I have known. We must get the people ready. Make them ready!'

Ishmillimech felt a shudder travel down his spine. He remembered the innocent beginnings of it all. Everything had changed since then; subtle changes had become downright, poke-you-in-the-eye changes. It had been just a bit of fun, the odd sheep, snatched and sacrificed, here or there. The feasting afterwards had always been what had drawn him. Now things had changed, sacrifices were made more often to aid all sorts of decisions and to all manner of objects, but Ishmillimech had been convinced of the power these acts of worship had given Bruja.

He knew deep down that he and the village were now caught firmly in Bruja's grasp. The ceremony now no longer took place in secret; anyone opposed to the rituals was ridiculed, cast off and neglected, and became unable to survive in the village. Ishmillimech had been there at the first and knew that he would be there at the last. Every time he had said to himself it would be the last, but each festival night, he was drawn out and sucked in by the atmosphere. He held to the excuse that he had no control, that his master had commanded him to take part. But deep inside, his heart was as dead as Bruja's; he would never want another to take his role in the upcoming events.

And so, Ishmillimech followed his master down the mountain side. Now was the time to prepare the girl for sacrifice.

4

Blameless

The night had been full of running, but now she slept, exhausted and drained. She had found an overhang of rock on the edge of a crop field full of red flowers. The smell was sweet and comforting. She had thought that it may even disguise her own scent.

Just beyond the field, there had once stood a large forest, but the trees had been cut over many years and now only small, weak or twisted specimens still grew. It was strange that she had found this place, it had a familiarity of a faded dream lost of finer details, but a real sense of knowing that it existed somewhere.

I sit on the top of the rock ledge, in the guise of man. I have chosen the appearance of a shepherd, wearing a loosely fitting tunic over a woven gown. It is comfortable for what use it is. On my back there is perhaps a bag almost the length of my upper body. Not everything is as it appears. My russet hair shimmers and my eyes twinkle. I sit casually and unseen atop the rock. The rock I told her about, the time she refuses to believe happened. She will believe again soon.

Scanning the sky, I can see far beyond human vision. To the human eye, the landscape is a patchwork of colours and textures, trees and cleared land. I can see so much more than this. To me, colours are truly vivid and flow from every living thing; they are not just surface decoration. Due to this depth, textures shimmer and undulate as these amazing life forms live. In the far distance, a volcano is stirring. It is an uneasy deep glowing red to my vision, with flecks of insipid yellow and bright gold conflicting the message that it sends, yet strangely working together, I do not understand what this means, but I know it is under control. It is in this direction that I look.

My role for the time being is to protect and to guide.

She looks so small and fragile, yet even she is not as she appears. She has faced so much and has proven to be strong and resilient. Not even she knows what she is capable of yet. Her colours are hopeful. As she lies there, she shimmers in shades of cyan and mint. Peace and hope seem to accompany her now. Even the deep brooding grey of fear seems to be subsiding a little.

Two butterflies, orange and black to the human eye, dance in the air before landing on a cluster of small purple flowers clinging to the rocks. The air flickers with gentle green ribbons of light where their wings once were.

There it is; a flash of light.

Standing up, I look to the point of origin of the flash. Shrouded suddenly in a gown of light, that would have scorched the retina and blinded the eye had anyone looked on it. I signal back.

In that moment of light, I am transformed into another being, my true form. My shepherd garb is gone and in its place, I look to be dressed for battle. In this moment, it is revealed that over my shoulder is slung a silver quiver full of arrows, perfectly straight and beautifully clear. The flights are argent in colour, yet they seem to flutter in the breeze. At the tip of each arrow a sharp golden point. The bow, to fire such powerful weapons, is caught over my other shoulder, where it glistens next to my tunic. My skin shines brightly. The light is gone as quickly as it came. I settle back to the rock, maybe not as casually as before. I sit in readiness for action. The plan is unfolding further, and this young woman has a large part to play in it. How exciting!

'My dear Kerim,' I say quietly as I look to the sleeping girl, 'your life is soon to change beyond all your dreams.' Her colours flicker about her. She hears me, I know.

My focus is now changed. I look to my left, up a small dirt track that runs through a dewy field of grass. I await another signal.

There. I see him in the distance, a dear friend of mine. If you were to see him too, you would note his large stature and his dark skin. I have known him from days grown old. I can see him focused on the human that he is following. Today, he has the appearance of a travelling man, dressed in long layers of thin material and holding a long wooden staff in his right hand. His keen eyes scan the horizon, and although he walks casually, he is not without purpose.

The human is distracted. Memories of teasing from both strangers and family occupy his mind. The stranger, dancing and mocking him, impressing everyone around. He thinks no one will take him seriously. Then his own brothers made remarks just before he escaped his home, said in jest yet taken heavily to heart. Oh, how it will all change!

Blazing colours of orange and red, the human in front reaches a fork in the path, my friend runs forward to bar one route. The man looks towards my friend but does not see him. Humans will do all sorts of things to not recognise a supernatural prompting. This man, I see, has decided to take the path that was not blocked, funny that! I even think he is muttering to himself, something about going a different way today.

The travelling man, shoots into the air, above the height of the scrubby bushes, and turns instantly into a blinding light, that shines for a split second. A glorious light, full of the colours found in this world and beyond. In that moment he is transformed. He is dressed in a white robe tied with a golden belt with a long, jewel encrusted scabbard hanging from it. In his hand he clasps a long sword with a solid gold handle. He looks to the east, where I am now standing upon the rock. I signal back. It will be wonderful to work with him again.

I restore the appearance of a shepherd and continue to watch their progress. My friend returns to the ground, light gone and traveller once more. He follows the human along the dew covered grass path that heads in that same easterly direction. As they draw nearer, although not close enough for human ears, I hear my friend's deep voice vibrating on the air.

'Don't you think it is a bit hot for that?' The travelling man smiles. 'Put it over your shoulder for safe keeping. There will be a need for that later!'

I can sense the anger in the human marching through the field, and it appears my friend does too. He shimmers red and puce with each step.

'That is enough of that Japh. You miss so much beauty that has been displayed just for you by stomping along in anger. Be at peace. May the Lord of peace himself give you peace at all times and in every way.'

'Indeed!' I think. The dark man cups his massive hands, and begins to rub them gently. He opens them slowly to reveal a golden ball of light that pulses with a heartbeat rhythm. Lifting it before his face, he moves his hands away and lets go, leaving it to hang in mid-air. Smiling to himself, he inhales the comforting scent of the field and blows the golden light towards Japh, where it settles just above his head.

'Be at peace.' He commands as he claps his hands. At that moment the ball explodes over the human and streamers twist in the air. The ribbons of gold light wrap around Japh. The ribbons dissolve the purple, red and brown pulses on contact and instantly his pace slows and even the small sound of a laugh comes from his lips. Japh casually runs his fingers over the flowers and looks at their beauty.

Bruja could be seen coming down the main track to the village with Ishmillimech running behind. The villagers were all out to meet him. They offered him gifts as he made his way to the meeting hut purposefully.

'Ishmillimech.' Bruja called to his servant lagging behind, and getting caught in the growing crowd. 'Go and get her. It is time to make preparations.' He smiled a cruel smile and stooped as he entered the cave while Ishmillimech was engulfed by the villagers.

Although it was daylight outside, the grotto was dark and lit only with a smoking fire. Bruja stood in the centre of the space as the villagers hurried in and clambered about. This was a spectacle they wanted to see, and they were keen to get the best places.

When the thrilled noise had settled down he began.

'The time has come once again to commit ourselves and to make this land fruitful. We will have beyond what we have ever had before.' Bruja announced to the appreciative crowd. 'I have made ready the altar.'

The crowd stirred with a mixture of excitement and fear.

'Who will provide our salvation?' hissed a woman near the back.

'Who will ensure our safety?' asked an elderly man clutching the hand of his grandson.

'I am willing!' offered a girl enthusiastically.

'Shush now my sweet.' her mother said smothering her own child's proposal. 'The master will tell us who it is to be.'

'I have been instructed as to whom,' he smirked. 'We shall be provided with a great harvest and salvation from the cold. The Mountain must be satisfied. The sacrifice should be that of the untouched, yet should be a sacrifice of punishment.' He paused to let the effect of his speech take shape in their impressionable minds.

'Who can fit such a calling?' they asked.

'We shall see Kerim the unbeliever, the untouched, the punishable become what she would abhor the most. I call for the sacrifice to be bought to ...' but Bruja never finished what he was to say.

'Master, master!' Ishmillimech charged in, red faced and sweaty. 'I must speak with you.' his panicked voice rang out over the gathered people.

Bruja glared down his long nose at the insolent interfering man.

'What is the matter? You will ruin it all.' Bruja growled angrily.

The crowd also turned to him obviously frustrated with this disruption.

Ishmillimech pushed his way through the tight crowd, and made his way to his master's side. He signalled to Bruja that he wished to whisper in his ear. Bruja stooped his tall frame reluctantly.

'She is gone my master. She is gone.'

'What do you mean?' Bruja whispered through his teeth, attempting to turn from the surrounding faces.

'What I say my master.' he whispered frantically. 'The cage is broken, she is gone.'

Bruja stood upright and watched the twisting smoke fill the roof space. Suddenly his expression changed.

'Our sacrifice is gone,' Bruja announced.

There was a gasp from the crowd. 'What now? We shall be ruined!' Panic began to spread throughout the gathering.

'Payment must be made for the loss of this sacrifice. We will find her.' Bruja reached inside his bag and pulled out a handful of herbs and spices. He raised his hand above his head, shouted an incantation and flung them to the fire. The flames spat and sizzled, as plumes of acrid smoke rose into the air. He waved his crooked fingers through the smoke, causing it to swirl about. The onlookers coughed and spluttered and many rubbed their stinging eyes. The smoke filled the cave and billowed out the opening.

Bruja was lost in his own world. He dropped his gaze to the base of the fire. 'The smoke has spoken. We must make payment with her father, and then retrieve her for the sacrifice.'

The crowd rallied toward the hut where Darius lay ill.

I focus now on the vision sent to me. I picture the scene unfolding. My friend is tall and wears dark clothes. He enters a hut on the outskirts of the rowdy village. He moves silently and with great care. He sees a pale, withered man curled up on a bed. Dark grey covers this man; his whole being seems ready for death.

'Darius, you must wake up! They will be here for you soon.' My friend is shaking the pale old man who lies in his bed. The room has one window, but this has been covered. In the darkness of the small room my friend has no distinct features.

'Who are you?' the sickly old man asks.

'My name is Liberate; I will talk more with you later.' My friend says. I smile to myself, what an excellent choice of name.

'You must again declare to the people the danger they are in.' Liberate states.

'They do not listen. Bruja has them. They have not listened to me for many years now. I stopped trying years ago.' The weak man replies, still shimmering in his dark grey colours as he turns away.

'I know, but you must do so again, one last time. They will come for you, but you must not be afraid.

You will not be taken by Bruja's method. Your daughter, Kerim has already been saved.'

'My Kerim!' Now he listens, now he gives Liberate his full attention. 'She is not hurt? How?'

'There is no time to tell it now. She will be safe.' Liberate looks kindly on this previously grieving man. 'Mercy and grace will be shown to you. Do you hear me?'

'Yes.' the old man replies. Do I see a slight cyan entering his colours now? 'But why should I bother?'

My friend looks directly at Darius. 'You must believe.'

In that moment, there stands before Darius, altered beyond recognition my friend, just as I would see him. In the dark room he glows a beautiful and comforting light, clothed in a robe that shimmers.

'I believe!' Darius whispered, dark grey banished from him.

'Be ready!' And the tall one vanishes from sight but the vision doesn't fade.

Then they come. Pushing and shoving through the narrow entrance of Darius' home, and burst into the dark room just as they had done when they had taken Kerim. Many hands grab at him, and pull him from his bed, rough and undignified. The people drag him to the village centre where they deposit him before their leader.

Bruja made his way out into the open. 'You are the fool who let her escape,' he hissed through his teeth.

Ishmillimech followed. 'But master the cage was secure, I have no idea how she got out.'

Bruja turned in his tracks. 'There's no excuse for incompetence. A new opportunity has a risen, we will track her down later.'

The village crowd was now making their way towards the tall figure of Bruja who stood central to the track. With them, they dragged the limp form of a man, which they deposited at Bruja's feet.

'What is going on Bruja?' The crumpled man asked weakly. 'Why do these people drag me from my death bed?'

'To die here.'

'What? I wish to die in peace. Away from this madness! Please, you do what you do, but leave me out of it. I am the last of my type here, you have already taken my daughter; I will not disturb you for long now.'

'You will not disturb me at all old man.' Bruja spat at the weak man in the mud. He raised his head and addressed the crowd. 'We will have a sign to destroy the foolishness of this man and his pathetic god. He is the last but the one remaining— and soon even she will be gone.'

Bruja looked down into Darius's face. 'Before you die, know this - your daughter will be sacrificed.'

'You must not listen to him.' the old man called weakly to the crowd. 'Can you not see the evil that he brings to you? Now it is me, who will it be next? None of you are safe.'

'Be quiet old man.' Ishmillimech snarled as he kicked him into the ground.

Darius coughed up a little blood. His chest burned with pain as he tried to straighten up to look into the face of Ishmillimech. He felt a deep sadness.

'We will have our sign.' Bruja called. He began to twitch turning his body to slowly face the place where a tethered cow stood ready for milking. Then he stood rigid, arms outstretched and his eyes glazed, the crowd transfixed by the show.

'Come here.' The leader commands.

A fat, self-indulged creature that oozes the stench of death, moves forward. Its eyes are red and hungry.

'Possess the animal tethered there.'

The evil servant crawls over the ground and up the cow's legs then up her neck. It claws at the cow's skin as it clings on and then climbs into the cow through her mouth. The horde screams with glee at the transformation. The servant inside the scaly animal bows to its master. It in turn hisses and roars in delight, the cow is being transformed into something that is other worldly.

The masses are beside themselves.

The cow lows and rolls her eyes. Something terrible begins to occur. The flesh beneath her skin begins to shift as if something were crawling there. Then, where there had been cow hide, scales begin to emerge, hooves became claws and her head lengthens. Instead of a gentle, passive face, a snarling, sharp toothed beast, glares at the crowd with blood red eyes. It takes only seconds to pull free of the tether. Men and women are screaming as others begin to run in panic.

'Stop!' Bruja commands.

Those that are close look on in terror while others turn back. Although most are filled with fear, they are also consumed with a hideous excitement. They look at their master as the beast lumbers toward him, lowering his head and then his body. It bows before them in a trance.

'We give to you this gift.' Bruja indicates as he steps aside to reveal the old man crumpled on the floor.

My friend now stands with Darius. His colours never fail him now, no longer grey with hopeless death. Cyan all the way, and even gold too! He sees the transformation of the cow with his own eyes, but even then feels peace. Liberate, now dressed as the white robed being does not leave his side, always speaking words of comfort.

'Not long now Darius. It is written that they must believe they have won this one. They will not see me until the last minute, and even then they will not believe.' The white robed being says as the beast approaches. 'Are you ready?'

'I am ready now. Please be merciful to me.'

In a flash of light Liberate acts and Darius is gone from his body.

The beast approached the man, but held back for short moment. Then it pounced and attacked. It took the body in its jaws and threw it up in the air. Catching the body by one arm, ripping it off. No one noticed the lack of screaming or the peaceful look on the lifeless form of Darius' face. The exhibition of power was enthralling to the crowd. They were mesmerized. Darius' body was eaten before their eyes and not one of them found it repulsive.

'This beast is in my control. We will now go and find our sacrifice.'

The beast sniffed the air and bowed once again to Bruja, although a snarl of a smile crept over its scaly face.

No one notices the steam rising, ever stronger, from the volcano over the village. Steam had begun to issue from the top of the mountain only two full moons previously. Bruja's host had of course used it to its advantage, but something behind the change in the earth's crust, is far more powerful than anything Bruja has ever experienced. Deep underground the once firm rock is thinning, moving and shifting. Pressure is building behind the fragile layer as the hot liquid rock grows thinner and hotter.

Far above, also unseen, due to the constant cloud covering the land, a large mass of rock and ice hurtles through space. The light from its burning leaves a long bright streak across the dark night sky drawing a dazzling line through the blackness. Ever growing closer, ever growing faster, ever unseen.

5

Found

The vision is gone and I stand ready to welcome an old friend.

'It is good to see you.' He claps me on the back. 'What name have you chosen?'

'Hope,' I state with a twinkle in my eye.

'Excellent choice.'

'And yourself?' I ask.

'I was thinking,' he says, 'Maybe Trust for this mission.'

'Ah yes. That would be an appropriate name.'

'Is she here?' the dark skinned being dressed as a traveller in his many layers of fine fabric, now known as Trust asks.

'Yes. She sleeps,' I reply. I get to my feet and stand by my friend. He is slightly shorter than me, a fact I often point out to him. 'It is going to plan. Just as it should.'

The human Trust accompanied sits on the large rock in the centre of the field where I stand, and pauses to take in the view. He sees the meeting hut, where he had listened to the villagers that had mocked him, sitting a little lower than his family's land. There are a few people moving with purpose, about their daily tasks through the village. The land he views, he knows only by sight, he has not ventured through the dense green foliage, and definitely not passed it into the yellow shimmering expanse. In the far distance to the north, the steaming mountain dominates the skyline. There is work to be done, but the human is mesmerized by the mountain. Dangling his long legs over the edge, he ruffles his mop of dark hair thinking on the things he is seeing.

'Shall I wake her?'

'No, he will find her, and take care of her,' I say as I look to the horizon. 'The volcanoes will soon erupt and the deep will burst open. Everything will change soon.' I tuck my short staff into my belt and casually wrap a loose thread from the jacket round a bramble as he slides from the rock.

'Very clever Hope! But oh so simple!' The other laughs.

The woven fabric of the jacket that the human had hung over his shoulder is pulled out of his hand and falls to the dusty ground.

Turning irritated, he reaches down to grab it, but he is distracted by a pair of small feet, covered in cuts and dry blood, poking out from a gap in the rock. Peering closer, he sees in the shadow of the rock, the huddled sleeping form of a young woman who looks frightened even as she rests. Her clothes are dirty and made of a fine silken fabric that is not warm. He is drawn to her beauty and fragility. Carefully, he unhooks his jacket, brushes off the dust, and lays it gently over her. He notices the scratches and smudges of dirt on her face.

'She will be in danger. You must stay here,' I whisper.

He walks a short distance away, checking if there is anyone else around. There is no one except my friend and I. He now sits within sight of the rock crevice looking at the woman. His colours are changing now. The cyan of hope seems to be intensifying, while other colours, he has never before displayed are beginning to flow. There is a hint of crimson and even silver now. He seems to understand more than I expected. His attraction is strong and his anger is righteous for what has been done to her. He wants to protect her and keep her safe.

He has a deep sense that she would be in danger if he leaves. He looks about for any impending danger, but his mind is distracted, and he focuses on the girl again. He sits on a patch of warm grass, spotted with small white and yellow flowers. Two orange patterned butterflies, flutter from flower to flower. He is ready to be a friend, someone to stick up for her, someone to protect her, I move to stand beside him but look towards the volcano once more. A pinpoint flash of golden light, quick but recognisable as a signal, flares from the foot of the volcano.

'It is done, her father has been saved,' I whisper. 'For in His great mercy He did not put an end to him or abandon him, for He is a gracious and merciful God,' I say with my head bowed and with eyes moist. 'They will now come for her. Everything must go just as instructed. We must make ready the family. All the others will be here within days. There is still so much work to complete.'

'What are your orders to me?' Trust asks.

'I must ensure they return safely to the family at nightfall. The human still has half a day's work to do. Maybe he can persuade her to help! Could you return to the family and oversee any early arrivals?' I ask taking the bow of glistening light from my shoulder and readying it with an arrow.

'Righto! Orders received.' Trust smiles at me and glances at the man before he disappears with a flash of golden light.

The heat continued, and the dew was gone. Kerim felt warm, but not comfortable. She shifted a little and pushed away the cover, stretching her arms above her head. They bashed against cold, rough rock. She was confused. The bed on which she lay was not remotely soft. Suddenly she sat up grabbing the jacket from her. She was not in a bed at all, the memories poured over her in a torrent. It was only a matter of a second before she was eye to eye with a strange man. She was unable to hide her fear.

The colour drained from her face. Her pale skin appeared paler still with the smudges over her cheeks. His face, warm from sitting away from the shadows of the rock, was a little red, as he smiled gently to her.

'Don't be afraid.'

Her eyes widened.

'It's okay. I mean you no harm,' he said kindly showing her his empty hands.

Her gaze darted from left to right. She swiftly searched for a quick escape route for fear of being caught again. There appeared to be none. Trapped again.

'You looked like you were cold,' he explained, 'so I lent you my jacket.' He smiled again at her. 'You can have it if you like. It will become quite chilly later.'

'What do you want?' Kerim asked suspiciously, her voice croaky from little use. She narrowed her green eyes. Aware of her flimsy dress, she lifted the jacket to cover herself.

'Nothing. Are you alright?'

'What were you doing?' she questioned. She took in the appearance of the scene. Could it be that he meant her no harm? Were there people like that still? 'Were you guarding me?' she asked.

'Er ... I guess so. I thought you might be in danger or something.' He tried to smile again.

'So, you're not with them?' Her eyes widening with fear. 'You're not going to give me to them?' She brushed her blonde hair away from her face, removing some of the briars quickly. She tucked her hair behind her ear, still glancing about nervously. The cuts to her face and arms were crusted with dirt.

'Are you in pain?' he questioned as he took in the injuries that looked soiled and untreated. Yet his question seemed to ask more. Did he care that she was hurt? Or worried that she didn't feel the extent of the wounds?

Kerim said nothing.

'Who do you think I'm with? I'm not with anyone except my family,' he said as he gazed at her intrusively. She then noticed the difference between them. He had olive skin while she had a pale complexion and freckles across the bridge of her nose. Maybe the gaze was not intrusive but more curious.

'Why are you helping me?' she asked suspiciously eyeing this young stranger before her.

'No reason really. I guess I'm just like that. I thought you looked like you needed a friend.' Sensing that she was calming a little, he tried a different approach. 'I'm Japh. My family and I live here. Well not right here, obviously, we don't live on a rock, but this is our land.'

'Sorry for trespassing,' she said nervously.

'No, don't worry about that. You can stay as long as you like. I didn't catch your name.'

'That's because I didn't give it.' She looked him over. He was unlike the others she had known from her village, the ones she had run from. He dressed differently; he was ready for work, not like the lazy men she had seen. Japh smiled at her. It was a kind smile and she decided he must to be a decent person, after all, what harm would it do to give her name? 'It's Kerim.'

He smiled again. 'Right. Nice to meet you.'

His smile was warm, so she returned it. 'So, where...' He started, but then appeared to change his mind. 'Do you want a look around? I mean you must be hungry; we could get something to eat. Just up there we have some really delicious strawberries,' Japh said encouragingly, getting to his feet and indicating the top edge of the field. He took a step away from her but glanced back almost immediately.

'Well, I am rather hungry,' Kerim answered nervously, but also getting to her feet. She shivered slightly. She looked at her dirty torn clothes and remembered them for what they had been, delicate and beautiful, but loathsome. She held the jacket up to cover the mess she felt she was in and then slipped it on. It was long, warm and soft. She felt comforted.

'Breakfast awaits. Maybe you'd like a look around after that?'

'We'll see,' said Kerim roughly. But she accompanied him just the same.

'He seems friendly. Why don't you trust him a little?' I say to Kerim as I stroll along behind the new friends.

The colours about them are changing. It is good to have friends when all around you seems dangerous. Kerim's sense of peace is returning a little, but still has a long way to go before her fears subside. Japh on the other hand is full of confidence. That passionate crimson radiates from him. He has a strong urge to protect her, I see that in the violet streamers that spark out of him. Humans are so fascinating.

'He knows you are scared. He'll protect you. Remember what I said before,' I whisper to Kerim, then turn to Japh. 'Don't you think she could be the one?'

Bruja carried only his sheepskin bag over his shoulder and a flint dagger tucked into his belt. He towered over Ishmillimech who scuttled in his wake carrying a large canvas burden strapped to his back that was almost as big as him. Behind him, the important men of the village followed, while their wives and any others stayed behind to ensure a hearty celebration when they returned.

Sniffing the air as it went; the horned scaly beast went before them all, looking for a trail to follow. Ishmillimech, although burdened, found relief in having to carry his master's things. It meant that he was not able to look at the monster that terrified him so much, because if he did so, he would be unable to walk at all. In fact, if he tried to look up, his balance became so unstable, there was a threat that he would roll backwards and end up stranded with his legs flailing in the air. He settled for following the scratches trodden into the path by the creature's claws.

The animal no longer resembled the unfortunate cow in any way. Its talons dug into the soil, and scraped across the rocks, as it swayed in its gait. Out from its mouth shot a black forked tongue, tasting the air. The red eyes searched the distant horizon, watching for movement. Suddenly, the beast's posture changed. It lifted the shrunken front legs from the ground and began to run.

'We have her!' Bruja shouted. 'Keep up.' The group ran urgently after the monster, energised by the thirst for blood. The hunt was on.

I smile as I watch the humans chatting. What strange creations they are? I lean on my staff as Japh bends low over the strawberry plants.

'There are some ripe and juicy strawberries under that big leaf Japh.' I instruct the butterflies to dance together leaving their emerald ribbons of light floating in the air, before landing on the large leaf. They will catch Japh's attention.

He manages to take his gaze from Kerim's face for a moment and peers under the big leaf and finds a selection of excellent strawberries. He picks them and hands the best ones to Kerim. She shows signs of being uncomfortable under his constant admiration.

'You can remember her beauty Japh!' I laugh melodically. 'She needs a little bit of time to grow used to you. Let her look at you without meeting her gaze.'

'So, you're not from round here,' Japh said as he handed Kerim another three strawberries. She felt the sudden colour in her cheeks. 'What is it that your family does?' he asked although his confidence seemed to ebb as if he instantly regretted asking.

'We used to be farmers. But not anymore.' Kerim took the berries but did not eat them. Again the answer would not reveal too much. He smiled at her, confidence instantly returned.

'Used to be?' he prodded.

'We kept animals. My mother and father, brother and myself. We had a large herd at one stage.' She was aware of his intense gaze, and felt slightly threatened.

'What happened?' Japh asked, suddenly looking away.

Maybe he was aware that she was uncomfortable. He made no more eye contact as they walked slowly into the felled woodland.

'Japh,' Kerim said cautiously, 'you don't appear to be dangerous. Please, if I am in danger with you, let me know.' she almost sounded like she was pleading. 'I have run far, but I'm not sure I can run further.'

'You think you are in danger from me?' Japh asked. He sounded shocked.

Kerim felt a little ashamed that she would think that of him. But still requested, 'Am I?'

'I don't think so. If you are looking for danger, you should head down the hillside.' He chuckled in his friendly manner. 'The village below might arrange that for you.'

'I'm not looking for it.' She scowled. Japh raised his hands as if to indicate that no harm was meant. 'I've had my fair share,' she finished.

'You were in danger? That is why you ran?' Japh questioned eagerly, then added, 'you don't have to tell me if you don't want to.'

'Yes, I was in danger,' Kerim said weakly, the burden of fear slowly lifting from her. 'My whole family had been in danger for quite a while.' She stopped and looked at Japh in the face. 'I feel safe with you. Are you like me?' she asked.

'What do you mean? Are you like me?' But even in saying so, Kerim had a feeling that he understood. 'I'm not like the others that I think you have met before, neither are the rest of my family.'

Kerim smiled, only this time it did not fade. 'I thought so.'

Japh met her gaze and she felt her face light up with relief.

One side of her mouth rose slightly higher than the other, and her deep red lips parted a little. 'We were meant to meet. I believe it.' The dream like memory replayed in her mind, the familiar setting, the young man sent to help and something else which remained out of reach.

'I think you are right,' Japh nodded.

Kerim lifted the strawberry to her mouth and bit a tiny morsel from it. It tasted sweet and refreshing. Japh had already eaten all he had picked. Feeling that there was no danger in doing so, she ate the others hungrily, as Japh observed. 'Have you had enough to eat?'

'Yes.' She smiled, 'Thank you.'

He smiled back.

'So, this is your farm?' Kerim asked peering over the small fields.

'Yes, of sorts.' He laughed at his private joke, Kerim merely frowned. 'Sorry! It's just that we don't really have a lot of time to farm the land. We've been involved in a rather long term project. We mostly only grow what we need. We don't tend to trade with others.'

'We used to trade livestock.'

'Really?'

Kerim nodded but didn't offer anymore.

'The people round here keep to themselves mostly. It just means we need to be self sufficient. We manage quite well.'

'It seems like a nice place to live.'

'It is most of the time.'

Kerim frowned again. Fear began to rise. Japh did not appear to be leading her into danger, he seemed genuine. Could she trust him?

He picked up her fear and added quickly, 'We don't always see eye to eye with everyone round here, that's all.'

She calmed herself once more. 'I know how that feels. We weren't all that popular either.'

'Is that why you ran away?'

Curiosity, that is all it is, Kerim repeated to herself. She looked at her sore hands and felt the sting of the nasty gashes on her arms. A natural question that was all.

Kerim was silent for a while, contemplating if she was indeed safe with him. 'Yes, I suppose so.'

'Have you come far?' Japh continued, obviously glad that she had trusted him enough to answer.

'Not far enough I fear.'

'It might be far enough. I'll protect you,' Japh replied eagerly. He glanced at his rather gangly frame. 'And I have two brothers and my father, they'll help.'

Kerim laughed a little. 'Thank you!'

'People round here don't think the same as us, but they wouldn't chase us away, I don't think.'

Kerim didn't answer, she just continued to stare out over the fields. I small bird rose into the air singing a loud and complicated song.

'Wouldn't it be great to be able to fly away from all your troubles,' she sighed.

'Oh, it's not flying away. That bird wants to distract us, it wants to lore us away from the nest on the ground.'

Kerim watched as the bird moved further away. It did its job very well. She was no longer aware of where it had taken flight, the bird's family was safe. Kerim was struck hard of how similar her own situation was. She was a lore, she was running in the hope that her father would be safe. She was drawing her obsessive captor after her. Her song was the one placed on her by that evil man, the promise of what he would do to her and gain from her sacrifice.

She was trusting Japh a little, and was glad he didn't ask what she wanted to fly away from, maybe he felt that would be one question too far.

'So, do you like animals?' Japh said and broke the song bird's spell. 'What did you keep?'

'Sheep mostly, but also a small herd of goats.'

'I'm not so good with animals myself. I guess I prefer working with my hands. More the creative type.'

'When you care for sheep, you have lots of time on your hands. I used to make all sorts of things while I watched over them. Their wool is really useful. I used to make all sorts, from clothes to blankets.'

Kerim caught him looking at the silken dress she wore. Hopefully he would see that it was not her choice then. She was glad to have been given his sheepskin jacket, something familiar and comforting.

'Does your family still keep sheep?'

'There is only my father left now, my brother ...' Kerim smiled weakly, 'he is no longer part of our family. My father left the upkeep of the herd to me.'

They walked for a few moments in silence before Japh asked, 'What happened to your family?' He looked at her as if realizing he suddenly overstepped a boundary. 'You don't have to answer that if you don't want to.'

'I will answer it. But it is a story that goes back a while.'

Japh nodded and remained silent ready to listen.

'Well,' Kerim began, 'all was fine for many years. Our herd grew well and we were blessed. Then suddenly members of the flock would go missing, they just disappeared.'

'Where did they go? What happened?'

'You see, a stranger had come into my home village and was beginning to influence certain members of the community, the younger men in particular; and unfortunately it started with my brother. He was taken in by the majority of the group in the village. They had been using our herd in sacrifices to the mountain. You see the mountain had begun to smoke - you can see it in the distance.' She turned to look down the track they had walked and saw the dirty smudge in the sky. 'The stranger referred to it as a god. It makes me cold to the bone to think that our herd was used like that of all things. Sacrificed to a false god.' She paused, remembering her friend Miriam.

'My mother grew ill with worry,' Kerim continued, 'and died in the early days. I don't know how she would have coped if she had seen the events unfold. My father, who had been highly respected, was now ridiculed by the village, and left without food or means to live. He was critically ill when I left. He is probably dead now.' Kerim fell silent.

'But he did not turn to them,' Japh stated certain of the truth. 'He didn't follow their ways.'

'No.' Kerim paused. 'Not even when they took me.'

'They took you?'

'Yes.'

'What to ...? To sacrifice?' Japh said his eyes wide in disbelief and horror.

Kerim lowered her head with shame.

'You have come to the right place. You will be safe with my family,' asserted Japh as he stopped walking and faced her. He reached out and took her hand. His breathing stopped for a brief moment. 'You will be safe. I can promise you that.' He was certain he would do all he could to keep that vow.

'How can you know for sure?' Kerim asked not wanting to remove her small hand from his. He showed strength but also tenderness. 'I know that I have been saved,' she continued, 'but for how long I do not know. They will come after me. I cannot allow you to be sacrificed too, because that is what they will do. Once I am gone, they will need others. Bruja, the stranger, he has a thirst for blood, and he will turn on any that do not do as he says.'

'You must not worry about such things, the plan for us is bigger than you could imagine.'

'I do feel safe with you. I don't know why, but I do.' Kerim squeezed Japh's hand; it was strong and calloused from hard work. 'What plan do you know of that I don't?' She laughed and released his hand.

'This one!' Japh raised his arm in a grand gesture of presenting something.

They had walked through the stunted and twisted trees, past the stumps where the felled trees once grew and now stood on the edge of a clearing with a deep basin in the centre of it. Kerim stood bewildered, her mouth slightly open. She shivered despite the heat and felt goose bumps spread up her arms so she pulled the jacket closer to her.

In the middle of the immense clearing, stood a huge wooden structure, stretched out into the near distance. It was taller than anything Kerim had ever seen. Had there been trees next to it, they would have been dwarfed. It had the basic shape of a very large box. Where the angled edges to the sides and underneath would have been, the sections were curved and smooth. Two colossal rectangular cut rocks, were tied to the end corners by substantial ropes as thick as a man's arm. There were others at the far end of the structure too, but from this distance they looked quite small.

It produced a substantial shadow, which the trees that had once grown there, would not have bettered. The lower parts and ropes were black with thick pitch, while the very upper level retained its honey coloured grain and had a small series of cut openings. The air was thick with the smell of pitch and sawn timber.

The structure spoke of years of toil, of amazing skill, and beautiful design.

'Remember Kerim, the things that I told you.'

She has trusted him so much already. I can see that in her heart she knows, but her head is still telling her to keep running.

'This is the place you have been running to.'

'You built this?' she asked astounded.

'My family and I did. Do you like it?'

'It is amazing. Beautiful.' Kerim was almost lost for words. 'How?'

'It has taken us a very long time!' Japh laughed. 'It is almost complete.'

'Why did you? What's it for?'

'Well.' Japh looked worried suddenly. 'My father was told to build it. He was even given the plans! It's for our salvation.' Japh waited for the familiar mocking, the jeering, the cruel words and disbelief.

Kerim had not taken her gaze from it.

'It is beautiful!' Kerim said again in wonder.

'You what?' Japh asked half laughing as he ruffled his dark hair. 'You mean you are not going to laugh at me?'

'It is beautiful,' she said smiling at him.

'Would you like to see the inside?' he said as if he could barely believe what was happening.

'Maybe,' she said dreamily walking towards it a little. Reaching out her hand she stroked the timbers.

'It is quite safe inside. The main structure has been finished for quite a while,' Japh stated. 'Do you want to take a look?'

'Alright, just a quick look.' Although Kerim had the strangest feeling that she had seen this somewhere before.

'Of course. Come this way.'

I follow the couple into the clearing. Ahead, the huge structure stands, made by human hands but with the touch of the Creator about it. It glows violet and gold.

It truly has been planned and built well. The proportions are balanced and the workmanship good. I am amazed at how competently they have fulfilled the plans.

I turn to Kerim, 'You should go inside. I think you'll like it!'

I have more work to do now, a little more business to deal with. I turn to watch the demons.

Weakness is spreading over them, a weakness that was bought on when she had met Japh. Her colours have changed and it has affected them. Excellent! Only two of them are able to hold on still, one with its long arms wrapped about her and the other being much smaller, its long twig like fingers tangled in her hair. The other two, scuttle along in her wake, occasionally shouting at her, but not being heard. As soon as he had shown her kindness their grip had lessened, and as she began to trust, they had fallen to the ground, screaming obscenities at him in anger, but not loud enough to be heard or have any impact. All of them have entered the clearing. The creatures see the structure built with human hands, but are taken aback by the light it emits. It glows with an essence not of this world. It makes their scaly skin itch uncomfortably.

'Your time is up here.' I state, transformed and glowing with the bow of light ready for use in my strong hands.

'What?' they both say as they jump at my voice. 'What are you doing here?'

'Where did you come from?' the one clinging to her body hisses, not so softly and sweetly now. Its tone is now threatening. But it is no threat to me.

'Never you mind.'

'I should have known your lot would be behind this.'

'Yes you should have known! I am here to work,' I state as I smile at them. 'But your work is done ... but not completed I see!'

'She is not yours! She is ours,' spits the one that drips slime from its oily skin as it crawls on the ground, flashing its red eyes towards me, the white robed one. 'I'll show you whose work won't be completed!'

'I know your names. I have authority here. You are Despair, you will leave her now, and you have no authority here!' I command. It has to obey.

'What?' it splutters. 'But she is mine. This is not fair. You cannot do this ...' But even as it speaks it begins to choke on its own breath.

'Leave it alone!' the other shouts, spreading its foul smelling breath over me. 'You can't do this! I will kill you first! You will die in agony at my will and beg me for mercy.' It raises its sharp talons about to attack.

'Fear, your place has been taken by Hope! You cannot harm me,' I state with supreme authority, 'or her anymore.' I see the feeble attempt at attack as if it is in slow motion. I am quick to deliver. I shoot the clear arrow, which flies straight and true, as I know it will, and pierces them, one after the other. Squealing, they take to the air, their bodies oozing, their hideous faces screaming at me.

'You have no authority here!' I declare. 'Tell your master that what he does is futile, you will never succeed. You will always be on the losing side!' I call to them as they flap away.

6

Family

I focus on my friend. He stands in the dimly lit room, in the place where Japh's family live. This room is not dimly lit to our eyes, the darkness is light here. The iridescent glow from him sheds light. He has made himself visible to the oldest human. There is a little fear that plays on his face, but his colours flash a deep blue with hints of purple. His fear is that of the reverent kind.

'The time has arrived.' My friend's voice rings out deep, clear and crisp. 'You must gather everything together just as you were told. It will only be a few days now.'

'Alright.' The man lowers his head, and his gaze from my friend's eyes. Perhaps he has seen the burning there. He replies with a strong voice. 'We will be ready.'

'Well done. You will have a special visitor today.' We are both impressed by this human. To us eternity stretches before us, yet this human, with his passing breeze of a human life, has been refreshing to work with. He has embraced the plan that was set before him all those years ago. My friend adds, 'Be prepared for a lot of guests over the next few days!' I can tell that Trust is smiling; his reaction makes me smile also.

Japh's father gets up from his knees, as far as he is concerned he is alone. He looks out to the stony track leading away from the house and then back to the empty kitchen. There is not a soul with him. The family have been trained well; they would work hard till the sunlight went. He will just have to wait to tell them.

He stokes the fire and hangs a water filled pot over the glowing embers, then takes his seat in the corner of the room and waits.

In a bright flash of light, the vision is gone.

The afternoon passed quickly for Japh and Kerim.

The pitch that covered the exterior did not mask the beautiful grain of the wood on the interior. Sawdust still lingered in the corners, walkways and ramps, but the overall appearance was that of a nearly complete project.

Japh had lit a lamp to show Kerim the lower decks as there was no natural light. The warm flame, flickered and danced. Kerim was drawn to the smooth texture of thick wooden walls and the amber glow of the timber.

The grand tour had not been completed before Kerim had picked up a tool and helped. Japh had been working on the pens, in between coating the exterior and any other jobs, on the first floor for the past fortnight, but had failed to come up with a catch to keep them shut. Kerim took a few of the off cuts from the pile in the corner, and put together a sliding catch with a peg to secure it. She worked fast and nimbly. She could tell that Japh was suitably impressed.

'How did you know how to do that?'

'There was one like that on the cage ...' she started, and suddenly stopped realising she was opening a topic she didn't want to discuss.

'Cage?'

Kerim bit her lower lip and rubbed away some dirt from her cheek avoiding eye contact with Japh. There was silence for a moment.

'It looks like a strong catch.' Japh said changing the subject slightly, yet still curious at what she had let slip.

'It is,' she said, then lowered her voice until Japh could barely hear her. 'You need to be on the outside to open it.'

'It is just what we need. Thanks.'

'You're welcome,' Kerim replied.

'Can you help make some more?' he moved away allowing her time to collect herself again.

'Of course. I'd be happy to help.' She felt as if there was a lightness to her that had not been there for a very long time. Her inability to mix with the people in her own village was long gone, Japh made her feel comfortable as if she belonged somewhere. He was like her.

As they worked together on the catches, they chatted and laughed with one another. She could tell Japh felt distracted by her presence, yet he still worked hard to impress. Each time she laughed; he would laugh too. He was the one who had made her smile, he had made her relax and with each passing moment she found a new peace.

As soon as Japh held out his hand to her, it had begun. I saw that.

She is changing. She had been so lost and frightened, but Japh is playing his part spectacularly. He is giving her confidence, although I know that he is very unsure. This is what makes humans so interesting. They live in a world that is broken and tainted, they are unable to do so many of the things that I take for granted, yet they adapt and change at a rate that is fascinating. They grow and discover, and yet it seems left to us to wonder at it all.

Her laugh is not high pitched like Helena's, nor is it quiet like Lellia's, there is a girlish giggle about it that is contagious. Japh notices as she tucks her hair behind her ear and exposes her smudged cheeks. He considers her beauty. Inside him there is a fierce need to protect her. Even her walk captivates him as she glides from one place to another.

He cares and shows care. He listens intently when she speaks and he offers her wisdom. He is strong but gentle, he offers her companionship.

That simple act of friendship has made it difficult for the others to keep a firm hold. The leathery creature I see clings on to Kerim, constantly having to re-adjust its grip. It winces at the affect hope and trust has in her heart. With each step she takes, the strength it once had, continues to ebb away. Its name is Suspicion.

The demon hisses and spits at Japh, desperate to cling on. It digs its multi-pointed claws into her side but Kerim seems unaware. She has grown immune to her freedom. The creature clambers up her back in a juddering scratchy movement, to rest on her shoulder. From there it can reach her ear. Its forked tongue flicks out of its snarling mouth, showing the double row of sharpened stained teeth. With the softest and saddest of voices, one which could not match its true identity, it whispers as she moves from despair into another much healthier horizon.

'How can he care for someone like you?' I hear it speak softly to her. 'He cannot make you happy. He does not understand you. He is not your friend. Why would you trust him?' It watches intently as she recreates the latch from the cage. 'You will not be safe with him,' it croons.

I can smell its reeking breath, and see the deathly grey attitude it has. But I also see it weakening. It knows I am nearby having seen its comrades dispatched. It nervously attempts to cling on. I see it falter and slip quickly to the floor, landing awkwardly and unceremoniously.

Japh and Kerim have reached the first deck. The creature seems shocked. It has whispered itself empty of new uncertainties. There is nothing that it can do.

Something strange has happened to her. When Japh had shown her the simple act of kindness, she begun to believe in him, to trust him.

It has become impossible for the creature to remain near her. She radiates something the creature has never felt before, and it is creeping under its skin and burning from the inside out. There is nothing comfortable for it here now. It hobbles behind her, injured by her new found strength to resist, shouting at the top of its voice, but no one pays attention to it. The creature is stooped in agony, powerless as she quickly fashions another catch for the pen not even thinking about its design.

Now is my time to act. A very enjoyable task.

'I suggest you get back to your master,' I declare loudly. 'You have no authority here Suspicion.' I make the creature jump in fear. This makes me smile. 'Now be gone,' I command, stringing a pure, clear arrow to my bow of light.

The creature knows there is no use in disobedience. It has seen its two companions injured and does not have the nerve to face such a beating. It has to go.

'Don't let her go little Loneliness.' It whispers to the tiny creature which has its long claws tangled in her hair. I hear every word. I know that the other creature is still relatively robust.

It hobbles down the ramp to the entrance, muttering to itself. 'There's something strange going on here. It isn't natural for these young humans to act in such a way. They should be making trouble.'

Summoning up its last ounce of strength, it spreads its long arms, revealing its rather weak wings, flaps them and takes off over the wooden structure, spitting sickly yellow sulphur as it goes. The acid is strong, but misses its target. The two butterflies that perch on the open door are unharmed.

'Thank you Kerim,' Japh said sincerely. 'You've helped so much.'

'You're welcome,' she replied fixing the final wedge in place while he hammered it home.

It had almost felt natural to have Japh this close to her. He turned and took a step back to admire the last latch along the long wall. His warm arm brushed against her and she instinctively backed away. Maybe, it wasn't that natural after all.

'So you must be hungry,' Japh said, assuming his own hunger was a signal for hers, not even taking note of her movement.

'I suppose.'

'Really?' he laughed. 'I'm famished!' He turned to see her face nervous again. 'What is it? What's wrong?'

'Nothing,' she said a little too quickly to be that convincing.

'Oh.' Japh gave her a crooked smile. 'So, do you want to come and have something to eat at my place?' Her eyes widened. 'My family will be there,' then he quickly added, 'they're friendly, you'll like them. The last thing I want is for you to disappear now. You will be safe with us.'

'Who is us?'

'My dad and mum, my brothers and their wives.' She gave him a horrified look. 'It really isn't as bad as that. Just give them a go. They're harmless.'

'Alright. I guess I am a little hungry.' But as for liking them, I think I'll be the judge of that, she thought. She was enjoying being with Japh. He felt safe.

The light had all but faded outside and the night air had a chill to it. Kerim pulled the jacket about her, welcoming the protection it gave.

After a short walk they arrived at an aged low level house in a grassy clearing.

Japh reached for the door and opened it. The aroma of freshly baked bread and warm vegetable stew filled the air.

'We'll never eat all that bread! What happened to it?' a deep male voice said.

'I don't know. I just got a bit distracted, and made double!'

'Did you say you'd made extra bread?' Japh called as he strolled in leaving Kerim feeling exposed for the first time since they had become friends.

'Yeah. Where have you been? It has been dark for over an hour,' a female asked.

Japh shrugged. 'Just got busy.' He stepped into the room. 'Can I bring someone else in for dinner?'

His mother, distracted from the stew, stared straight at the wall. 'Someone else?' She looked over her shoulder.

'Of course you can bring a guest,' his father sounded inquisitive. His chair creaked as he got up. 'Show them in.'

Kerim swallowed and folded her hands. Her nerves had been rattled enough for one day. Now she was meeting strangers, what had she done?

Japh returned to the door, where Kerim stood like a statue.

'It's all right,' he beamed with pride. 'Come on in.'

Her body felt rigid and she could not move. 'I can't.'

'Yes you can.' And he held out his hand. Kerim reached for it clasping onto him like a lost child.

Japh came in slowly, pushing the door closed behind. Kerim trailed in his shadow, as if he dragged her out of some pit. The room was full of strangers.

'Well hello.' Japh's father tugged on his silver whiskers. 'Welcome.'

All but two of his family sat around a large table, their mouths hung open in shock. Her tattered appearance was exposed in the warm light of the hearth.

Kerim cleared her throat, as she stood like an exhibit for all to see. She noticed his father's warm smile and shared her own. The man was tall, with long white hair, and kind eyes.

'Sit down dear.' The oldest woman showed her to an empty chair.

The family had gathered around the hearth after their day at work and continued whatever they were doing before she entered. Kerim thought that the old man, Japh's father could have easily dozed in the wooden recliner in the corner. His wife was busy stirring pots over the fire, adding handfuls of chopped carrots, sliced onions, roughly cut potatoes and couple of leaves of fragrant basil. A rich aroma spread throughout the room.

The two younger women present were very different in their appearance. One had long, light coloured hair and an olive complexion, her eyes studied Kerim in what appeared to be a critical manner, the other had darker skin and dark hair, but she only appeared surprised.

The dark haired woman sat at the table, dipping into the woven basket, taking a handful of dried plants, and separating the seeds. Her husband, Japh's brother, sat with her, talking quietly, as he put the seeds into pots. The table was full of assorted size containers.

'That is the last of that sort. Can you seal it Ham?' she asked.

'Sure.' Ham took the pot, and forced a wad of cotton into the remaining space, before securing a fabric top to the pot with twisted twine.

'Supper is nearly ready. Can you clear the table Lellia?'

'Of course mother.' Lellia quickly sorted the seeds left on the table, as the critical looking one placed a bowl overflowing with bread in the centre.

'She can't sit there,' she said plainly to Japh.

'Helena!' Japh exclaimed angrily.

'No ... no... I didn't mean that,' she replied apologetically. She turned to Kerim. 'Look at you. You must be frozen. Let's get you something warmer to wear.'

'Oh right. Yes, that would be good.' Kerim pulled the sheepskin jacket tighter around her.

'Kerim, this is Helena. You can go with her.'

'You are daft boy.' The other woman chuckled. 'I'm Lellia.' She got up from her chair and took Kerim's hand. 'Is there time to change before we eat mother?'

Kerim shyly looked at the others in the room.

The men, either side of these women were related, there was a family likeness, although Kerim saw that the darker skinned one was also more muscular than the shorter stouter brother. The muscular one, wore a large grin across his face, friendly and not menacing, it was almost contagious. She would have returned the smile if she hadn't felt so nervous. The older woman stood by the fire stirring a large pot of bubbling food, Kerim was now certain that she was Japh's mother; her gentle face seemed to mirror his.

'Yes, go ahead. Don't be too long, I don't want the stew to spoil.'

Helena took her by the other arm. Lellia followed giving Japh a little wink as she went.

'Be gentle with her,' he whispered, but it was loud enough for Kerim to hear.

The kitchen went quiet behind her. Kerim could feel their eyes on her. She listened intently as Japh explained to his parents where exactly he came across this female stranger.

She heard their voices from the other room. It was only the silver haired one that spoke. 'She is very welcome Japh. I take it she is like us.'

'Yes father,' Japh replied.

Kerim could tell he was smiling. 'She thinks like us and believes like us. I think she has run from her own people because of it. She has had to deal with her own kind of persecution,' Japh then said quietly to himself, 'I've never met anyone like her before.'

'That is good. Well, let us welcome her into the family then. I am sure Japh will explain all later. I don't want questions now.'

The door sealed her off from their conversation. All went quiet. Helena was studying her.

'Would you like to borrow a dress?'

'Not that what you are wearing is wrong ... just a bit cold for this time of day,' added Lellia.

'That would be lovely. Thank you.'

'Helena,' she said in her musical voice.

'Helena, thank you.'

'I'm Lellia and I'm not sure what you have been up to, but I think there is half a tree in your hair.' Kerim tried to pull her hair into a more manageable state, but failed miserably. 'Now that can't be comfortable. Here let me comb it for you.'

As the women worked they chatted away as if they had known Kerim for years. She had missed this. It had been a long time since she had female companionship. Suddenly Kerim felt a pang of grief for her mother and for Miriam.

Her eyes began to prickle and as soon as tears began to swim in her eyes, she blinked them away.

Helena had found a dress that was very much to her liking and Lellia had cleaned and dressed her wounds. They were gentle and kind, offering a bowl of water to clean her face. Perhaps they had seen her eyes reddening and were making opportunity for her to recompose herself.

As Helena helped to fit the dress to her more slender figure, Lellia brushed and tied up her hair.

'There,' Helena stated, 'you look beautiful.'

Kerim blushed.

'Perfect touch!' Lellia said laughing. 'Come on.' As she followed Helena out of the room.

The cooking had continued. Kerim noticed the younger men kept trying to make eye contact with Japh, who kept his gaze firmly on the floor. When Helena returned he looked up quickly. Kerim thought she saw relief spread across his face. It took a few seconds before he finally smiled at her.

'Wow!' he mouthed.

'Although the jacket was truly beautiful Japh, we felt that maybe something a little more feminine was required.'

'No. You're right!' Japh winked at Kerim and nodded. 'You look great.'

'Last of the great compliments!' laughed Helena.

'It's a bit long.' Kerim commented as she smoothed the front of her skirt.

'Well you're not as tall as Helena. That can be sorted out later,' Lellia said lifting the lower hem to adjust the length.

'Kerim, is it?' Japh's mother said kindly, 'take a seat, I hope you are hungry!'

'Kerim, that's my mother,' Japh said as his mother smiled and loaded the table with food. 'Glad there's plenty of bread. I'm hungry!'

'I'm Tabitha,' she smiled kindly. 'Vegetable stew, I hope you like it!'

'My father.' Japh gestured to the oldest man there.

'Noah. A real pleasure to meet you my dear,' he said kindly.

'That's Ham and his wife Lellia, but you've already met her!' Japh continued badly. Ham stood up briefly. He was shorter and stouter, more like his mother.

'Hello, welcome.' Ham winked at his brother with a slight grin.

'And finally, Shem. He's married to Helena,' he said as he gestured towards his older brother. He was by far the most muscular but his cheeky smile made it hard to feel threatened.

'Smooth bro! Nice to meet you,' Shem said as he drew closer to the table.

Japh sat down next to Kerim. Noah closed his bright eyes, raised his hands and gave thanks for the food before them. Just that small act made her feel at home. As they ate their evening meal, many things were discussed, but no one asked where this female had come from. Kerim was grateful not to be interrogated; without all the awkward questions she was able to relax.

She hardly said a word throughout supper, but watched and laughed with the family. Often she noticed Japh's brothers' affection to their wives. Everyone laughed when Shem said something funny, yet it was never at the cost of another. Noah led the others in being grateful for the spread of food set before them, each one was thankful for the hard work that Tabitha and Helena had gone to.

Once or twice she even caught Japh looking at her. He did not make her feel uncomfortable, but the gaze seemed to linger longer than from the others sat there. It was always she that broke the contact, perhaps just with a quick smile, a downward glance or nervous smoothing of her clothes. She felt well dressed in her borrowed clothes and soft warm slippers, but was aware of her broken nails snagging on the fabric, and her blistered feet rubbing on the woollen insoles. She was determined not to let this ruin the joy of this company; it was wonderful to be with friendly people again.

As the meal drew to an end, Kerim began to wish she did not have to leave but the last thing she wanted was to put these kind people in danger. She was about to speak to Japh when his father stood at the head of the table.

'It is so lovely to have a guest with us,' he declared, while the others agreed. 'I do however have some news, but before I get to that, Japh my boy, have you shown this young lady around?'

'Yes father.'

'And what did you think Kerim?'

'If you are referring to what you are building, it is truly amazing. You have done such a beautiful job.'

'Thank you my dear,' he said, pulling at his whiskers as a hint of a smile showed in his eyes. 'In that case, I believe it is the right time to speak.' The room went quiet; the family it seemed, was rarely this formal. 'Earlier today I was given a message.'

'Excellent!' Shem exclaimed.

'Message? What kind of message?' Kerim whispered to Japh. 'From who?'

Japh jumped as he felt Kerim's warm breath in his ear. He turned and she found his face very close to hers but it no longer bothered her, she trusted him. She bit down on her lip, who knew she was here? 'I think it is a special message. You mustn't worry. Listen!' He smiled quickly to her and turned his face towards his father, yet he gave the impression not all his attention was there.

'Not so fast Shem!' Noah laughed. 'He came as he did before. A man dressed in the finest white. I say man, he looked like one, but I know it was a supernatural being. He told me,' and he looked to his sons, 'we are to be ready in a few days time. Everything must be complete.'

'But the seeds aren't done yet,' Ham argued.

'Well actually,' Lellia said, 'I only have three baskets left. That may take one more day if I can just concentrate on it.' Her husband shrugged his shoulders and smiled.

'We haven't finished the latches, or gathered all the food,' Shem said.

'Let alone the animals,' added Helena.

'Well Kerim and I fixed the latches today,' Japh replied.

'What all of them?' Shem asked, his brow furrowed.

'The majority.' Japh stated. 'Kerim came up with a very good design. Simple but very strong.'

'Great!' Helena smiled widely at Shem.

'And I've been told we are to be ready for our many visitors. It appears they have been gathered and are on their way,' Noah said.

'What work would you have us do father?' Ham asked seriously.

'Shem, Ham and Helena, it will your job to gather in the remaining food stores and to move the existing. Lellia you must complete the seed bank. Japh, you and Kerim seem to work well together. I think any carpentry and last minute finishing touches. Plus we will need all men to help move the furniture. Your mother and I will organize the moving in of all the animals. Of course, when you have completed your job, as always assist someone else.'

Kerim looked about at the faces of this family. Even having shared a meal with them, she felt obtrusive in their plans. It was time to leave.

'I thank you so much for being so welcoming, but...'

'There are no 'buts'. You are welcome to join us.' His kind gaze scrutinized her expression. 'If you feel however that you need to go, then you must.'

'It's not really my place ... here ... with you,' she replied almost wishing it was. It had been a long time since she had seen this much harmony in a group of people. 'You remind me a great deal of my own family,' then added, 'I don't want you to end up the same way.'

Noah's interest seemed piqued, 'In what ways are we like your family?'

Kerim sat back and inhaled a deep breath. 'From what I have seen, you do things in the right order.'

'The right order?' Lellia chided.

'You know ...' Kerim was suddenly unsure of what she had witnessed. 'I see you giving respect to your parents and to one another, you work hard for the benefit of each other.' Then Kerim turned and looked at Noah, 'I heard you pray. You pray to the one true God. It has been a long time since I have been with people who worship like that. My own father gave up some time ago, I miss it.' She bowed her head, suddenly overwhelmed with the shame of dishonouring her father.

The room seemed still for a moment, the only noise was the crackling of the fire. Kerim lifted her head to see the family exchanging nods and smiles.

'You are different to the rest of the human race,' Tabitha said with a gentle smile, dimples rising to her cheeks. 'You are like us.' Then she added, 'Your place may well be with us.'

'What?' Kerim asked turning to Japh.

'Mother is right,' Japh said, wishing he had been quicker to verbalise his thoughts. 'You fit in so well. Beyond that really. You are perfect for our family.' Kerim felt the focus of all the others on her, but she was determined to look only at Japh. 'I've never met anyone who described our lives work as beautiful before. Now 'hideous' or 'waste of time' or 'insanity', that's all I have ever heard. You aren't like the others and besides, you will be safe with me.' He smiled at her. 'I want you to be safe. I can give that to you.'

'Well said son.' Noah's white whiskers bristled over the gentle smile. 'You would be very welcome to come with us. But the decision is entirely yours.'

'But how can you be sure?' Kerim was overwhelmed by the bewildering words, but feared that her old life would catch up on her. She feared what would happen to these people. 'You hardly know me. In fact, you know nothing about me.'

'That is true,' Lellia said glancing at the others around the table. 'So why don't you tell us.'

'Lellia!' Japh admonished protectively and gave her a dark glare. 'What does it matter about what has gone on before?'

'It's alright Japh.' Kerim said, patting his arm. She did not want to cause a rift in the family. 'It is a long story,' she explained.

'We have all night!' Lellia laughed unperturbed by her brother's glare.

She turned to Japh, unsure of what to say. 'I don't think I can. Could you?'

Japh smiled at her gently, 'Are you sure?' Kerim nodded. He turned to his family and began to recount the story he heard earlier that day. As Kerim sat and listened, her head remained bowed and her fingers fiddled with the shawl. She smiled sadly, in amazement at details Japh had remembered and peered at his family. He told them of how Kerim's village had been influenced by a stranger. He explained the sacrifices performed to the mountain, the missing herds, the smaller animals and then those of the human kind.

Helena and Lellia sat motionless with tears running down their faces, while the men had fierce anger in their eyes. He continued with his father's permission to tell of Kerim's mother and Miriam and how they both died, leading to her ill stricken father and the betrayal of her brother. The whole family sat in silence until Japh had finished. Kerim raised her head unsure of their reaction. She had expected looks of horror and fear, but was taken aback. Japh's mother was the only one who showed nothing. Instead she spoke up.

'You, my dear,' she said in a soft maternal tone, 'have been exposed to a most horrific evil. I do not want to let you go back to that place. I want you to stay here with us. I believe that there must have been someone else at work to free you from such a place.'

Kerim gazed at her soft face in silence. 'Yes there was.' Her voice barely louder than a whisper.

'What?' said Japh clearly surprised by this new information. 'You never told me someone else had helped you.'

'I thought you would think I was mad if I told you how I was freed,' she said apologetically. When she saw that Japh was not offended, just confused, she turned to look at his mother in the eyes. 'You are right. I had been locked into a cage, like a wild animal, and ... stripped down.' Her gaze fell to her hands twisting the fabric in her lap, she felt ashamed. An angry snort broke the silence. Kerim peered at Japh quickly. It was him who was angry, but she could see it wasn't directed at her, more at what she had said. She was distracted a little by his reaction, but focussed again on her lap and continued.

'I was given the white dress to wear for the sacrifice. There was no way out. The cage was in the stranger's hut, and he had left to prepare the altar. He took so much pleasure in describing what would happen to me.' Kerim's eyes widened in sick horror of the thought, before they began to fill with tears. 'He left me there, alone, without food and water.' She raised a hand to wipe away the moisture on her cheek. 'All I could do was pray. I knew that I was not clean enough to call on the name of the Lord, but I had no other choice. It was soon after that, that a man dressed in the purest white, a white that made the sacrificial clothes I was wearing look filthy grey,' and made me feel filthy grey she thought, 'stood before me. I did not see him enter, but he was there. He bent down to me and told me that I must run far from the mountain, to run and not turn back. He looked kind, and he was because he unlocked the cage, the same lock that I had pulled at and kicked at and given up on. I don't know how he did it!' She remembered. 'He took my hand; he had warm hands.' She looked at Japh and thought of the similar warmth of his hands. 'He told me not to worry but trust in the Lord. He guided me out of the hut and through the village. I was so scared, the other villagers knew I was to be sacrificed, but not one of them looked at me as I walked past them with him. It was as if I was not even there.' She remembered how confusing that was. 'He took me to the edge of the village, spoke to me once more, he told me of the rocks where I should hide, the place where you found me Japh. Then he was gone. He didn't walk away or run or anything like that, he just disappeared. So I ran.'

I remember the time well.

Demons had flocked to their leader once he had established himself in that village. The leader had taken hold of a wandering man, who had destroyed many human lives over the years. This village was no different in its eyes, but it was very different in the eyes of the Creator.

Kerim, distraught over the loss of Miriam had been hidden by her father. A man who still believed deeply in a mighty one. His colours had faded over the years of suffering, and now at his moment of fear, they virtually disappeared. Kerim was trapped— Firstly inside the village, then inside her house and finally inside the cage.

The cage in which she sat, cold and exposed, which she struggled to escape from. She could not do it alone. The evil that the demon spoke of, stripped her of nearly all she had. Each time he approached, I had to stand back. It was difficult for me to let this go unchallenged. But I was obedient.

The man and demon went away to prepare for the hideous festivities of which this one of the Remnant was to be subjected. I remember now the images that she imagined. Of the brutality she expected, the filthiness of the acts against her, the hopelessness she felt. Of course I had seen the images of what was planned and was glad that her imagination could not go as far as the evil ones hideous intentions.

Now was her moment. I had to wait until she did it.

'Help me!' she cried.

The Creator is merciful and just. My command was given. 'Help her.'

She was alone, dressed in that evil stained sacrificial dress, crouched in the cage. I approached, glimmering in glory.

'Don't be afraid!' That line always makes me laugh. As if a great glowing being appearing from nowhere telling a human not to be afraid will actually make them not be afraid. I spread a mist of green throughout the room. Peace filled the space and she stopped trembling.

'What do you want?' she asked me. She is brave indeed.

'I am here to help you.' I bent low to the cage door. It was such a small place to be trapped. The latch which had been so secure when she had struggled feverously with it, comes undone at my touch. She crawled out, looking undernourished and ill.

I produced a small loaf of warm bread, a goblet of milk and chunk of cheese and offered them to her. She took them, showing complete trust to the one who had freed her.

As she ate I spoke to her again.

'You must find a place to hide. A large rock with a cool space below an overhang. It will smell sweet there, a comforting smell. You will be safe.' I allowed images of an overhanging rock next to a field full of red flowers fill her imagination.

'You will find safety there until a new place of safety will be shown to you. Do not be afraid. You can trust them. They are like you.' I quickly flicked images of a smiling gangly young man into her subconscious.

'A new place of safety of salvation is waiting for you.' The last image I revealed was one of a huge wooden structure in a vast clearing, it shimmered violet and gold.

She has eaten all the food. Immediately she looks better. My food has a habit of nourishing more than the body.

I took her by the hand and led her from the hut. She was fearful. I hid her under my wing. No one saw her. The villagers were out on the track but they were blinded to our presence.

When we had passed the outskirts of the village I turned to her once more.

'Remember the overhanging rocks Kerim, it is there you will find safety.'

I smile at her. 'Run!' Then I blind her to my presence also but continue to follow and guide her the whole way.

'Wow!' Japh stood back in amazement. 'You were always meant to come with us.'

'How do you know that?' Kerim said gently amazed that he did not think her crazy. 'You were as surprised to see me as I you.'

'Japh, when you showed Kerim your handiwork, didn't you tell her anything else?'

'Shem, give him a chance!' Helena admonished. 'He'd only just met her, why would he do such a thing?' Kerim had no idea what they were talking about.

'We used to tell all that would listen about the prophecy,' reflected Ham.

'But that was before all the abuse,' Lellia stated.

'I am part of a prophecy?' Kerim questioned looking slightly fearful, and biting down on her lip. 'What prophecy?'

'Well, maybe.' Japh smiled reassuringly. 'It's nothing to worry about though.' He nodded at his family and they smiled in reassurance. 'Look don't be worried, I'm pretty sure it is you now. It is about you being part of our family.'

'Noah, why don't you tell it!' Tabitha said with a hint of girlish excitement.

'Yes Tabitha.' Noah looked across the table and into the face of the bewildered girl sat there. 'Many years ago, before the great building project, God spoke to me. He didn't come with a booming voice, or out of a strong wind, but came as a man of light. The light was bright and I couldn't look into it, yet I knew He was beautiful.'

Noah now looked beyond all those sat in the room, even as they focused on him. Kerim thought he looked younger than he had before. He was remembering the moment as if it were a heartbeat ago. 'He spoke to me much the way I sit here and converse with you now. He warned me of events to come, a wave of degenerate evil would rise in the land. He said the earth would be overcome with wickedness, violence and greed.'

Noah sat back contemplating what it is that was happening around them. He heard stories, they all had of what occurred in villages and towns, and the tribes that ran about them.

'God is holy,' he inferred. 'It is because of this lawless living that He has sworn to put an end to mankind. He will destroy the land and bring a flood to cover the whole earth. Everything will perish.'

The table grew restless, the family looking at Kerim awaiting her reaction. Her knuckles were white as she clutched the side of the table. Noah spoke softly, 'I too was frightened, but God has made a way. The vessel you see was made to His specifications, it will hold pairs of animals and will save my family, and all that we hold dear. I made rooms for my sons and their wives, planned three of them before they were even born.

'When is this flood, as you say, going to happen?'

Tabitha looked away. 'As soon as the promised one arrives.'

Kerim sat back. 'And who is that?'

'We're not sure,' Japh added.

Noah raised his head. 'The flood will not begin until every son is married. Japh is the remaining lad.'

'Right.' Kerim looked at Noah's serious expression. 'Right ... I see.' Kerim glanced at Japh who appeared unshaken by such a story.

Her mind was racing. How could she escape one lunatic bunch just to find another. 'So I've only just met you and you think I am sent here to marry your son. But if I say no, I am going to die.'

'Well,' Noah continued. 'You won't.'

Kerim began to squirm. Japh exhaled. 'I know what you are thinking. But this vessel would not be possible unless the Creator ordained its work. For a hundred years my father has worked on this vessel. The trouble alone it has caused my family is proof that the end is nearing.

Tabitha poured some milk into a goblet. 'People look on us as those who have lost their minds. But now you have come.' At that, Tabitha finished abruptly as if it would convince Kerim of her purpose in being there.

She was more confused than ever now. Not fear like that of her own home, but a fear that this was too fast and too soon.

She gulped the milk before Tabitha set it down. 'And you think I am the fulfilment?'

The family just smiled and nodded. Kerim smiled weakly back to all their faces then focused firmly on her hands clasped tightly on her lap. Slowly the others turned away and started to speak of all the work left to do. She was confused. How could she be the fulfilment of a prophecy? There was nothing special about her. The amazing stories could just be coincidences couldn't they? She looked up, hoping all the attention of the others was far away. Only Japh looked at her now. He leaned forward and took her shaking fingers into his strong warm hand.

'I want you to come with us,' he whispered. 'If that makes any difference.'

'You have done all the work. You and your family. I'm not sure I can offer you anything except trouble.'

'Don't give me an answer now. Stay for a while.' Japh suggested. 'Maybe we will grow on you.'

'You are all very kind but ...'

'I'll sleep in the barn and you can have my room,' he stated quickly. 'I'll just grab some clean linen.'

Before Kerim could protest he had rushed away from the table.

7

Belonging

The evening had quietened after the story telling and revelation of the prophecy, and everyone had retired early. Kerim was glad of it. She felt exhausted. Somehow relaxing earlier in the company of Japh's family and then all the confused emotions, had bought the weariness she had carried for days to the surface. Before Japh headed to the barn to sleep, he had shown Kerim where she would be staying.

'Use whatever you need.' he offered ruffling his hair. 'Sorry about the mess.'

'Thank you.' She peered about; it was no messier than her own room at home. 'I'm sure I will be very comfortable.'

'See you in the morning! Sleep well.'

'Hmm, thanks. Good night!'

Kerim closed the door. The catch that held it shut was not as nimble as the ones she had helped to make, but it served its purpose. A lit lamp had been left on the small cabinet by the bed. It spread a dim, flickering light throughout the room. It wasn't a large room, but she would describe it as snug. The earthen floor was covered with an assortment of woven reed mats that brushed the floor with gentle hushing noises as she stepped on them. To walk from one side of the room to the other would only take a few paces. A small window, cut into the far wall, was partially covered with a drape of dark heavy fabric. The whitewashed walls were thick and strong unlike the wattle and daub of her own home. Her own home, how she missed it. How was her father? She sighed. Kerim moved over to the bed and sat down. It was comfortably soft, smelt of clean crisp linen and had several woollen blankets lay folded at the end.

Memories of the events that had bought her to this place filled her mind. Kerim took in a deep breath as she felt tears springing to her eyes. Here, in this quiet, private space she was free at last to cry. What would happen when they came looking for her? 'There is no way I am going to put these good people through that.'

She could not doubt the kindness and acceptance that this family had lavished on her. It was difficult not to respond to such affections when it had been such a long time since she had experienced them. She craved for them. How she missed having a mother who fussed, a father who doted and a brother who protected her. Time had obscured and history had destroyed all that inheritance. She longed for it now, now that she had witnessed it firsthand again, but her fear for them made her resolute not to let her presence threaten them. She whispered. 'I will sleep for a few hours, and then leave before morning.'

Oh Kerim! I see her conflict. Her longing for peace and love, but the unrest in her too. She wants safety for them. She has not heard, not in her heart anyway, that this is the place of safety. You have come so far. Now is not the time to run away. You have a purpose here. He has planned wonderful things for you. Now is the time to step into those plans.

She is certain she knows what is right. But I see that she is not. All the decisions she makes are based on her fear and feelings that are only on the surface. She refuses to look deeper, to trust what her soul is saying and what her Creator says. Her colours betray her. Although they are foundationally violet, proving that she rightly longs for Japh's family to be protected, they have become corrupted by her own desire, to protect them in her own way, and the pureness is impregnated with murky ribbons of maroon. It twists and swirls about her. She feels anguish over them, a common human reaction, but are they not in bigger hands than hers?

'See how these people have given you comfort.' I state as I gaze at her changed appearance. 'You need to see these people for what they are. They are genuine and true.' I point to the wall opposite. 'See how Japh thinks. He is like minded with you.'

Shivering, she wrapped the shawl about her shoulders.

'I wonder if they would really hate me if I took these clothes.' she looked down at her slippers and wriggled her toes. 'My feet are so enjoying the comfort!'

At last, she smiled. She lifted her gaze and noticed the opposite wall. It was covered with thin strips of something, different shapes and sizes fixed to it. She reached over to the lamp, got up and tiptoed over to inspect it.

Dozens of thin slices of wood, which curled at the edges, had been pinned against the wall. On the surface of each, charcoal images had been made. The larger pieces had drawings of the vessel she had been in today, details of how it was put together, beautiful designs. She traced the lines with her finger, slightly above the drawing so as not to smudge the charcoal. She could tell that some had been laboured over and reworked; others had been adjusted and altered here and there.

Near the door frame, she noticed several smaller strips with catch designs with various faults. The images were captivating. Tiredness, now a memory, she studied and understood the workings and makings of the lifelong work that Japh and his family had created.

As she returned to the bed, Kerim felt a connection with Japh she had not felt before. Now, everywhere she looked in his room, she could see his creativity. Even the small cabinet had the strong lines, gentle subtleties and attention to detail that the drawings had shown.

Slipping off her outer clothing, she clambered into the soft bed. As she relaxed, sleep came quickly, but so did her dreams.

I see it there, weaving its web of lies. It tangles its hideous fingers in her hair as it stokes her head in mock comfort.

I am commanded to stand back, to watch. I want to string my bow, to pierce its body, to banish it forever, but I will follow my commander.

Loneliness knows her weakness. It attacks her where she is vulnerable.

I watch, but I do guard. This demon will not overstep the mark. There are limits that have been set. I am commanded to protect her and I will not leave my post.

The damage that Loneliness is doing will be turned and used for the Creator's glory. My Lord and Master knows all things.

The light was bright, too bright. The glare hurt her eyes. Before her there was nothing except the landscape that stretched out before her. Turning she saw the same landscape mirrored behind. There was nothing, nowhere to go, nowhere to hide. As that thought caught hold, a strange panic began to rise in her heart. She felt like she was being watched. She spun around fast, too fast that she felt dizzy, but her eyes caught a movement, a shape growing in the distance. Kerim knew what it was, who it was, even then she could not force her feet to move.

The shape grew ever more distinct as it drew closer. Then suddenly, he was there, his harsh eyes and sallow skin close enough to touch. He smiled his sharp toothed smile. Still she could not move. His eyes had been fixed on her, leering at her, she felt exposed, then he was distracted, something had caught his attention behind her.

Kerim turned very slowly now. As she turned, horror began to take hold of her. Japh stood firmly before his family, they were all there. Helena and Shem linked hand in hand, Ham held Lellia protectively about her waist and Noah and Tabitha stood either side of their small family group. Details of their appearances were blurred but the expression on their faces was sharp. They were full of fear.

As Kerim watched, Bruja, with his sneering grin sauntered around her and approached the terrified family. Before he even reached them, they fell one by one to the ground, leaving Japh standing last. Bruja approached him. Kerim saw him raise is hand above his head and saw the glint of a blade held in his fist. She flinched and then she screamed as the blade plunged into Japh's unprotected body.

She woke up with the scream still in her throat.

She leapt from the bed and dressed quickly. Quietly she slipped out of the house and sped through the night.

8

Rescued

Japh bolts upright. He hears a scream. 'Kerim!' He throws the blanket to one side, shoving the clothing he had removed back into place as he runs towards the house. A shadow moves away from the building, speeding into the darkness. Japh notes its direction, but what was inside the house is of more importance to him now.

There is little sound except for the snoring from his parent's room. He quickly takes in the surroundings, checking for things out of place. It is then that he notices his bedroom door standing open. Rushing forward, he worriedly looks in. There is no one there. Kerim is gone. He races out into the night and heads in the direction the shadow had disappeared.

He worries that they have come for her.

The night is still and the gentle light that filters through the clouds illumintes the path along which Japh runs.

Japh's breathing is laboured, not out of exhaustion, but of worry. Over and over in his mind images flash of Kerim being dragged off to be tortured, violated and sacrificed. As the moments drag by, Japh becomes increasingly anxious. Desperation is rising in his spirit. Adrenaline pushes him faster and focuses his mind to the fearful acknowledgement that he has lost his kindred spirit. The image of her damaged by evil, brakes him, and injures his very soul. Japh knows that Kerim has unashamedly become part of his life. From the moment he had seen her, she was not just to be part of it, but essential to it.

Panic flares within him in wave after wave.

He is at last making sense, although I think he still feels confused. To me the air around him vibrates with his intense colours. They flit from tainted flashes of ochre and murky blue to vibrant, clean yellow and rich red. He fears for her, that is very clear but intermingled and twisting through all of it I see the passionate love he has for her. He seems to be coming to that conclusion all by himself!

He is not alone. The indefinite form of another follows him. I see it changing, shifting into differing forms, merging one with the other.

I have encountered spirits like this before. Their changeability conceals them, makes others think they are harmless. I will not, however, be fooled.

I follow silently, cautiously. An arrow strung, ready to fire. The arrow must pierce them both. My friend, Trust, would be useful right now. His sword is made for this kind of creature. I have, in the past, seen him cut down such spirits.

It does follow, but is having trouble keeping up. Japh seems to have shaken this one off himself. And it is about time I finish the job!

'Hey you!' I bellow.

The spirit turns, shifting quickly into a larger model of itself.

'What do you want?' it yells back, but in taking in my appearance, it changes its own. Now it looks weak and small, almost insignificant. 'I mean no harm,' it mumbles.

I will not be deceived. I have seen its forms. From massive and burly, to spine covered and now this.

'Insecurity,' I begin in a threatening voice.

'That's not me.' it lies.

'It is. You will …'

The spirit changes again, taking on a form that is dangerous. Its body covered with spines, oozing poison. It snarls menacingly at me and crouches as if to attack.

I am quick but also patient. I have to time this right.

As it leaps for me, its shape shimmers into a form with massive jaws and razor sharp fangs. I fire my arrow.

It flies straight. It pierces the spirit mid change. Sickening shrieks fill the still air as the arrow pierces its multiple pieces. Sulphurous gases explode from its body before it disappears.

Japh will not suffer from insecurity again!

Kerim heard the hurried footfalls behind her and turned, noticing her pursuer, and then put in extra effort to run faster. Unfortunately, in her eagerness, her foot caught on the hem of the long skirt, and she tumbled to the ground. She landed hands out in front of her, and then rolled head over heels on the rock strewn path. She lay still.

Kerim sighed and then, in the pale light, her frightened eyes flickered open. The fear quickly became shame. Japh was leaning over her, pain and worry in his expression.

Tears spilled from her eyes and rolled into her hair. She lay defeated, not even trying to get up from the ground.

'Kerim. Are you hurt?' Japh asked his voice full of concern, not sure how to help.

'I don't think so, not really.' She pushed herself up to a sitting position and quickly wiped away the moisture from her cheeks. The salt water made her palms sting. She looked at them quickly and saw that the skin was grazed. She rubbed her thumbs over the broken skin.

Japh sat next to her, resting on a flattened rock.

'What are you doing out here?' he finally asked.

'Japh please?' She looked pleadingly into his sad brown eyes.

'What's happened? What's wrong?'

'I can't,' she said, 'I'm sorry.'

'Sorry for what?'

'I don't belong here,' she replied hooking her hair behind her ear. 'I have to go.'

'*Have* to go?' Japh had found the true meaning in what she had said. 'You don't have to go. We want you here.' He paused. 'I want you here.'

'I can't.' Her voice shook.

'Again with the *can't*?' Japh's brow furrowed in confusion. 'Why *can't* you?'

There was silence. Kerim rubbed her palms not answering.

'You can't do this! You can't just leave and run away without saying goodbye!'

'I am truly sorry,' she whispered.

'No you're not.' He scowled.

Darkness of night is not darkness to me. I see her run, I see her turn. I tuck the hem of her skirt beneath her feet. I quickly shift threatening rocks before she tumbles, and I break her fall. Everything is done in a moment.

Japh is worried, concerned. But he hurts too. I will observe. I watch closely. Japh is confused right now. He refuses to see it from Kerim's point of view. He is so caught up in what he feels; he has failed to notice her torment.

'Japh, she needs you. Open your eyes and see it, unstop your ears and hear her,' I admonish. 'Selfishness is not a trait you should strive after.'

Japh took a deep breath and exhaled slowly. 'Why are you running away?'

Kerim heard that his voice was quiet and undemanding.

'I need to leave for your sake. Don't you understand?'

'But I thought you liked us?'

Again Kerim rubbed at her palms. It sounded like madness even to her. But there was no other way. 'I do, but that's why I have to leave.'

Japh turned his head. 'Because you like us?'

'Yes.'

'That makes no sense.'

Kerim sighed and another tear rolled down her cheek.

'Look, you're sad about going,' Japh stated as he gently wiped the tear away. 'Something that makes you this sad and doesn't make sense can't be right.'

'But it is right. I have to go.' She looked fearfully again into his sad eyes.

'That's it,' he said, almost triumphant. 'You're scared.' He reached over to take her hand. 'It was you I heard screaming wasn't it? What are you scared of?' He gently brushed his hand across her grazes. 'You know,' he hesitated, 'I'll protect you.'

'But who will protect you?' she asked seriously.

'What do I need protecting from?' He smiled at her softly.

'Don't laugh Japh. He'll come.' Her voice flickered in fear. 'He won't stop until he finds me, and he'll hurt whoever is in his way.'

'We'll be gone, and so will he before that happens.'

Kerim squeezed his hand, urging him to understand. 'Why don't you believe me? Bruja will come after me. He will stop at nothing.'

'I can't let you go Kerim. You are my future.'

'Stop it.'

'I can't believe you feel nothing.'

Kerim blushed at the memory of Noah suggesting they should be married.

'But you don't see it do you?'

'See what?' she asked.

'Ever since I knew about that prophecy there has always been that nagging all my life. Then when my brothers married, well, the pressure intensified didn't it. I've tried to find the right woman; I have been pushed away and spat at by a few. You have no idea how much pressure I have been under, especially as the project is nearly finished.' He smoothed his fingers over her hand. Kerim could not fail to hear what he was saying was real. 'I could do nothing to make it happen. I had given it all up on the morning before I found you.' He made his face serious. 'I know my Dad was too much, but you really are an answer to prayer. My prayer.'

Kerim sat quietly, listening hard to what he said. It seemed only to make this harder. She didn't want to hurt him further. She didn't feel like any answer to prayer that she would want. All she brought with her was danger. But Japh's words softened her.

'Don't you feel the connection between us?' he asked.

'Please don't pressure me,' Kerim said pulling her hand from his.

'You don't feel it?'

Silence filled the air. Japh stared blankly at the ground. How could he make her understand?

'That's not strictly true.' Kerim admitted. 'I do feel something.'

Japh perked up. 'You do?'

'Yes, but I don't want to disappoint you, or lead you to think that I care in a way that I don't.' What do I feel? She asked herself.

'I won't push you.' Japh pulled her hand into his lap again. His hand was warm and his skin rough, but his touch was reassuring. 'I just want you to be safe.' She knew the truth of his words and had to look away. 'Please let me protect you.'

Kerim thought about what it might be like to have Japh protect her. It felt warm. It felt happy. It terrified her.

'I don't want you to be in danger,' she breathed and he shrugged. 'Japh,' she urged, 'I put you in danger.'

'What do you mean?'

She only uttered one word, shaking slightly. 'Bruja.'

'The one who put you in the cage?'

Kerim nodded.

'Why would he come after you?' Japh took the other hand and tried to steady them. 'What he did was wrong, it was evil, but won't he just move onto another victim.' He spat out the last word, hating that Kerim had been that at one time.

'No Japh. He will come after me.'

He clasped her hands tighter. 'You don't know that.'

'I do.' She stifled a sob. 'I heard him recant his desire while I was locked in that cage.' Kerim dropped her head. Was she ready to speak what she heard?

Kerim looked into Japh's face. 'I was pure.' She gripped his hands, desperate for him to listen. 'I was going to be a special sacrifice.' She sighed. 'What he said he would do to me would be a new thing for my village, not only to witness but be a part of. He told me, smirking, enjoying the torment he could see in me. He said I would be under the influence of some herb,' she remembered the bone like fingers caressing the necklace he wore, 'So that I could not fight.' Japh sat motionless. 'He will come after me. I was the significant one who would open up all sorts of evil for him. He wanted that more than anything. You have no idea how wicked this man is.' Kerim tilted his head back so that she could look into his eyes. 'He will stop at nothing Japh.'

Japh looked into the frightened face before him.

'I hate this man. What right has he got to make you feel this way.' But then stated in a soft voice, 'I will not lose you.'

Kerim sat silently.

'You can't leave,' he growled taking her hand in his once more.

'I have to,' she answered shaking her head.

'No, you can't.'

'Tell me why Japh. If there was a way to stay I would.'

That was all he needed.

'You can't go, because if you do,' he said seriously, running his finger from her cheek down to her chin. 'You will die.'

'I will get away from him.'

'He won't kill you.' His voice softened in sorrow. 'The flood will.'

'The flood that will arrive after the promised one comes?' Kerim said, her stomach squirming at the thought that they believed she was that promised one.

'The flood that will be sent to destroy everything,' Japh said quietly, 'Accept those that are in our Ark.'

She sat very still, absorbing what he had so obviously stated.

'But if I stay, you will be in danger.'

'And if you go, you will die.' Japh cupped her delicate face in his rough hand. 'Let me protect you. I'm certain I don't want you to die.'

'But the danger I will put you in...' she stuttered, almost breathless.

'Let me and my brothers deal with that,' he laughed. 'Besides,' and he raised his eyebrows, 'I think I know someone who might have a plan about that anyway.'

'I've hurt your family now though, by running away.'

'They don't know you're gone, and I'm not going to tell them.' He sighed. 'Which reminds me, aren't you tired? Don't you want to sleep?'

'Yes I'm tired,' Kerim admitted.

Japh got to his feet and offered his hand to Kerim. She took it and rose to her feet.

'Ow!' Kerim lurched back and grabbed at her foot.

'What is it? What's wrong?'

'My ankle.' She winced as she tried to put her weight on it.

Before Kerim could object, Japh had swiftly lifted her into his arms.

'What are you doing? Put me down!' she protested weakly, grateful for his support.

'I'm taking you home,' he whispered, 'where you belong.'

Kerim knew there was no use fighting. Japh was strong and fast. She could not escape with a twisted ankle. She put her arms about his neck in the hope it she would make the burden easier for him. How embarrassing, having to be carried. He looked down into her apologetic face and smiled his crooked smile. She felt safe again.

'I knew God would have a plan to make you stay.'

'God may have arranged my injuries,' she smiled shyly, 'but you've made me stay.'

Japh leaned toward her and pressed his cheek against her forehead, lingering for a moment, before looking down into her face.

Kerim's shyness disappeared as they made eye contact.

'I am so glad that you are coming home,' Japh whispered.

She rested her head on his shoulder. It was strange how easy she fell into place. She felt the nudge in her spirit, this did feel like home.

Japh strolled back up the track, triumphant, Kerim firmly in his arms.

The house was silent when they entered. Japh took Kerim straight to his room and laid her gently on the bed. 'Will you be alright now?'

She nodded shifting herself into a sitting position. 'Thank you for everything you've done.'

'No worries. Good night!'

'Good night,' she whispered back as he crept to the door. 'I'll see you in the morning,' she promised.

Japh turned to beam at her. Then shut the door noiselessly and returned to the barn.

9

Build

Kerim awoke having rested well. As she dressed she thought again about the things Japh had said. Her mind tugged at her to leave, but her heart was split. She wanted to be certain that Japh, and his family, would be safe, which would mean leaving them to their peace. She could argue this point very well.

There was a long list of reasons why she should disappear, with their lives intact at the top of that list. But there was a smaller section of her heart, a place that she felt at ease, the part that said she would be safer here with him and his family. But mostly with him. He had made it clear that she would be secure, or at least his intentions were for her survival. She shivered when she remembered that Japh had said that all were doomed to death outside the ark. There appeared to be hope then, if Bruja could be included in that. She had to put her hope there then.

She remembered his touch. That was a very pleasant memory.

Kerim wrapped up her ankle to support it, and the long skirt covered all signs of injury. She was ready outwardly, but anxious about her choice to stay.

The family were enjoying their breakfast when Kerim entered. She was still for a moment as they turned to look at her and greeted her. She smiled briefly and quickly scanned the room for Japh. He wasn't there. Her heartbeat increased and her breathing became shallow.

'Come and have something to eat,' Tabitha said kindly.

No one seemed to notice Kerim's slight worry that he wasn't there.

'Where's Japh?' she asked timidly.

Shem laughed loudly, then stopped abruptly as Helena elbowed him and scowled.

'He's probably sleeping in,' he added still chuckling at Helena's look of disapproval.

Helena passed the bread basket to Kerim.

'Don't mind him,' she said still glaring at Shem, 'He thinks Japh is making a little more effort this morning,' but now with a hint of a smile on her lips. 'I'm sure Japh will be here soon.'

'Is everything alright?' Lellia asked from across the table.

'Fine,' Kerim answered a little too quickly as she pulled apart a section of bread.

The door opened behind her, Kerim spun quickly to see Japh framed there. His hair even more dishevelled than usual. Her heart skipped a beat before returning to a reasonable pace.

'We were just talking about you,' Shem emphasized with a grin.

'Oh really?' Japh replied not rising to the bait.

He crossed the room to stand behind Kerim in four easy strides, and bent low to speak to her.

'Is it alright to get some things from my room?' he asked quietly.

'Sure,' she said blushing at his attention.

Shem's laugh was cut short again by another elbow in the ribs from Helena.

'Come on you!' Helena said grabbing Shem's arm. 'We've got work to do.'

Kerim watched Japh go into his room, he seemed to take a deep breath as he entered. She hoped he would not mind that she had made the bed and tidied away a few things.

When he returned, he wore a fresh tunic and his hair was flattened a little.

'It smells of you in there.'

'Sorry,' Kerim replied looking horrified.

'Oh no, don't be sorry. It's a good smell.'

Kerim nervously tucked a loose strand of hair behind her ear and smiled. Japh looked a little pink as he took the open seat beside Kerim. Both relaxed in each other's presence, unaware that they had tensed in the minutes apart.

'Hmm,' Lellia mumbled noticing the new couple.

'What?' Ham asked worried about his wife.

'Nothing,' she answered happily. 'I think we have work to do too.'

The family set their hands to the jobs still complete at the ark, just as Noah had arranged. Lellia took charge of sorting the seeds and finally securing them in manageable baskets. She supervised the packing of them into larger crates which she insulated with straw. Ham filled an extra crate with rich soil; carting the soil up to the living area was backbreaking but satisfying. He sealed the crate shut. Noah and Ham carried and loaded the majority of the furniture, while Tabitha carried the more fragile items inside.

The thick walled dwelling was now nearly bare; only the essentials were left ready to pack. Lellia dug up several plants and transplanted them from the farm garden, into baskets, and sat them neatly outside the door.

Japh and Kerim had worked hard. Japh kept his word and his family were not aware of what had happened the night before.

They laboured harmoniously together. When they were alone and none of the others could overhear, he asked how her ankle was.

'It's fine,' Kerim replied, 'Sorry about that.'

'About hurting your foot?'

'No!' she giggled. 'About last night,' she said seriously. 'What you said made a lot of sense.'

Japh looked at Kerim. She was being cryptic and she was sure he was trying to gauge whether she really meant it. 'If you have any worries, you know you can talk to me.' Then he added, as he seemed unsure of himself. 'Don't you?'

'Yes.' She smiled at his nervous expression. 'I know.'

They got back to work with enthusiasm. The latches were all finished, as were all the partitioning walls and ramps. Kerim had suggested fixing lengths of rope along the walls and down the ramps to help steadiness. She had suggested many projects, some of which she took a large part in completing. Japh had not dismissed them but had thought them worthy ideas, and seemed glad to have her nearby.

She hoped Japh would find her to be an inspired woman, yet not afraid of working hard. The more time she spent with him, the more compassionate she discovered he was, and the more she wanted to be with him. She didn't want to consider that she might have to leave again and fall to the fate of the all the rest.

Later that morning, as they measured rope for the lowest deck, Kerim again raised her concerns. 'Japh?'

'Hmm,' he acknowledged engrossed in the knot he was tying.

'Do you really believe all that your father says?'

He straightened up and could not fail to see the doubt in her eyes. 'You have seen heavenly beings Kerim; surely you can see what he said is true.'

'But, well,' she hesitated, 'it's just that trouble seems to follow me.'

'Not where we are going.' Japh was confident as he tried to reassure her.

'But this structure, this ark, I mean, will it really save you?'

'Us Kerim, and yes it will.' He looked down at her. She stood eyes wide, like a small child asking for reassurance. 'Look, God has given us the plans for this thing and we have followed them exactly, so do you really believe it will fail?' Kerim found it difficult to be convinced. Japh tried a different approach. 'God bought you from your village to be here. He has plans for our future. He wants you to place your hope in him.'

'I want to.' Kerim felt ashamed.

'But?'

'Japh, you've lived with this all your life,' she paused, unable to say exactly what she wanted. He deserved safety, it was his ark. She would only lead Bruja to him and his family, and all sorts of evil would follow. She wanted to know why she should be chosen and why Japh's family had so readily accepted that fact. Instead she said feebly, 'I've only just arrived.'

'But God has had this planned all your life.'

'Japh that is easy to say, but somewhat harder to come to terms with.'

'I know,' Japh said quietly as he returned to his knot, but Kerim did not believe him. How could he know what she felt? Where had he really been when the real world out there was so different, so damaged? He could not know as she did, his life was far too sheltered. He had a family that cared about each other, that looked after one another. That wasn't real, not in her world.

People from her world took what they wanted, no matter who they hurt. They would pass it off as the best thing to do, well, best for them anyway. People never really went outside of themselves to think of what was best for another person. Even her own father had done that. Yes, he had protected her, but what was his motivation? Love? Yes, mostly. But he was selfish too. Was it love that let her brother go off into that evil world without a word of discipline? No. Even in her father, she saw that he acted out of self-preservation. He wanted to stay friends with her brother, rather than be his father. If only her mother had lived. She had managed the difficult combination better.

Japh had a life that was so different. He was part of a family— a family that if she was honest with herself, she was envious of. Noah took the lead, Tabitha helped him. Then Ham and Shem had also modelled this with their wives. Kerim couldn't fail to see the amazing design of that kind of family structure. Respect given to all.

How could she be destined for such a life? How could she possibly fit into something so alien to her? It was uncomfortable to comprehend. She would be a misfit, this she knew, but it still drew her in. She longed for it.

She remembered the touch of Japh's fingers on her face the previous night, to wipe away a tear. She reached up to her cheek to caress the spot. If she was going to be honest, she longed for that kind of affection too.

10

Protection

The heat of the day had passed and the evening was cool. The family had retreated indoors for the evening meal. The near empty room echoed. Only the very large items of furniture were still in place.

'It was good to see that the pitch dried even after the heavy dew this morning,' Noah said to Shem as they washed the grime from their hands before sitting down to eat.

'I thought Ham had applied it to too thickly.' Shem patted him on the shoulder. 'Good call!'

Ham smiled at the compliment before adding his own encouragement. 'Those ropes were a great idea Kerim.' She nodded.

Noah beamed with pride. 'I think we've all worked hard today.'

'Is that why I am so tired?' Lellia yawned. 'I think we'll turn in early tonight.'

'First we must eat. Who would like to bless the food?' Noah directed his attention to Ham.

'Thank you O God, for a productive day, and this mouth watering food. We ask again for safety tomorrow and deep sleep tonight as we rest. Amen.'

The brothers laughed as they quickly filled their plates with bread, potato salad, a selection of roasted vegetables and stuffed peppers. It was good!

When the meal was finished and everything cleaned and cleared away, Lellia said good night and went off to bed. Ham followed soon after. Everyone else seemed tired and peaceful as they sat around the fire. Noah and Tabitha were chatting quietly on the far side of the room, giving Japh ample room to recline beside the fire. Kerim felt relaxed sitting alongside him. He looked very content and carefree, something she wished she had known back at her home.

Helena, was watching the two and nudged Shem in the ribs. 'Kerim,' Shem suddenly asked, 'Do you like our country?'

'Erm, yes,' she stuttered. Shem hadn't really spoken to her before tonight. 'It's lovely.'

'Lovely?' He laughed. Japh scowled at him. 'It's not exactly that. I see it as rugged and impressive. You should have seen it when the forests were still standing. Of course, I didn't see it when all the forests were standing because father had already started the work before I was born. But it was definitely impressive back then.'

Kerim smiled. Shem was a character, the most assertive of the family.

'What about you, where you are from?' Helena asked more kindly than her husband.

'I was raised in the valley, beyond the mountains of the south.'

Helena nodded. 'Do you think you'll stay here?'

Kerim shrugged and suddenly didn't feel quite so relaxed. She looked down at her hands in her lap. She clasped them anxiously.

'Well, you will be very welcome if you do decide to stay,' Helena said quickly.

Japh stood to his feet, brushing off the morsels of hay from the cushions. He extended his hand to Kerim. 'Would you like to go for a walk?'

She took his arm and rose to his side. 'Sounds perfect.'

The night air was cool and refreshing compared to the questions Helena hurled at her. Why she let such innocent questions make her feel confined, she did not know. But the scent of mint and lavender lightened her mood.

Japh led them down a path toward the rocks where they first met. The sound of chirping insects filled the air.

'I'm sorry about Shem and Helena,' Japh said crossly. 'Sometimes I think that they think that they rule the place.'

'That's not very kind.'

'Oh come on! You must have noticed it.' Kerim frowned at his harsh words. 'Shem always bosses Ham about. And Helena can be a bit rude too.'

'Shem is older than you" Kerim replied. 'I expect he feels some responsibility in your decisions.' She strolled on ahead of him. 'And Helena, well she only says as she sees. I think that can be a good thing.'

Japh was silent. His steps slowed. 'You're right,' Japh sighed, 'It was unkind. I shouldn't have said it. They're not that bad. I suppose I just want to have something that is my own without them interfering.'

They walked on wandering down the trodden path. 'I wish my brother was more like Shem,' Kerim said as she tightened the shawl about her shoulders.

They were approaching the flower fields; she was certain of it. The scent was strong and sweet. She placed her hand in Japh's. 'Is that why you asked me for this walk?'

Japh glanced her way. 'Because of them? Partly! I couldn't bear to hear you answer unfavourably.'

'I was not bothered by their insinuation. I welcome their feelings about who I am and if I belong.' Her voice trailed off. 'It's just that I started to remember my home and my father. I wish I could know if he was alright.'

Japh squeezed her hand. 'I wish you could too. I don't want you to be sad.' His energy rose. 'It's strange, but I somehow think he is being protected. I know it doesn't seem possible, but I just have this feeling, you know?'

'I hope you are right.'

'We are getting off the point though Japh,' Kerim said, 'Why do you think I need protecting from your family?'

'Pardon?'

'Should I be scared of them?'

'No,' he said quickly. 'Well, I don't know. Are you scared of them?'

'Not at all. You have a lovely family. You don't know how blessed you are.'

He laughed sarcastically.

'I like them!' she defended herself.

'They don't freak you out?'

She dropped his hand. 'Really Japh, it won't be them that scares me away.'

He walked closer beside her. 'I'm sorry.' Then carefully wrapped his arm about her waist. She looked up at him and smiled girlishly. Japh shortened his stride to match hers. He sighed happily.

Kerim was surprised by his touch. He was gentle with her. She thought she understood his reason for stepping in regarding his family. She felt comforted by his fierce protective nature. She felt safe with him.

'Can I ask the same question that Helena asked then?' Japh said tentatively.

'And what is that?' teased Kerim.

'Will you stay?' he asked.

'I've not decided yet.'

'Is there anything I can do to help you decide?' Japh said, then added. 'I do want you to stay.'

'You are doing a very good job right now.'

They had made it to the rocks. They walked around the side until they were sheltered from the breeze and sat down. Japh's back was against the hard stone, but Kerim was snuggled up against him. He didn't seem to mind. The dim light that filtered through the clouds, took the colour from the surroundings. Everything was tinged with grey.

'I could believe almost anything of this land of yours,' Kerim said dreamily.

'You seem happy here.'

'I am.' She could tell that he was satisfied with her answer. Somehow, being back in the place where they had first met bought back the realisation that she should be fearful. But she wasn't, at least not nearly as much she thought she would be. Japh was a safe person and his family were ready to accept her. But Bruja was certain to come after her. She shivered at that thought.

11

Every Kind

Kerim had only been working with the family for two days when the first animals arrived. They came in pairs, one male and one female. Familiar ones arrived at first. But after a while unusual and weird species came wandering into the clearing.

The family already had a few animals that lived with them. The sheep and goats were led to the top floor, the area next to the family space, and were settled into their stalls by Kerim. The farm cats were already inside, they had found the warmest spots to curl up in weeks ago. The vessel was teeming with new arrivals. Rabbits, foxes, cougars, parrots and monkeys, camels, crickets and frogs; they all needed to be housed.

The longer they waited the bigger the task appeared. Now a whole host of unusual creatures arrived each hour. Some were covered with scales while others had smooth soft skin patched with assorted pigments. The ones covered in fur came in many patterns. The design and beauty of their fur was an awesome sight. The largest had tough hides, but were just as gentle as their smaller counterparts. There were two of each kind, one male and one female, except for those that were ritually clean— the goats, deer and sheep, then there were seven.

The animals were calm and seemed to know exactly where to wait. Shem and Helena took charge in placing the animals in their stalls, holes and dark corners. The largest were given space at the lowest part of the structure, as taking them up the ramp proved difficult; middle sized ones were given stalls above the hold, while the mass of insects were housed near the top. Gaps and holes were filled by what seemed an endless flow of small creatures. As each animal was settled, they became quiet and still.

Kerim stood by as Helena carried a pair colourful lizards, while the two tan rodents she was guiding dashed about her feet, standing on their hind legs to peek at their surroundings.

'Are you alright?' she asked seeing Kerim's wary glace at the lizards. 'They will not hurt you!' Helena said not unkindly.

'I'm fine.'

'You sure?' Helena asked as she allowed the lizards to walk slowly from her arm onto a thick branch wedged into the corner of a rapidly filling pen.

'Yes,' she replied quietly.

'You seem a little distant today.' The lizards were cuddled up, clinging tightly to the branch and peered at the women, both of them at the same time as their eyes swivelled in opposite directions. She smiled at the eccentricity of their design. 'There's nothing bothering you?' She pulled the headdress from her head, tidied her sandy hair and looked at Kerim.

'No, not really.'

'Don't you think this is amazing?' Helena stuffed handfuls of hay into a series of small boxes that lined the walls of the pen. 'I mean, all these animals, where are they coming from?'

Kerim looked about her. The peeking rodents jumped into the hay filled box and disappeared. She had no idea where these exotic creatures had come from. Nowhere near here, of that she was certain. 'Why do you think they have all come? How did they know how to get here?' Helena giggled to herself. 'I guess God has it all worked out.'

'Yes, I guess,' Kerim said fastening the latch to the pen.

'Just look at them. They are so funny. Have you seen that huge animal below? Why would it need such a long nose?' Helena shook her head in amazement.

'Oh yes, I've seen it.'

'When it boarded, the male was touching everything. It even blew dust into Japh's hair with it.'

Kerim laughed. 'I was wondering how he got so grimy earlier. No wonder he wouldn't say.'

'How about the spotted ones with the extended necks.' Helena drew the latch on the next pen.

'I saw how they were stripping the twisted saplings out in the clearing" Kerim said nodding. 'Their necks are useful for reaching the leaves that others couldn't reach.'

'Don't you think it is amazing that Noah knew exactly how big to make this building?

'He didn't know,' Kerim corrected. 'God told him.'

'Yes. God did tell him!' Helena smiled triumphantly. 'I think we are safe in God's hands, don't you?'

'Yes.' At last Kerim smiled. Yes, she could trust that everything was taken care of.

'Are you sure you are alright? You seem,' Helena paused as if to take in Kerim's appearance, 'I don't know, just little distant.'

'Maybe.' Kerim was shocked at how Helena picked that up. Lellia seemed to be the more sensitive of the two women. Together they walked silently down the ramp.

Kerim noted how Helena didn't push the issue and this gave her confidence. Maybe Helena was the right one to ask. Her answer would be blunt, but it would be truthful.

'Do you think I'm the right one for Japh?' she suddenly blurted out.

Helena stopped in mid stride and leaned over to grab hold of Kerim's hand.

'Of course,' she said with a laugh.

Kerim froze. Was Helena laughing at her?

'What?' Helena asked seeing the hurt in Kerim's face.

'Why are you laughing at me?'

'I wasn't laughing at you.' Helena chuckled again. 'I just can't get over fact that you still don't see it.'

'But you are still laughing at me.'

'No!' Helena tried hard to keep her face straight. 'I guess I've seen Japh go through so much. I've seen him try to find himself a ...' Helena thought about her use of word, 'girl. And seen that fail miserably!' She took Kerim's hand in both of hers. 'You have no idea how transformed he is.'

'What do you mean?'

'He smiles.' Helena seemed to think that was the only answer required. 'He smiles a lot.'

'Yes ... and?'

'Look, I've seen him, worked with him, and been part of his life for quite a while. I've not seen him this happy. Ever.'

'Ever?'

'You do that.' Helena patted Kerim's hand. 'So,' she said with a little laugh, 'I've no doubt that you are perfect for him.'

Kerim looked away and let her hand drop from Helena's. She started to walk again.

'I guess,' Helena began and Kerim turned responsively toward her. 'The question is though; do you know you are perfect for him?'

Hundreds of figures dressed in simple clothes, with staffs in their hands and packs on their backs, are guiding the animals towards the vessel constructed by man but designed by the Creator. Large beings, dressed for war, encouraging the smallest hopping, scurrying, creeping and crawling creatures towards the entrance, alongside what would naturally have been a predator. All moving on in peace with one another.

It has been a long time since I saw so many different kinds of animal in one place. They filed past a human then too. The memory saddens me. Yet here we are again.

I check each creature as it passes, talking animatedly to each being, thanking them for their work thus far and stating any new orders.

'Champion, it is good to see you.'

'Thank you.' Champion booms in his deep African voice. 'I have some field mice and long eared bats for you. Oh, and a couple of woodworm. Where would you like them?'

'The mice have some warm boxes along with all the other rodents. The bats can be housed there too. As for the wood worm well,' I laugh and the melodic sound carries into the ark, 'they need to be kept away from the main structure! There are a number of insects that have an appetite for timber. A special enclosure has been set up for them with the other insects.'

'Great.' Champion moves on.

'Just one more thing.'

'Yes Hope.'

'Could you take my charges with you?' I beckon with my hand to the two orange butterflies. They flutter from their resting place, the solitary clump of flowers, the only clump left un-nibbled, and float above Champion's head.

'Of course. I'm glad to see we each had charges that we could handle!'

'All need to report back here by dusk.' I tell him, playfully ignoring his last remark.

'No worries,' he booms and carefully creeps up the ramp persuading the tiny creatures before him.

My friend stands with me. Together we laugh at the spectacle before us. Mighty warriors engaged in this unusual preparation for battle.

'Love, will you keep watch over the others and bring back to us a warning when they approach.'

'Of course Hope,' he replies.

'Just one more thing. Remain unseen.'

'I am on my way.' In a flash of golden light he is gone.

I remain at my post. Each creature is guided to its place, and its guardian stands over them, whispering to each animal and each other. All is safe. All is quiet. All is calm.

Bruja dripped with sweat. It ran down his forehead, through his eyebrows and into his eyes, making them sting. He did not slacken his pace. He knew that he had to keep up with the possessed creature lumbering through the thick vegetation. It tasted the air, following the trail the girl had set. With each step, although it brought agony, it had the irresistible hunger for power attached. As he pushed aside the low branches, his fingers were once again drawn to the claw tied about his neck; he continued to caress it as he stumbled on.

The pack on Ishmillimech's back grew heavier with each passing moment. He struggled to keep up with his master, gradually dropping behind the main group. He cursed under his breath at the speed this creature travelled. If it could move so fast, maybe it should be the one to carry all Bruja's things. Deep in his heart though, he was glad to be playing such a vital role. After all, nothing could take place until he arrived. His self importance pushed him on.

12

Wife

The screaming preceded them. Bruja was drenched in sweat; his long hair clung to his forehead. His normally pale skin was blotchy and red from the exertion of his exercise, but he had not allowed the beast to travel too far ahead. Many others behind him complained of tiredness but continued to keep up their pace. Each and every one of them felt an indescribable excitement rising inside them.

The first scream was followed closely by others. The beast had entered the village, and those ahead had encountered it. It rose to its hind legs, flicking its forked tongue and sniffing the air. The scent of the girl was near, but maybe not in this place. There was something about this place that confused it, another presence in the air, a presence that threatened, but would not attack. Not yet.

The track had cleared and doorways were being blocked by the scared inhabitants inside. Down at the far end of the village a small gathering of men stood behind a large fire, brandishing clubs, axes and torches.

Bruja came panting up the track towards the beast, and stopped a few steps behind it. Seeing the men about to attack, he shouted out to them. 'I wish to speak to the head of your tribe. Show yourself.'

Tarlin, the village leader, desired to be anyone but leader at that moment. He had never been invaded by others before, and was shaking at the sight of the creature between himself and the one that spoke. He breathed deeply and stepped forward with as much confidence he could muster.

'I am here.' His voice fighting to be strong. 'What is it you want?'

Bruja walked casually around the side of the creature, his fingers again reaching for the claw about his neck, while the other hand pushed his hair from his face.

'Let us hope you will be able to give us what we want,' he threatened, indicating towards the beast, 'or we will all be sorry for your loss.'

The mob behind him laughed crudely, while many fearful villagers cowered inside their huts and looked to Tarlin to offer what was needed.

'Well,' Tarlin began, 'we have a few supplies. They might help on your continuing journey.'

'Journey? Yes, we could do with rest and food, but that was not our prime reason for intruding upon you so!' There was no apology in his voice, and he was not going to leave with such meagre pickings. 'We are hungry and thirsty now.'

'Get some wine and food out here!' Tarlin ordered his wives. Several of the women ran in various directions. 'Please, be our guests and sit for a while before you must be on your way.' Tarlin hoped these invaders would eat and leave his village intact.

'We will move when we are good and ready,' asserted Bruja as food and wine was handed round by the nervous women.

Tarlin waited until his wives were a good distance away before he spoke again. 'What is it you want from us?'

'A girl,' Bruja declared. Behind him, the men stuffed bread and cheese into their mouths, guzzling down every bit wine. He had failed to eat his share, which he left at the feet of the creature. It sniffed at the food but would not eat. Instead it lapped up the liquid, looking round eagerly for any more.

Tarlin was shocked by the spectacle but was unable to take his gaze off the beast. The creature, he believed would of course only eat meat, and without a full belly it could very easily attack and kill. He whispered to a woman nearby, to fetch meat for the beast. She appeared quickly with a squawking chicken held firmly in her hands, and handed it to Tarlin.

Taking the offering he walked a little closer to the creature. Its red eyes were fixed on the chicken. He threw it into the air, and the creature caught it in its mouth, crushing it between its teeth with a series of cracks. The taste of meat sent a spine chilling quiver over the scales, and its eyes flared brighter at the taste of blood.

'You want a girl? Any particular type?' Tarlin asked hoping that there would be one in the village that would suit such a request.

'You want to offer me one of your girls?' Bruja smiled.

'Is that not what you wanted?' Tarlin asked with a degree of hopefulness.

'It was not my intention,' he gawked at one of Tarlin's own young dark haired wives who was transfixed by fear, 'But I'm sure we could come to some arrangement.' The laugh that followed was wicked. Bruja felt immense power over this village. 'I am, however, looking for a particular girl.' He focussed again on Tarlin, 'She fled a short time ago and we believe she came this way.'

'And if she did, and I was able to help, what is your offer?'

Bruja sneered, 'Your life and those of your people.'

Tarlin's confidence was gone in a flash. 'There was a girl, but she didn't come to us. She preferred the company of the family over the hill and near the forest. She arrived a few days ago and I believe she may still be there.'

'Show me,' he commanded.

Tarlin looked around and spotted a scruffy haired youth. 'You!' he said summoning the boy to him. 'You take them up there.' The colour in the boy's cheeks disappeared quickly as he stared in shock.

' You don't seem to understand.' Bruja smiled at Tarlin showing his threatening row of pointed teeth. 'You show me,' he instructed.

Tarlin reluctantly did as he was told. He had hoped that the offered information would have given him freedom. Still, at least he had the chance of seeing this intruder made a fool of at the top of the hill.

I stand silently behind the silver haired man inspecting the far side of the structure. He is impressed at his family's hard work. They have all worked so tirelessly for such a long time and now it is completed. He pulls on a small crate door to close it as the two chinchillas snuggle into the hay tucked away in the corner. They close their eyes and are asleep. He sighs at the wonder of it all and turns.

His eyes widen as he sees me. I am dressed in a long white robe. Not my full battle attire. This is not a time to warn him: after all, I come with a good message.

'It is nearly time,' I say to him in a gentle voice. I can see the shock on his face. It almost makes me laugh. Shock is a reasonable human response, I know that.

'Everything is done?' he stutters.

'Not quite.' I allow myself to smile at his courage, although I do see him quaking in shimmers of indigo, the right kind of fear for this moment. 'All the animals are now here. But there is the matter of your son.'

'What matter would that be?' he asks with a tinge of acidic green. He worries.

'He is to be married before you are sealed in.'

'That hasn't happened yet,' Noah says, 'But he has met someone.'

'Yes,' I smile a little. 'I know.'

Noah is certain she is the one now, his canary yellow colours are glowing brightly. Before, I think he felt that Kerim was some kind of test. He is happy now that he can see the completion of his task.

'I will go and find them,' Noah says, 'I know they are ready.'

He is so eager to do the will of the Creator. This is something that he should not be in control of. 'No, he will come to you.' My gentle voice contains authority. 'The moment they are wed, the seal will be made.'

Tarlin was forced to march before the beast which drooled as its tongue flickered in and out, occasionally catching the edge of his jacket or arm. Tarlin glanced back in horror as he stepped up his pace; this was truly a daytime nightmare. Bruja cackled at the fear.

Tarlin, the beast, Bruja and his band of men took the path out of the village and then headed up the hill towards the forest. The people left behind heaved a sigh of relief.

The hill was steep. Tarlin panted, his substantial frame having not worked this hard in years, but he did not let the slope defeat him, the fear of the beast kept on pushing from behind. The climb led to an outcrop of rocks and to some sweet smelling fields, the beauty of which was wasted on this crowd. They trampled through the red flowers, no longer keeping to the path. Tarlin was eager to get them to their destination.

He led Bruja and the mob round the bend, and past a large mud clad barn. The low laying buildings stood before them. 'She went here,' Tarlin wheezed, stepping aside.

The beast pushed past, brushing him with its scales. The beast had caught a strong scent, it ran from one place to another, licking the ground and flashing its red eyes in all directions. It was energised, and Bruja was feeling that same energy seeping through his body like some gas feeding his muscles and brain.

Bruja saw the central hut had been extended with two or three smaller additions affixed to it by a fence and thatched canopy. The central hut would be the first point of attack.

The door was shut, and there was no movement by the small windows. 'Bring her to me!' Bruja shouted, and the men fell over each other in their desperation to do his bidding. They ran at the door, which collapsed under their weight.

Bruja stood next to the beast starring into the opened hut. Tarlin retreated. He was not sure that he was finished with yet.

A shiver went down Kerim's spine.

'Are you alright?' Japh asked, catching hold of her under her arms, as her footing slipped on the ramp.

'Yes ... I think so.'

Kerim looked pale. Japh took her by the hand and began to lead her up to the top floor where the family were rearranging and organising the furniture from their home. She followed the gentle guiding, but found it difficult to put aside her uneasy feeling.

'I wanted to ask you something.'

'Yes.' Kerim did her best to turn her attention to Japh. 'What's that then?'

'You are coming with us aren't you?'

'I had hoped to. Are you asking then?' she teased with a straight face.

'Yes, that goes without question!'

Kerim enjoyed his look of shock. Fancy having not asked her before, or at least checked what she had intended to do.

'Great. I'll come then.' Kerim smiled and walked on thinking that was it. 'I just can't shake this odd feeling,' she muttered.

'That wasn't what I wanted to ask you,' he said quickly, his cheeks flushing with colour.

'Oh! I wasn't fishing for an invitation,' Kerim teased, tucking her hair behind her ear.

'I know. I just thought you'd come with us anyway.' Japh took a sharp intake of breath. 'I wanted to ask you something else.'

A shudder went down Kerim's spine. 'Is it cold in here? I feel cold.' She thought quickly, but no it wasn't that she was cold, it was something else. She glanced at her body. 'I'm shivering. But on the inside.'

Japh loosened his clothing from round his neck. 'It isn't cold. It's rather hot actually.'

He turned, gripped her hand and halted. She stood and looked up at him unaware of the reason he had stopped. He looked into her green eyes. He looked at her as if he had not noticed, until now, that her eyes were flecked with differing shades and intensity of green, or that the freckles swept slowly up her cheeks, or her skin looked soft and smooth.

She noticed him catch his breath and refocus. 'I know we don't know each other that well, but we'll have plenty of time for that. You bring out the best in me, you make me smile, and you are very beautiful.' It was Kerim's turn to blush. 'I can provide for you a home and protection. I think God bought you here to me.'

He paused and took a sharp intake of breath and gazed almost fearfully into her striking eyes. Kerim held her breath.

'I want to be your family Kerim. Will you be my wife?'

The sound of her name when he spoke it made her smile. Her eyes widened and her thoughts of uneasiness banished.

The shaking stopped. 'Japh?'

'Kerim, please say yes. I love you.' She could hear the begging tone. Why would he need to beg?

She stood still and silent for what felt was an eternity. 'I wasn't expecting that!'

Japh worried. 'That didn't come out the way I had planned it. I'm sorry.' He began to doubt and in turn started to pace. 'I haven't convinced you that I love you. Why would you say yes to something based on practicality?'

Then Kerim began to smile. 'Japh! I think it's a great idea. We should be married. I think that is what God had planned from the beginning.'

Japh laughed out loud. Relief spreading across his face. 'Excellent!'

He raised her hand and rubbed it across his lips, then gently kissed it. He couldn't help but smile. He felt like she was the most beautiful woman he had ever, and would ever see, and she had agreed to be his. It seemed impossible. Amazing!

'All the love I have felt burning inside from the moment I saw your scared little face, I am now free to shower you with!' He took both her hands and looked at them carefully. 'You are so soft and warm. And look at these blisters from hard work you have done here.' Japh touched them tenderly along with the scars from her previous life. He bought them close and kissed each one tenderly. 'Now I can protect you properly.

'I love you!' he whispered. And he kissed each hurt again. His gaze lifted from her hands to her face.

Kerim stood with tears flowing down her cheeks.

'What? What have I done?' With his free hand he tenderly wiped away the tears, but they just kept flowing. 'Kerim, please?' he said cupping her delicate face in his hand. 'What have I done?'

'Everything,' she sobbed quietly.

Japh was confused. Kerim saw the hurt in his eyes. How could she take it that way? She didn't want him to hurt.

'You have rescued me.' She smiled through the sobbing.

'No Kerim,' Japh raised his other hand to hold her face. 'You have rescued me.'

'I don't know how you can love me.' Kerim dropped her gaze away from his. But he held her there gently and firmly.

'It's very easy!' Japh said seriously. Then smiled her favourite crooked smile. He felt no need for an explanation. It was, after all, obvious to him. Kerim was still a little unsure, but left that unanswered.

The couple began the slow walk up to the family quarters hand in hand. Kerim seemed in a daze. She knew that this was right, it had been planned but she still felt lost and out of control.

They had reached the lowest ramp when the boys came bustling past.

'Father thinks that we have all the assigned animals inside,' Ham called over his shoulder.

'Give us a hand with these doors Japh,' Shem added.

'Hang on, more are coming!'

'Well hurry them along!'

Ham picked up a rich amber coloured shelled creature in each hand, and led the two hares behind them up the ramp.

'And they got back in time!' he laughed.

Japh reluctantly let go of Kerim. They pushed away the rocks holding the heavy doors open and pulled them shut. They closed with a sharp thud, as the wind outside the vessel caught them. Not a chink of light penetrated the passage. Together they placed the long plank that held the doors shut, into its holdings.

Ham and Shem walked on ahead laughing with each other, a trimmed oil lamp giving them light.

Ham tucked the two tortoises and hares into the hay of a nearly full but quiet stall.

Japh took Kerim's hand once more and rushed to keep up with the jostling point of light ahead.

'Well you are definitely stuck with me now!' Kerim said with a rather shy and worried smile.

'I wouldn't have it any other way,' stated Japh confidently.

'What's that brother dear?' Shem said turning. He smirked at his little brother holding Kerim's hand.

'I wasn't talking to you,' Japh said, 'But now that you asked; there is something you should know.'

'Really! Enlighten me!'

'Kerim and I are going to be married.'

Wow!' Shem laughed, 'That has enlightened me!'

'Congratulations Japh!' Ham said striding down the ramp to him and clapping him on the back. 'It will be lovely to have you as part of the family Kerim.' He nodded.

Kerim giggled nervously.

'Shem, I don't want to hear any rubbish from you.'

'Well thanks for the confidence!' Shem muttered. 'But I actually think it's great.' He began to smile again. 'Helena will be pleased. She was wondering when you would get round to asking!'

Ham, Shem Japh and Kerim entered the well lit family room.

'Good I'm glad you are here.'

'Father I have some news!'

'You do.' The silver haired one smiled.

'Kerim has agreed to become my wife.'

Helena and Lellia jumped from their chairs and hugged the couple. Everyone, it appeared was so happy.

'No time like the present,' Noah said. 'Japh, take Kerim's hand.' He did so.

'What? You're going to marry us right now?' Kerim asked.

'Why not?' Japh replied squeezing her hand.

'Well ...' she hesitated. 'I don't look the part.'

Lellia shook her head. 'A bride deserves to look her best.' She ran over to the soil filled toughs and quickly picked a handful of sweet pea flowers. She came back to Kerim and starting threading them into her hair.

'Now you look the part,' she whispered then she kissed her cheek.

'Alright,' Kerim said smiling in thanks to Lellia. Then turning to Japh. 'Let's do it!'

Helena pulled the embroidered sash from her hair and handed it to Noah.

'Thank you Helena. That will do very nicely,' Noah said as he wrapped it around Japh and Kerim's clasped hands.

'Do you Japheth take this woman to be your wife; to love her and cherish her, to treat her with kindness and consideration, to lead her and show her the unconditional love God has?'

'Yes father I will.'

'Do you Kerim take this man to be your husband; to love him and obey him, to give him respect and treat him with kindness and consideration, to follow his leading where ever it may take you?'

'Yes, I will,' Kerim replied her eyes flickered to the ground then back up to meet Japh's face. Why shouldn't she? Japh was a good man and he would look after her. She had to trust her God.

'Let the blessings of God pour over what God has bought together.' He raised their linked hands so that they could all see the union. 'Excellent! May God bless your union.' He hugged his son and his new daughter in law.

Japh gazed at his wife. She was truly radiant, a beauty far beyond all other women. She was his.

Kerim saw his intense gaze. She caught her breath; no one had ever looked at her that way before. His love was accepting and gentle, yet she saw that he desired her. It was both frightening and delightful. Suddenly she felt a wave of guilt. Did she love him that way? Could she really return what he was ever so willing to give to her? He was her friend, her best friend. She felt certain of that love for him. But his gaze was adoring and passionate. She gulped. How could she possibly live up to that?

Japh bent to kiss his wife tenderly, her soft mouth like sweetness to him.

Kerim felt the gentleness of his lips. He was more than a friend; she could feel it in her own response to his kiss. What could be better than to marry your best friend? How could she feel his love and not return it? She was surprised to feel she was able to return his affection. The kiss was over before she was ready for it to stop. She was disappointed that it hadn't lingered, but something had interrupted that sweet moment.

The sound of a strong wind lashed against the outside of the structure. Everyone turned startled. Something spattered over the wooden exterior, and then the noise was gone as soon as it had started.

'God of all,' Noah prayed when the room was silent once again and their focus had returned. 'Keep this couple as strong as a three stranded cord with you at their centre.' Then he added, 'Remember your promise to us. Do not forget us in the destruction to come. Amen.'

'It is done!' I shout and celebrate.

The multitude around cheer and dance. Music and melody came out of their laughter. As they celebrate their appearances change from peasant, farmer and shepherd to radiant beings clothed in garments of purest white.

A strong wind blows across the clearing, lifting the debris from the ground and twisting it in swirls of leaf, dust and vegetation. It circles the vessel, setting a whisper among the angels and disappears.

'We have been given instruction to seal them inside.'

The robed ones begin to circle the vessel, I am at the head. We travel at ever increasing speed, rising from the ground and surrounding it with a blur of light. In our flight, we seal over the closed door, and over the pitched timber walls blocking all the tiny gaps. It is now watertight. The safest place on earth. The only safe place on earth.

Slowing and landing gently on the ground, we gather together to await further instructions.

'What are we to do now?' Champion asks, eager for more work.

At that moment a flash of light fills the centre of our throng. A deep voice rings out before the one that spoke appears. My friend is coming to join us.

'The others are coming for them. We are to be ready.' The golden long sword, raised and ready in the firm grip of my towering friend.

'Station yourselves around the chosen ones,' I command. 'We will be ready for the attack.'

I see the others quickly move to their posts their swords unsheathed, bows at the ready and their faces full of vigilance.

'And by the way,' I add with confidence, 'we will be victorious.'

13

Droplet

The majority of the host are stationed here with me, but there are others set about their tasks. Time is out.

At the foot of the volcano, near Kerim's home, there is utter confusion. I watch it unfold.

'We can't wait any longer!' shouts one woman. Men and women are urged on by the creature that she carries. 'That mountain demands it of us.'

The oldest man is gazing at her barely covered body. 'What would you have us do? Bruja will return soon, we must sit it out.'

'You are a fool Julio, to believe that he is coming back. He took all the best with him. He has only gone off to another place to start again. He knew that without a sacrifice we were all dead.'

Steam and smoke have been rising from atop the mountain for quite some time. The town below understands so little of it, they had looked to Bruja for the interpretation. He is now gone on his search for their run away sacrifice. The mountain has taken to shaking a little and the people are concerned. One of their so called wiser members had said that it was because the mountain had not tasted the sacrifice that Bruja had promised. Behind closed doors all the people now talked of performing a sacrifice without his help if he did not return soon.

'What shall be done?' Julio asks in a rather weak voice, now looking more like a stooped old man after contemplating the mountain with fear.

'We should make our own sacrifice. One that would out do anything that Bruja could have ever done,' said the woman in the group smoothing her eyebrow with her finger tip. She smiles. 'Our offering should be made from our own flesh and blood.'

'Are you saying we should sacrifice ourselves?' Julio asks, shocked.

'Not quite.' She pauses. 'The innocents should be sacrificed. The children.' There is a gasp from the men that surrounded her. 'What is the matter with you?' she questions, 'You can produce more! It is either your life or the children; which would you choose?'

At that moment the mountain shudders so harshly, and smoke billows from the top in deadly threat that all there are knocked to the ground.

'So? What do you say?' she asks as she takes one of the many willing hands helping her from the ground.

The decision, they say to the wailing and fighting mothers, is out of their hands. The mountain had spoken; it demands sacrifice.

The crowd are filing up the rocky serpentine path, the wicked woman at the lead. Children are dragged by the older men of the community, forced to walk or in some cases are still carried by their mothers. At the end of the snaking people the old man known as Julio is pulling a young girl behind him.

'What have I done?' the girl cries. Her fine clothes dusty and ruffled.

'Be quiet Jabari!' Julio scowls and pulls a small dagger from his belt. 'Or may the mountain stop me; I'll cut off your tongue.'

Further up the trail they climb. Julio, due to his robust size is sweating profusely. Beads of sweat drip from his forehead and off the end of his pointed nose. He is falling behind the group.

'Father!' a breathless woman calls from behind. She wears a similar style and quality of clothes as the girl.

'Mamma, you've got to help. He's gone mad,' Jabari begs.

'Father, you can't do this!'

'I have to,' Julio says.

'No father, you can't take her, she is mine.' She grabs her father's wrist and begins to prize open his strong fingers. 'Let go of her.'

'I have no choice Urshia. The mountain.' He points a shaking hand towards the smoking mountain top.

'Who cares about the mountain? She is your flesh and blood. You will not do this.'

'I have no choice,' he repeats.

'There is a choice,' she whispers. 'We could run away from them. They wouldn't know. Look we are at the back of the group. We could sneak away.'

'Grandpa, please,' Jabari whispers hopefully, 'Let go.'

Julio pauses. 'Alright,' he whispers and drags Jabari into the greenery.

'Wait for me,' Urshia urges.

The sombre, crying, weeping and wailing trail of children, mothers and grandparents continue to snake up the mountain led by the sore covered creature and its human host, taking several hours to reach the summit. Many have collapsed out of heat exhaustion, fear and poisonous gas along the way, but every child has been carried, dragged and pulled to the overhanging edge of the smoke filled hole. Visibility is very low, many have covered their faces with shawls and cloth to cut out the choking smoke and now stand perched on the edge of reason.

Consumed in her bitterness at being childless, used and unloved for all her years, the woman, Hussana gives the command. 'Throw them over the edge!' The children old enough to understand and fight, grab at their mothers while the older men drag them from safety. One boy is grabbed either side by strong hands. He kicks and shouts, but it was no use. Their grip is firm. They lift the struggling boy off the ground and swing him back and forth until they have enough momentum. Letting go of him mid air, he screams as he plummets through the vile smoke and into the depths of the mountain.

Screams flood the air. Some are prised easily as mothers stand emotionless and in shock. Many children cling tightly to the humans who had once loved them and a few of them are being protected.

'Mamma, save me!'

One after another are thrown, pushed and dropped over the edge.

A few mothers block the attack. They are shoved aside, falling into each other or the ash covered ground, while their children are snatched.

'Take your hands off her!'

'Leave them alone. They are innocent.'

A girl who had been thrown in was strong enough and quick enough to catch hold of the heated rocks just below the edge. She clambers back up further along the ridge. Hussana sees her. She strolls over to the spot where the girl's tearstained and sot blackened face appears. Hussana kicks her, with all her brute force, in the face. The girl seems to hang in mid-air before she is thrust to her death.

Older men, some weeping at the loss of their grandchildren refused to join in, but in their passivity to help the vulnerable they have played their part. Small babies are torn from blankets and dropped into the pit. The horror is other worldly. Others join the death plunge. Distraught mothers jump after their stolen children.

'Let the mountain take me!'

Despite the momentary and futile scuffle, all the children are tossed to their death. Then there is silence. A deep and thick silence. No one cries or screams. All emotion has been sucked out of them, and they feel nothing.

The silence has also crept over the mountain.

The woman, Hussana, stands, her back turned at the death and she smiles once more, now they would feel as she does. 'There you are! See and hear what your sacrifice has accomplished. The mountain is silenced!'

I have my command, just as the angels do there. They have been told to let the humans do as they feel. These human lives are led by false gods and sick hearts. They fear for their own lives but had not shied away from sacrificing others. They have been judged.

Stillness fills the scene. Gold dust shimmers in the air. I see it sparkling. Holiness is shining all around. The ground is now holy. Nothing can stand in the Creator's presence unless it is as pure as He is. The command is given.

A line of angels flank the humans. They create a barrier. There is no means of escape. They flame into beings reflecting the holiness of the Creator.

The ground trembles and shakes in the Creator's presence.

A crack runs the length of the ledge, destabilising it where the wicked adults stand. A narrow breach begins to form as little puffs of dust rise in the warm thermals, and then a mighty crack rents the air. The ledge shifts with such speed there is no chance to jump. The crowd screams as one voice, selfishly wanting to save themselves. Rock and human flesh tumble into the fiery pit. A moment after they have been pitched to their death, the massive explosion sends a colossal cloud of burning ash, gas and molten rock into the air.

Another friend weeps at viewing the scene. He sees something quite different but gold gleams in the air before him too.

The valley is quiet. The grasslands here are lush and nourishing, yet all the animals have gone. They had sensed something long ago. The ground trembles, something it has done here before, but this time there is a greater force, a higher frequency to the rumbling. It is building from deep inside, and the ground moans at the onset of what is yet to happen.

Leaves quiver at the tips of branches, dancing as if some unnatural breeze touches each and every one of them. There are no startled noises or scurrying creatures. This place has the mark of death written over it.

The trembling in the valley deepens. The trees and plants shake until many fruit drops to the floor, shaking any last birds from their branches. Pebbles that sat high on the valleys rim become loose in their setting. At first stones roll away, gently pattering down the hillsides. As the shocks grow, the loose rocks begin to shift and shake. The pitching of the rock becomes too much for the destabilised footings to bear, they break free and massive boulders are lost to the valley below. Skidding down the slopes, crushing all in their way, smashing themselves into hundreds of pieces at the base of the valley.

Then it begins. With trembling, a small gash appears in the earth. It remains unchanged for a moment then spreads fast to the left and to the right.

Through the grasses, the earth is splitting open. The tear spreads. It slashes through the lush valley, ripping one ancient tree cleanly in half; one side now clings to the valley that shifted eastwards, while the other speeds westward. The wound extends itself by each passing second. It reaches into the mountains that are shown no mercy, and tears them in half as if they are made of cloth. The ground scrapes the edge of its opposite broken wall, dragging and grinding, cracking screams from the earth itself. The sound fills the air and valley. It is a self-destruct message. The sound would have killed any living thing that remained there through instant madness, yet there is more.

A deeper roar now joins the throng; not only deeper in sound, but deeper from the earth, deeper than the fabric had torn. The pressure is immense, the ground bracing itself for more onslaughts. The trapped beastly roar has built into a crescendo as it bursts from the mutilated valley, a gushing tower of water, rising to above the highest mountain. Seas from the very depths of the rock are pouring forth. Oceans piling up behind to be released. The water continues to spew out as if it will never stop. Water that falls to the ground smashes and pounds any remaining rock to powder with its tremendous power.

The water now takes on a life of its own. Gathering at first in the broken valley it searches for a way to escape. This huge monster forcing its way out, pushing aside and churning up all in its path. In its jaws it holds trees torn from their roots and chunks of mountainside. It swirls about, churning the valley hidden below its depths. This valley will never hold it back, neither will the next.

I watch the burning rock and ice draw closer to the cloud covered earth. The long journey though the blackness of space will end soon. Its tail of light burns brightly as dust and rock were consumed. It is struggling to hold itself together. Many large lumps break off and speed along in the wake of the largest piece. All these shards are entering the earth's atmosphere far from where I stand, burning ever brighter and glowing with heat. The smaller fragments burn up on entry, sending heat shockwaves down to the earth below, but the larger rocks are still heading for a collision course. The heat is intense, so supreme that it begins to react with all the gases in the atmosphere. Vast explosions take place as the large rock hits an all-time high temperature level. The blasts generated spread far and wide. They reach down to the earth's surface melting rock and sand, setting ablaze and destroying plant life, animals and humans alike, the heat does not distinguish between them. The detonation of these fiery clusters is so intense, so powerful and awesome that the whole earth trembles and shakes. The rotation of the earth is disrupted and altered forever.

One more friend stands far away, on the edge of the land. Men from another village have set out to sea in long log canoes. They are hunting for their main source of food. The fish off the coast are exceptionally tender and are used to trade with neighbouring villages inland.

Not one of the men has caught a single fish; the morning has been incredibly quiet. Many bowed in their boats, praying to the small wooden statues of fish monsters tied to the tips of the canoes, to supply food.

The smaller boys are in the water, diving for fish. One after another they came up for air, wide eyed and pale. Then there is a vibrating deep below them, so awesome that it stops the waves, and for a moment the surface of the ocean is as still as a pool. The feigned hush is followed by a low level boom of sound. Some of the fishermen are tossed from their boats as the water begins to rise in a wave a short distance away. Within seconds it is upon them, dragging them to its peak. The wave pulls at the sea, sucking the water from the sea bed.

The wall of water grows as it moves closer to land, piling up ever higher, picking up rocks and gathering small sea life into its grip. Its towering bulk is sweeping towards the land.

The women on the shore notice the rapidly retreating tide and are the first to see the tsunami. They scream and run to grab small children, heading inland as fast as they can carry themselves. Their effort is pitiful against such a force. The wave pours over the beach, engulfing the village, rides through the tropical forest, smashes the rocky mountainside and surges over the land. The roar of the water is all that is heard. There is no more screaming, no panic left in the air. Everything has been overwhelmed. The wave shows no mercy or distinction to living things, it takes everything.

Much closer to me now, the stream bubbles over the pebbled bed, gurgling along its way. It deepens among the weeds and silver fish dart to the surface to pick off the flies. It is the only movement inside the village where Japh's family had once lived before they were called to create the ark. Within moments, small things are changing; no one notices it at first.

The air is still, deadly still. No bird or insect buzzes in the heat of the day. There is only the gentle sound of trickling water, splashing over the steam's bed. The sound of the gurgling stream is becoming harder to hear, it is slowly being over taken by another much more threatening sound. Far away and yet not sourced is a growing roar of water, constant in its pitch, a deep grumbling. As the sound grows louder, the pebbles begin to skip and jump under the influence of the vibrating ground. The air is pulsating as the people stop at whatever they were doing. The smash of a large pottery jar is followed quickly with a scream.

'Run! Get out of here!'

Others enter the panic although the roar that grows closer is now muffled and obliterated with the terror stricken screams. People run here and there, some run to their huts hoping beyond reason to find shelter there, others flee towards the highest ground while a few even attempt to use their own roofs as a high point. A lone child, forgotten and abandoned stands in the main track crying for no one to hear, fear written over her face.

Then it comes; a wall of water rushing, on its own devastating path, ever building, ever deadly. It sweeps over the weak wattle and daub houses, bushing them, and all that is within, away, as if they are twigs. And yet it still comes. Those that had run, even those that seemed to reach the high ground are cut off now from escape and are quickly consumed, struggling in the torrent. But it is a worthless fight, the whole village is destroyed in a matter of passing seconds, in a catastrophic event that had taken years to build.

Now I am witness to the experiences of many of the host all over the world. Ash spreads through the cloud cover. The heat and heavy dust settles inside the cloud. As it settles, things begin to change and something begins that has never happened before, droplets of water form in the vapour barrier above the earth.

Fluffy wool like clouds are building in the sky. As they speed over the land, thrown by the wind the darker they become. The cloud is turning from white to grey and from grey to black. The soft appearance is changing. The gentle billows were shifting and growing, expanding and swirling. Like lumps of clay, thrown, one after the other, by a potter and then squeezed and moulded until it oozes and bulges.

The air temperature drops quickly and is now moving in swirls about the cloud and towards the ground. It gathers speed as the cold air from above buffets and dodges the heat from the ground. Faster and faster it twists, gathering in breadth and velocity. As it corkscrews to the ground it carries away dirt and sand, lifting it into the air and dumping it unceremoniously.

Growing stronger as each moment passes, it feeds on itself as it spins eastward. People caught in the path of the tornados are plucked from the ground and tossed about as if they are mere rag dolls. No one hears their screams over the howling of the wind. It grabs at trees with such force that they are ripped from the earth, their roots still clinging to the last remnants of soil, and swings them round before throwing them away weighing no more than twigs.

Water is spreading everywhere.

Spurting from the ground, overflowing from the rivers and cascading over the beaches. The level is rising as if filling a cup from a jug only this is filling valleys and vast plains. Those that had managed to escape thus far, scramble to the highest places in haphazard groups. The sound of crying and weeping fills the air as their tears only added to the ever pressing flood. The lower ground, softened by the waters traps heavier beasts, and they struggle against the death that creeps towards them. Engulfed not only in water but silt and mud.

Then it begins. We all witness it fall.

A single droplet of water falls from the sky.

It hits the dry path and a small cloud of dust explodes. Then another droplet falls, joined by another. They land on blades of grass that dance under the impact. More drops fall, falling on the leaves of the trees which bow under their pressure. Droplet after droplet, one after another. Gentle splats of water fall. First a hundred, then a thousand, now a hundred thousand. Soon, millions upon millions fall from the sky. Everything bows under the onslaught.

On the outskirts of the swirling wind, rain is falling in long strong canes hitting the earth and pounding it into submission. Any plants and trees that had been left, are battered so that limbs were stripped from them. All life that could move is running, scurrying and flying for their lives. Fleeing from this new phenomenon will be futile. The water droplets are now caught in such a chill air that they freeze as they drop to the earth. Hailstones that sting as they hit fur and scales are soon growing to the size of small boulders before pelting small and large animals to death as they run for cover. Even those that are not killed instantly, are caught in the icy mud soup, unable to run, with the energy being dragged from them, death will soon be upon them.

The humans that have managed to escape so far are the ones that have headed for high ground, found shelter in strong forms such as caves. Such places of safety soon become overcrowded.

My friend from the mountain quickly catches up with Julio, his daughter Urshia and granddaughter Jabari running from Hussana and the monstrosity she had planned. They find an easy path that leads far away from the smoking mountain. As the first groan rents the air they increase their speed.

'What is happening?' Jabari screams.

'I don't know,' Julio pants, 'But keep moving.'

Sudden light streaks across the sky and the air vibrates with a deep roar. They are terrified. They think the anger of the mountain is great indeed. How foolish.

14

Destruction

Celebration of the wedding had faded quickly.

From the moment the ark had been sealed a different ambiance had entered. They looked to Noah for instruction.

'There will be time to celebrate, but now we must wait on the Lord.'

'What would you have us do father?' Ham asked.

'Pray.'

It was a simple instruction and required a simple response. Inside the vessel the men and women were on their knees. Japh and Kerim were still joined by the sash tied about their hands.

As they prayed, Noah told again of that first encounter with God, and the promise that had been made, he was certain he and his family would be saved. Faith was built up.

Bruja stormed into the clearing atop the hill, a vulgar anticipation etched over his face, unaware of the destruction of the world. They had left the dwelling. It had been inspected and found frustratingly empty, but Tarlin had told of this other place.

Bruja was followed by the scaly beast that constantly tasted the air, and clambered over the tree stumps and soft earth to keep up with Bruja. Behind the creature, the band of distant villagers dragged Tarlin over the unforgiving land, while Ishmillimech, wheezed heavily at the rear weighed down with the pack, but strained to raise his head a little to see the spectacle.

A vast structure stood in the middle of the clearing, towering over the ant like people below.

Bruja approached the vessel slowly but confidently. He knew she was in there. Taking a deep breath, he shouted inhumanly loud.

'Bring her out. The girl is mine. Do this or you will all die.'

There was no reply. The others had by now caught up. The monster boldly moved towards the thick timber walls blowing out the sickly scented breath in coils of gas. As it roared its breath caught alight and fire poured from its jaws. It reached out a long clawed foreleg, to scratch at the wall; it would stroke the ark before it would burn it to the ground. Before its putrid skin could touch the beautiful wood, it was thrown back with such force, that it flew over the heads of the onlookers, its legs kicking in the air and its jaw roaring out fire as it went. It landed with a back breaking crack on a stump of a large dark felled tree, and remained deathly still, its legs splayed and with a dullness to its red eyes.

Bruja stood unmoving, there was something else there, something very powerful.

I will not let this creature touch the place where the precious cargo is kept. I flare into glorious light and kick the monster into the air as if it were only a twig. Like I said, nothing will touch His precious cargo.

'You are not welcome here,' I breathe, but my voice still echoes though the clearing with authority. The human carriers cannot hear my voice, but each of their burdens do. I see them quake. 'Make yourselves known!' I command the others surrounding the ark. They should see what they are up against.

Dozens of flashes, light the clearing. One after another, the figures dressed in white make themselves visible. They no longer look gentle, but have fierce and dangerous postures and blazing eyes. They are armed as warriors and ready for battle.

The demons stare at the scene with fear, a few try to flutter away. They have been taken by surprise. Deathly grey cloaks them, but they appear nervous and anxious by our presence here. And so they should!

'You will stay! And we will fight!' screams the creature at human's back to its horde. 'They are not many, we will defeat them!'

It seems to think that it is in charge. What utter foolishness.

I see their numbers. They are many. It will be a fierce battle.

The men in the clearing began to shift draw back.

'You will stay and fight!' Bruja commanded, 'Let us get what belongs to us.'

After a few moments a loud voice could be heard outside the ark.

'We knew this would happen,' Noah said. 'Be strong.'

Kerim's eyes opened widely as she looked to Japh for support and her face drained of all colour. Her emerald eyes began to fill with tears.

'We are safe.' Japh said gently to his new bride. 'People will come now,' he explained cautiously. 'Now that they know we have the only means of salvation.' He squeezed her hand bound to his. 'Father says we are to be strong. They were given a thousand chances. At some point, those chances must run out.' He put his free arm about her waist and pulled her close to himself. 'This is that time. Be strong my love.' It was only then that he looked at her and saw her struggling with her own fear. 'What is it? What is wrong?'

'That voice. I've heard it before.'

'Where?' asked Noah and she turned her face towards him.

'The stranger from the village,' she whispered. 'The witch, it is him.'

Helena began to weep too, Ham consoled her.

'You are not safe when I am with you,' Kerim sobbed. 'You must let me go,' she begged. 'What if I am not supposed to be here? What if we were wrong? I'm not the one from the prophecy.'

'You are,' Japh declared, and pulled her tighter to him. 'You are my wife; you do not belong to him.' Kerim's heart swelled at the strength of her husband.

'There is no way out, we have been sealed in.'

'But you are all in danger because of me.'

'No, Kerim we are in no danger,' Tabitha said with authority. 'Anyone and anything outside this ark is in danger.' She turned to Noah. 'What do you say my dear?'

'There is nothing left to be added. You stay here with us, under the protection of your husband, his family and the one true God.' He stroked his whiskers in a familiar way. 'Let us keep praying.'

Although Kerim still struggled, she pushed through and prayed for the safety of the ones so faithfully behind her.

The prayers of the others were not fearful or demanding, but simple and worshipful, declaring the promise out loud.

I see the demons draw close using the backs of the humans. Some even slither to the floor. They unsheathe their swords that scrape and grind on their scabbards.

The swords are lifeless; deep, flat obsidian that reflect no light at all; many still bear the stains of previous use, human blood. What vile instruments of death.

They willingly move before their leader does. Maybe, it isn't willingness; maybe they fear the reprimand they will face. It is the leader that is the coward. He will not step up and fight, but would take all the glory of the crown if the battle goes his way.

It will not.

The battle victory is ours for the taking. We will be victorious. They have been judged already.

'For the God of all! Attack!' I command.

The other angels echo, 'For the God of all!'

We fight as one. Unity is our strength.

There is a moment of pause before the battle begins. The angels' swords are fast and accurate to their targets, taking many, but still the demonic army come. Screams and shrieks of blasphemy pour from their foul mouths, but the host are strong and attack with wisdom. They see the captains and ring leaders and attack them first.

The demons weapons are quick but not quick enough. They fly with sharp swords but are parried away by the superior Lord's army.

The ground is littered with the injured. Many demons are fighting for their lives now and not as a structured unit. It is easier for us to break the ranks with our fast blades. Many demons limp and moan in agony, oozing wounds with seeping acrid yellow gunge. Insipid green gases swirl in the air with a rotten acerbic smell.

With each slice of his sword, Love destroys the demons in a mixture of putrid sulphur and black smoke. I see him take off wings and limbs with each swipe.

My arrows fly straight and true. They pierce the enemy. The fetid gases swirl in the growing wind, as the demons disintegrate and return to the place where they belong.

'Get over here!' Bruja roared.

Ishmillimech shoved his way forward, through the pack of villagers, past the broken body of the creature. The frenzy fed his ambition.

'Set up a fire,' Bruja pointed to a spot on the ground. 'I will make the sacred circle and at my signal, you light it.'

'Yes master,' he yelled. Ishmillimech's eyes brightened at the mention of fire. Perhaps his time had come. He too wanted to take part in the sacrifice and to be the one who took life for his own gain.

Kerim turned in shock. There was another voice outside, not just the one of the stranger, another she knew well. 'He's out there.'

'Don't worry Kerim, we are safe,' Japh said gently also listening for voices outside.

'No! You don't understand.' Kerim desperately pulled at Japh to get to his feet. 'My brother is out there, we must save him too.'

'What?'

'I heard his voice. He is out there still doing that evil man's bidding,' she said pointing to the outer wall, tears springing to her eyes.

'Kerim we can't help him.'

'But we must.' She pulled at her wedding cloth to release her hand. 'We have to help,' she begged. 'How can I let him die?'

'We are sealed in,' Japh said grasping her. 'We are as trapped in here as they are out there.'

'But he is my brother,' she wept.

'He has done nothing for you,' Japh replied harshly. 'He sold you for evil Kerim,' he continued angrily. 'He was willing to corrupt you in ways no human should ever be treated and then sacrifice you so that his master would be satisfied'

'How dare you!' she spat as she pulled away from him. Tears sprang to her eyes. Tears of sorrow or anger? She did not know. 'You are willing for me to be saved, but will not take him?' she accused trying to free herself from his grip. He let her go. 'Let me out of here!'

Japh approached cautiously, his words spoken tenderly, 'Kerim?'

She straightened her back and clenched her fists. 'If you won't save him I will!' she stuttered through her tears and rushed over to the shutters pulling on the bars that held them shut.

'Kerim, we have our orders.'

'And who gave you them?' she lashed out angrily, 'Why not spare him? He is my own flesh and blood.'

'Don't you remember what he did to you?'

'That wasn't him. Not the brother I remember anyway. It's all that witch's fault.' She turned to Japh, her face wet from tears. 'Help me,' she pleaded.

Japh walked to the shutter and twisted the internal catch. When Kerim saw her husband's willingness she allowed him to help. Together they pulled at the shutter which opened a little but was immediately snatched back into place.

'Again.'

Japh pulled harder. 'I can't move it.'

His brother rushed forward. 'We'll help you.'

Kerim stepped aside as all three men strained, but again it opened just a peek and then snapped back into position.

'You've got to open it!' she begged.

'It's stuck. There's no way to pry it any further.' Shem was weary from exertion.

'What about the others?' Kerim said rushing to another shutter and trying again. It wouldn't open.

Time had run out for the others. Fresh tears flowed painfully. 'Run Ish! Get away from here!' she shouted, 'I'm sorry. Save yourself!'

Kerim rested her head against the unyielding wood. She bowed her head, defeated.

'How can He let this happen? All that death, all those people. What about the little children, what have they done to deserve this?' She collapsed sobbing. 'Why can He,' she said pointing at the ceiling, 'not choose my brother too?'

'He,' Japh pointed to the ceiling, 'as you put it, has the right to choose. The moment you can create life out of nothing, is the moment you can decide what lives and what dies,' he said just as his own father had said to him many years ago when Japh had struggled with the same question.

Kerim looked to Tabitha, who nodded slowly at the truth.

Her knees gave way and she dropped to the floor. Japh crouched down beside her. 'My sweet Kerim,' he said quietly and leaned forward to stroke her hair. 'The fact that you can forgive him for doing what he did, is a quality that God has given you.' His finger then slowly pointed at her heart. 'Surely the God that gives you such grace, is also abounding in love. Let Him decide what to do.'

'I don't understand all this.'

Japh enveloped her in his arms. 'None of us do.' She wept into his shoulder. 'We don't know why we were chosen.'

I hear the command, and quickly dispatch the order.

'Hold the shutters in place!' Those nearest do as I say immediately.

Kerim is finding this more difficult than I expected. Japh will help her, I am certain they will get through this.

Bruja reached into his pouch and removed a handful of herbs and spices, then took the necklace from his about neck. He held the dead claw between his own, and drew a large circle on the dry ground making a slight indentation through the dust. Then standing in the centre of it, he began to chant, scattering the mixture for magic into the air.

An arctic breeze swept through the clearing. The people there shivered and pulled their cloaks about them.

'What's happening?' some asked.

The light had suddenly grown dim as the cloud covering began to turn from pearly white to a deep and threatening grey. The wind was beginning to howl about them as it rushed from one course to the other tossing hair, clothing and dust in all directions.

Bruja continued to chant, calling on the names of ancestors, helpers and guides. The villagers were mesmerised by what they witnessed. Bruja danced before them, a dance that some of them recalled having seen before.

Ishmillimech busied himself with preparing the fire. He had placed a large flat stone; one he had carried all this way, in the centre of the circle and was even now, dodging Bruja, laying dry kindling on the stone bed only to be thrown about by the wind. He cursed the wind with profanities. It would not destroy his moment of glory.

Bruja turned toward the men holding Tarlin. 'Bring him here!' A cold shiver flowed through the group; they seemed to know what would happen next. Bruja took some small stones from his pouch and was now pounding them to dust. Tarlin stood, held firmly by three men. He was terrified. The darkness and wind seemed only on the edge of his reason for fear. He could not understand or see what else lay so heavily on the clearing.

Bruja approached and snatched at Tarlin's jaw. He poured the dust he had created into Tarlin's mouth, followed by a few drops from a leather flask, then shut it tight and clamped it with his long fingers. As Tarlin wrestled, Bruja pinched his nose, ensuring that the contents were swallowed. Then he let Tarlin fall to the ground.

The man coughed and spluttered for a moment and then got unsteadily to his feet. Suddenly Tarlin was seeing something beyond anything he had seen before.

A wild, swirling cloud was flying closer, drawing nearer to the clearing; a hissing and eerie beating of leathery wings ever coming louder. Drawing his gaze from the sky, Tarlin caught sight of the creature clambering higher to stand on Bruja's shoulder.

'You see that! You puny host of heaven— that is back-up. You will be destroyed!' the creature screamed to the ark, billowing putrid smoke.

The fore runners of the cloud sped to this creature, their master, spreading dust and dirt in all directions in their landing. Their mismatched bodies oozing black substance and smelt of rooting flesh. Tarlin drew his hand over his eyes.

'The world has gone mad. He, the creator, has gone mad. He is destroying it all oh great one!' said one jumping up and down in morbid glee.

'There is no one left to torment, they are dying in their millions!' another announced, only just noticing the battle going on about it.

'It is glorious!' said the third, grinning widely revealing a row of mismatched razor sharp teeth.

'Do you hear that Captain of the host of heaven? Your so called all powerful god has gone mad and He is being destroyed. You should give up now!'

'We know what is happening. But don't count on us giving up!'

Tarlin turned and stared at the bright white beautiful and fearsome being. He ripped the demons around him to shreds with his bare hands. 'Why do you stay back there? Will you not face your destruction?' His ringing voice attacked Tarlin's ears.

The hideous army crawled, flew and clambered to the attacking front line. The white beings seemed overwhelmed by the numbers that just kept coming in an endless tide of evil.

'Keep them safe,' another being of light with a bow shouted in short bursts. 'Stay by your posts.'

Sword against sword; the battle was unevenly matched.

Black creatures, with appallingly misshaped bodies and deep staring eyes were clambering and fighting the other beings that were too bright to look at. The brightness and purity of these beings hurt not only his eyes but deep inside, his body shook in fear of them. He felt something on his back and turned slowly to look, terrified at what it might be. The long and slender creature gazed into Tarlin's gaping eyes. His razor sharp teeth and penetrating stare drew the life right out of him. The creature's tongue lashed out of its mouth and ran slowly over its gaping jaws. 'You are mine!' it whispered. Tarlin crumpled to the floor, curling himself up into a ball.

'Death! Bring me death!' he begged. The creature was pleased to oblige.

Bruja dragged the cowering man to the fire. He screamed in torment as the others looked on.

Bruja slit the flesh of the frightened one and breathed in the aroma of human blood. 'Now into the flames!'

Tarlin's body twisted before the crowd, the ferocious flames eating away his life. The wind howled and buffeted the furnace until a powerful gust put out the flames, but it was too late for the charred body.

'Let the other humans see the worship I have,' Bruja commanded in an unearthly voice. 'Show them their families!'

Each human in the clearing is covered with the evil servants. They obey the command of their leader. They rush to their task. They probe the humans' minds and show them the scenes from the mountain. They see their own flesh and blood perishing.

The men in the clearing began to wail. Some fall to their knees with the weight of their visions.

'No!'

'My daughter!'

'Leave them alone, they are innocent!'

Some ripped their garments in anguish and grief.

'NO!'

I see the violence and evil intent. It will not continue. The air is thick with it. The creatures poison each breath they take. Our battle will not fail. The air around the host is tinged with cyan; hope is still in my ranks.

Protection of this precious cargo is in our hands.

I wait. I know that it will not be long now.

From the west, a flash of light precedes the coming of the army of heaven; with loud trumpets the host declares their arrival and readiness for battle. Thousands upon thousands of bright white angels armed with blazing swords and pure bows pour forth. Suddenly the clearing is filled with glorious light.

Suddenly from the west of the clearing a bright light flashed. It shot from the sky to the ground, followed by a deep and threatening rumble. The villagers, shaken from their horrific visions, looked towards the sky, then towards Bruja. Fear had filled them to the point of numbness. Then it happened again, a fork of light split the sky and touched the ground, and the sky thundered so loud that the earth vibrated. Men began to turn, to move away, only slowly at first, but when the third bolt struck, they ran, full of fear, away from that place. Bruja shouted and screamed his commands, but to no avail, all but one fled. Ishmillimech, now so consumed with the spectacle of sacrifice, dumbly thought it was Bruja's power that caused the sky to scream in such a way. Craving for the same anointing as Bruja he stood arms raised to the sky.

'I want the power. I am worthy. Give it to me!'

The fourth lightning bolt moved slowly from above, arcing and focusing its power to one small space on the ground. The full force hit Ishmillimech full in the head, leaving nothing but a pile of smouldering ash where he had stood. Moments later, that was tossed about in the growing wind.

The angels have them surrounded. The demon crouched on Bruja's back shouts out commands. The commands seem less sure than they did before. This demon appears to be panicked.

'Fight!' it screams. 'The human race is all but finished. This is the last place to find them.' It jumps about demanding its lackeys to continue their pointless sacrifice. 'Just this lot and then we are done. We have won.' But even as it screams out these words, defiance is spreading through its own ranks. They see the battle for what it is now. They scream abuse at their leader, demanding it to do more. Their leader is discovering the problem with having an army of selfish, obstructive, disreputable creatures, ones that are now not offering themselves up for their cause in case they could not gain the glory.

'We are outnumbered!' whimpers a small hairy imp amongst the main body.

'What can eight humans do anyway?' another replies.

'They will die as this world self destructs. We aren't needed here; let their god kill them if he wants.'

'He's let thousands of their race die today; this lot are heading the same way.'

'We've won anyway!'

They are flying off in their droves, but the command of the angels is not to follow.

'Let them leave. We are called to protect this cargo.' I spread word through the ranks.

The demons soon see that they are free to go, unhindered, or fight to destruction. Within a short time only one demon remains.

'They will burn for an eternity! I shall have my glory!' Bruja screeched.

He bent down to take hold of the piece of dry tinder that lay at the centre of the circle. Striking two flints, the spark caught hold of the fuel immediately. The flame danced and flickered unnaturally in the howling wind but did not go out.

'Give them room,' I say quietly, and the other angels let them pass. 'You will not harm these treasures,' I state calmly.

'What a complete idiot! Flame and pitch equal what you stupid angel?'

He continued to draw close; he was only ten paces away when water was torn from the sinister cloud above. It fell in an endless outpouring. It came, extinguishing the flame, turning the ground to mire and washing any remains of sacrifice away in a matter of seconds. Bruja reached out to cling to the vessel, but the roar of what was to come made him turn. A towering wave was throwing itself towards him. Rising over the treetops it barrelled toward the ark. The roar announced its violent behaviour and the angry waters carried massive boulders, trees and debris to warn of its truth. He frantically stretched out his bony fingers to grab the wooden ark, but there was nowhere for him to grasp.

He saw the thick long ropes tied to the corners of the ark with large man sized stones attached to the other ends too late. He scrambled along the extensive length, desperate for survival. There was no time left, there was no hope given, there was only moments of life left to live. The torrent was nearly upon him threatening to sweep him away as if he were nothing.

'No!' Bruja screamed in his feeble human voice reaching out for any salvation he could seize before the swell overcame him. He was swept away in the torrent, pounded by the ferocious wave and drowned. 'I want my glory!' the remaining creature yelled as it launched itself into the buffeting wind. 'She belongs to me and will not be taken.'

All that remains is the ark and the swelling waters.

15

Flood

The torrent of water crashed into the end of the ark at great speed. It carried within it the debris from the land along with any animal that had once breathed air that dared to be in its path. The dark water poured over the land, engulfing the small cluster of buildings, and blowing out their walls, swamping the tree stumps and the clearing.

Only the leafy branches bent over in the force of the current, and the solid structure of wood stood firm in the surge, but there were signs of even that changing. The ark creaked and shook a little, and then suddenly it listed to one side before it lifted from the place it had rested for many years. The massive structure had been picked up and it was floating for the first time.

The vessel suddenly lurched to the side, followed closely by several crashes and loud bangs. Nothing inside was damaged, just tossed about and strewn across the floor. The noises from outside; trees, rocks and other matter carried with the current that had lifted the ark from the ground. The wave tossed and bounced off the structure.

Those onboard shouted and screamed, more out of shock from the sudden movement. The screams quickly turned to laughter at the sight of the men laying sprawled over the chairs and floor.

The only ones with any dignity were the eldest couple; the silver haired man had tied his favourite chair down, and was sitting snugly. His strong arm encircled his wife. 'Well then. It appears to have begun,' Noah said smiling through his whiskers.

'What is that sound?'

'It's probably just things from the ground.' Noting the horror on the faces around him, 'Just branches and objects like that.'

Lellia struggled toward Ham who clung to a wooden partition.

They each clambered about, crawled around the open space, trying to find a place to sit still.

'What about that drumming?' Kerim shouted.

Japh wanted to comfort his wife. 'Maybe we should take a look through one of the windows?'

'Do you think the shutters will open now?'

'We can try,' he offered. 'I think just one shutter should be opened, and only a little, if we can, I can hear wind behind that noise.'

They gathered themselves off the floor with difficulty as the vessel rolled, lifted and dipped. A little giggling continued for a while, dying down as each of them began to feel queasy with the movement.

Shem was ushered forward; being the strongest they felt it best as he could put his force behind the shutter if necessary to close it. He twisted the catch and the shutter blew in on the wind hitting Shem hard in the face, then flying across the room taking them all by surprise. Water splashed in through the opening, pouring down in hard and fast droplets, lines of water streaking the view. The overhang of the roof above the shuttered openings offered little protection as the water was being carried inside the family space on the fierce howling wind. Ham dived on the board that skidded across the floor and under the chair. The others stood blinking as the water smashed and splattered their faces and blasted into the room. Ham lifted the board to the window and with a great deal of force Shem was able to secure it back into place.

'What was that?' Ham asked breathlessly.

'The water was everywhere,' Helena stuttered.

'It looked like the sky was falling in on us,' Lellia whispered. Ham pulled her securely to himself.

'Where was all that water coming from? Do you think the sky was collapsing?' Helena said fearfully to Shem.

'Now you need to be calm,' Noah said wiping the water from his head and settling back into his chair. 'We were told that the flood would come. This is it. It truly has begun.' There was silence for a while. 'Perhaps we should give this phenomenon a name,' he suggested. 'I think we need not fear it.'

Everyone began to think, some screwed up their faces in the process.

'What about a name that says it destroys?' suggested Shem.

'I'm not sure that is a positive way to see it,' Noah said thoughtfully.

'But it is going to destroy everything father,' Shem stated almost coldly.

'That it is.' Noah sighed.

'Demolish ... iser?' Ham said with a half smile.

'Ruiner?' Lellia threw in.

'What about Judgement Juice!'

'Ham!' Shem playfully punched his brother on the shoulder. 'There has to be something better than that. I'm not sure I want to live with that name forever!'

'I think "geshem" is a good name for it,' Kerim said quietly grateful for the distraction.

'Geshem?' asked Helena. 'I don't know what that means.'

'Well it has destroyed...' Kerim begun.

'Definitely!' Shem laughed. 'In a somewhat extreme manner!'

'But, I think the sound it makes on the roof, it says geshem. We will know what it is doing, but do we need to remember it for that? We should perhaps remember the fact that we experienced it from the other side.' Kerim laughed uncomfortably.

'Too true!' Noah nodded. 'How is that with you Shem? I think it conveys what you wanted, but has a little feminine subtlety to it.'

Shem shrugged and nodded. 'Sure. That sounds about right.'

'Geshem it is!' Noah said almost sadly. The faces showed no sign that their fear had gone. 'I would like to add,' he said with a slight smile. 'We have also received a promise.'

'You are right father,' Japh spoke quietly nestling in closer to Kerim.

There was very little that could be done, but sit and take deep breaths each time they rose high knowing that the inevitable dip was about to come. Kerim was the first to feel at ease. She did her best to hand out small cups of fresh spring water to her new family, smiling at each one in turn. They mostly sat in silence.

'I think I'll just check below ... if that's alright with everyone?' she said after a long silence, although now a member of the family, she felt uncomfortable in the small place and the lack of conversation. Receiving a small nod from Japh, she picked up a small lamp and quickly left the room, lifted the hatch to the lower decks and scurried down the ramps.

Once below, she could see the steam of her breath caught in the light of the lamp. The chill felt unnatural, with so many animals the air should be warm, but the coolness only encouraged the animals to sleep. Kerim was glad of it, she needed the fresh air in her lungs to make her feel alive. Everything had happened so fast and with such finality too. It was strange how torn she felt.

Part of her wished that she had been destroyed along with the rest of human kind, just so she could escape the searing pain of their loss. But she was also glad to have survived, to be chosen. How odd it was to think that way. Out of all mankind, she had been chosen to be saved.

Kerim could not understand why and did not feel that she ever would. The fear that perhaps she had taken the rightful place from another was banished now. Japh had told her that she was the one, but it wasn't until this moment that she really believed him. Having glimpsed the destruction that was going on outside, Kerim had no doubt that if she were not supposed to be here, she could be wiped out in a moment. It was the fact that she could feel the cool air filling her lungs time after time that told her she was in the right place.

Stall after stall was still and quiet. A few animals looked up at her as she peered in, but other than some loose boxes or hay that had been thrown from their place, nothing had really changed. Everything was quiet, but not like the uneasy silence from the living space above, it was peaceful here. She checked the walls for damage, of which she found none, and when she felt that perhaps there was nothing else to keep her below and she had spent a little too long away, she decided to return. Climbing up the ramps as the ark listed on the rolling water, was far harder than coming down. She bumped the sides and missed her footing a couple of times; again it was only seen by a few sleepy creatures who would have smiled if they were able.

'Is everything alright below?' Japh asked as she staggered in.

'All is fine. In fact they are faring much better than us.'

'There is no damage?' Shem questioned.

'No, not at all.'

'It sounded worse than it was then. That is good.' Ham nodded to himself.

The room relaxed and conversation began among the couples.

The tension eased a little, they would not be drowned. Kerim moved towards Japh who sat in a now secured space in the corner. He made room for her to sit with him as she approached.

'How is it down there?'

'Cold,' she sighed.

'What is it? Are you alright?'

'I was just thinking, that's all.'

'What about?' Japh asked patting the seat next to him.

The room was full of noise. Everybody was involved in their own conversations.

'What about the others Japh?' Kerim asked hesitantly. 'What will happen to them?'

Japh sighed sadly and shook his head. 'Sit here with me.'

'They never had a chance,' she said slowly as her eyes filled with tears.

'They had the chance. They were warned to change. They could have saved themselves.' He put her hand in his and pulled her towards him. 'Our God is not a reckless God. He is merciful.' She shrugged as the tears flowed down her cheeks, she did not wipe them away. 'He is. After all he could have destroyed the entire world and everything in it and us too.'

Kerim was aware all the others were now quietly listening. She looked at each of them in turn and one by one they bowed their heads. No voice disturbed the relentless drumming. Each person was lost in their own thoughts. Helena began to weep.

'But we have a promise?' Kerim finally asked breaking the self imposed silence of the room.

'Yes,' Japh said firmly, looking at her, his eyes burning with intensity.

'And so do all these animals,' Shem said looking up once more.

'And the plant life contained in the seeds,' added Lellia 'They have the promise of new life inside of them too.'

'He has given us a hope and a future, each and every one of us on this ark,' the silver haired one said with a smile as he twiddled his beard.

The host have positioned themselves round the vessel although it has floated from its construction site.

Several large trees, carried by the surging water come close to damaging the exterior.

'Protect the vessel!' Love shouts, over the sound of rushing water and the pounding ... rain ... hmm unusual idea for a name.

The host work as a team buffeting dangerous objects out of the way with careful hands.

I am on board with many others. Most patrol the lower decks ensuring the animals continue to sleep and are not plagued by their instincts. There is a deepening peace spreading throughout. A deep emerald green colour in the air. Someone has been a little over cautious.

I return to the outside, to inspect the host. They are magnificent. They surround their Lord's treasure, His remnant on earth, protecting and ensuring the enemy will not have his way.

Hours passed by.

The ark pitched and rolled unpredictably on the mounting waves. The family grew restless. Having worked tirelessly for the past few days, and steadily for months, years and decades, sitting idle was great agony.

'Let me set you some tasks!' Noah finally said. Everyone looked toward him eagerly, and he laughed out loud. 'Right, well I think we could be here for a while, so ...'

Within minutes everyone was busy. The sparse furniture that had been bought on board had to be tied down, pots, blankets and crates that had been thrown about had to be cleared, the animals that would produce food and drink had to be cared for. Eggs needed to be collected, there was grain to be ground, new seed to be sown and young plants had to be watered. All these jobs were attempted as the vessel rocked and sailed through the rising water.

Tasks took longer than normal but the distraction eased the sickness. They went about it in solemn quietness, letting their minds linger on what would be happening outside, the destruction of villages, farms and ultimately the human race. The fact was hard to get away from as the water hammered on the roof and tossed the ark.

The scent of warm food, cooked over the stone lined fire, drew them all back to the central room, with its shuttered windows and dim oil lamps. The homely smell of leek, potato and onion cooking and warm bread wafted through the upper deck. The aroma was delicious, a refreshing change to that of animals.

Cushions and rugs were now neatly arranged in the largest alcove, tightly packed, so that they wouldn't move.

The bright earthy colours of the fabrics bought home into the space. All the mess caused by the relentless rolling of the vessel had been cleared away and secured. Simple earthenware plates sat in the centre of the rugs laden with bread, cheese and milk, along with a large pot of hot steaming broth.

The family gathered, and Noah prayed.

'Thank you Lord for your abounding mercy to us. We are so grateful to you. We heard you speak and then acted in faith by building this ark. You have preserved us. Thank you for preserving us. We thank you for this food. Let it nourish us and build us up. Amen.'

'Amen,' they all agreed.

The food was distributed, although maybe not the usual amount to each plate as they were all still feeling a little ill.

Kerim looked about at this new place. She felt snug and secure tucked away in the corner, sitting cross legged on an abundance of cushions. The eating area was tucked in between the plank partitions of two bedrooms. Noah and Tabitha's to her left and her own, which she would now share with Japh to her right. She tried not to dwell on that fact. It sent butterflies in her stomach. Next to her own bedroom, along the short wall of the ark, was a long stabling area for the flock animals, the ones used for milking and other necessities. The heat they were generating warmed the upper level nicely.

Across from her, against the opposite wall, were the planting toughs, only just filled with fresh rich soil. A closed trap door nestled between two of them in a sizable gap midway along the exposed floor. At the opposite end to the stabling, two more bedrooms, belonging to Lellia and Ham (closest to the plants) and Helena and Shem.

The fire burned low in the centre of the space over a layered stone hearth. Ham had fixed a ledge to the edges of the hearth to ensure no hot embers could roll off with the movement of the ark. He now sat, his arm wrapped around Lellia.

Kerim was almost comfortable on the cushions, although she still felt like she was intruding. The broth was comforting and the bread still warm. Her new husband lounged beside her and kept turning towards her with a smile or a wink or two. How could he be so relaxed with outward signs of affection in front of his family? What would they all be thinking of them?

Kerim was shaken from her thoughts as Japh offered up to her mouth a small chunk of cheese, she took it in her fingers and smiled at him. She sat back, defeated in a simple task to please her husband. She looked about her and to her amazement, no one was watching. In fact each of the brothers were showing simple forms of affection to their wives.

The wall vibrated at her back. Her ears had grown accustomed to the drumming of the rain, though it fell harder at times. Inside the vessel, she was warm and dry, but she dared not think of what was happening outside. She could only imagine the devastation that had occurred. Surely the mountains would be high enough to offer retreat. If only her father could reach them.

The night lagged on. A few hours of chatting in the firelight had been enough for all of them. Each couple retreated to their individual rooms.

'Are you alright?' Japh asked as he sat himself among his belongings.

'I will be,' she whispered.

He reached for her hands. 'What is it?'

'Nothing. I'm fine.'

Japh pushed at a large wrapped bundle of clothes with his foot to make room. 'No you're not,' he stated. He pulled her gently down to the edge of the bed near him. 'Please Kerim, tell me what's troubling you.'

She looked down to the floor and started to trace the wood grain with her fingers.

He carefully cupped her chin and raised her face so that he could see her sparkling eyes. 'You're upset. Let me help if I can.'

Kerim took a stuttered intake of breath. 'You have your family here. I don't know what has happened to mine,' she said sadly.

'I'm sorry.' He rubbed his thumb across her cheek. 'I don't know what to say,' he said defeated.

'There is nothing anyone can say.'

A tear rolled down her cheek. Japh let it fall to the floor.

'You are part of this family now.' Japh leaned forward and kissed her cheek. 'I want you to know I will do all I can. All I have is yours.'

Kerim's heart fluttered at his kiss.

'I can't offer anything in return. I have nothing, not even the clothes I wear.'

'I don't want anything, except you.'

'Well, you're stuck with me now anyway.' Kerim half laughed.

'And like I said before, I wouldn't have it any other way.'

Japh released her and turned quickly at the sound of murmured voices.

'I want you to be happy with the choices you have made,' he whispered. 'I know you don't think so, but you have everything. You have safety, new family and my love and admiration.'

She smiled, but she feared that Japh would see that her eyes stayed sad. She knew that he couldn't convince her. She would have to come to that conclusion.

Japh moved over to the corner and removed his jacket and shoes. Then he went over to the bed, pulled away the blankets, and climbed in. He propped himself up on his elbow. 'From the second I first saw you, frightened and hidden; I knew you were different.' He sighed, and lay flat. 'You did not escape by chance, it was indeed a miracle. And neither was the fact that I found you an accident. By all rights, you shouldn't be alive but you are.'

Kerim listened as his thoughts were spoken. 'I hardly ever venture toward that field, but that day I did. It was meant to be.'

Japh sat up, suddenly realizing what he had done. He looked at the small bed and then at her. He saw the worry in her eyes. 'I'm not expecting to be anything but a friend right now.' He moved over. 'We have all the time we need to be husband and wife.'

Kerim was pleased. Truly his words eased her tension. 'I think I ... I think we will be very good friends.'

'I think you are right.' He yawned and covered his mouth. Now if you don't mind, I would like to get to sleep.' Japh lifted the woven cover to make space for her then lay down and closed his eyes. Kerim smiled at his generous gesture. She quickly removed her shawl and slippers and carefully climbed in beside him.

'Thank you,' she whispered toward him while nestling into the bed. The room was still and no other voices could be heard. Her heart felt right. She was surrounded by family, and for that she was thankful in a way he wouldn't understand.

Kerim felt him turn his head towards her and heard him fill his breath with her scent. He sighed. She wriggled slightly, pulling herself a little closer to him. Gently but deliberately he allowed himself to kiss her cheek, but only once. She felt his body relax and she could imagine that his eyes were closed, simply enjoying her warmth next to him. Japh drifted off to sleep in happiness.

It was not long before he was breathing slowly and deeply, fast asleep. Kerim lay still for a long time, waiting for sleep to carry her away. But it didn't.

The heavy thudding on the walls and roof filled her mind. The room had a smell of animals and cooking, and the bedding was rough to the touch. She could not sleep.

She sighed. Everything was so different to what she was used to.

Japh's body, rising and falling to the rhythm of his breathing, was warm and strong. Kerim was sure he was deeply asleep. She touched his fingers and felt the tough calluses from hard work and the rough skin. She lifted it and placed his palm to her lips and kissed it. In that short passing moment, she tingled and discovered that she had held her breath. Something about her was changing. 'I am so grateful for your patience ... my love,' she whispered.

She slipped from the warmth of the covers to the cool air of their bedroom. All around there were noises of deep breathing and one or two snores. Kerim found the small oil lamp and easily lit it. She found her small slippers beside the bed and wrapped Japh's jacket about her. It was long enough to keep her warm and smelt faintly of him. How she would have loved to walk out in the fresh air and open spaces of her old pasture to clear her mind, but she was not able to do such a thing. The next best thing was to walk the lower decks and take in a different scene.

She left the bedroom and crossed the living space. The fire glowed orange in the centre, sending out slight shimmers of heat. Lifting the trap door with her free hand, Kerim descended into the dark lower decks.

Why did she feel so uncomfortable? What was wrong with her? She was safe, alive. She had a husband who showed her so much respect and love and what does she do? Kerim tried to reason it through until she found herself near a large pile of hay and collapsed into it. As she rested, her mind became still again.

'But it must be wrong to feel this happy and content when I should feel so much sorrow too.' As she spoke out, it somehow released her. To put it into words allowed her to inspect it. There were two very different and conflicting feelings. Of course she could feel grief. Her father and brother had died, along with so many others, but she knew that her father would have been happy that she was to be safe. She had seen the fear, anguish and sorrow on his face when they had taken her. He would have been happy to know that their God was faithful and had rescued her.

Her thoughts turned to the other feeling, what was it? It was happiness. Of course it was happiness, only she had not recognised it before. Japh made her happy.

'I will allow him to love me,' she commanded herself. 'I even think that I already do. I know that I love him,' she whispered and curled into a ball on the hay. She felt herself relax, but why? She thought for a while, 'I have privacy,' she concluded. 'All these years I have been by myself with father. I have been living in solitude and loneliness. Then, all of a sudden I am the object of everyone's gaze. I don't like it. It's shameful. But here, down here in this smelly, cold place I have found some privacy.' Her mind finally and peacefully concluded and she fell sleep in the warm hay.

16

Rescued

I stand somewhere between the decks neither restricted by the physical world about me, the lack of light nor the rolling of the ark. A large angel girded with a long sword at his side draws near. My friend and comrade in arms!

'The larger animals on the lower deck are all secure. There is nothing to report. The enemy has not been able to tamper with anything on the inside of the ark. There have been no extra enemies allowed to board.'

'Excellent. Keep watch.' I smile and rising to the higher deck, I turn to another angel, of golden skin and hair, 'What news of the smaller creatures?'

'All sleep. There must be thousands tucked into every nook and cranny, all species of the world are represented in this one space, such amazing design each and every one of them.'

'Too true! There are thousands here, but of course, not all as big as the elephant! This higher deck carries the bulk in terms of numbers. The swelling seas, however now contain a mixture of both fresh and salt water beasts and fish. Only the ones that keep closest to the ark are thriving in the strange mix. Their design miraculously able to cope with the rise or fall of saltiness.'

'The Creator even thought of all this when He first designed them.'

Just as the angels around me begin to marvel at the Creator's work, there is a disturbance as another appeared suddenly.

'One of the chosen is not sleeping. She is coming this way.'

'Kerim?' I ask, yet knowing who it will be. I have been waiting for her.

'Yes Hope. What would you have us do?'

'Just stay at your posts. She is quite safe to wander. That is what she needs to do.' I turn again to the golden angel who had been speaking to me before. 'Humans are above all, the most amazing of all creation. The Creator took such joy in making them.'

Kerim shivered a little under Japh's woollen jacket and awoke. She got up from the hay. The decks in which the animals were housed were colder than she had expected. The warm glow of light from the lamp spread orange flickering patterns over the walls, gates and hiding places. The dark shadows danced as she moved. Darkness had so long been a place of evil and fear, but here on this ark, the darkness felt peaceful.

She wandered around the deck, leaning over the enclosures, and spreading the light from her oil lamp as far as she could reach. All was still and all was quiet when it came to the animals. The ark however, rocked from one side to the other, occasionally lurching unexpectedly, while the falling water could still be heard hammering on the walls or splashing on the sides. She imagined the sound up in the living space to be much louder than below decks where she wandered.

She made her way down the ramp. The smell of the animals here was stronger as were the slight sounds of breathing or shifting in their sleep. Neither was unpleasant, but comforting instead. Here the boat moved differently, the rocking seemed more steady and controlled but the biggest difference was the lack of noise from the pounding rain. This lowest deck was below the level of the water, the stillness of the echoing silence hung in the air, and Kerim was grateful for it. She had not really understood her unsettledness until now, stood here at this moment. The constant hammering of the rain had scared her, it made her think of all the lives destroyed just by being the thickness of the ark wall away from safety. It had been a relentless reminder of death.

Finding a pile of clean straw, she sat and listened to the silence.

'Kerim.'

Turning quickly, she had expected to see Japh standing behind her, but there instead was the one who had released her from the cage, wearing the purest white tunic.

'Don't be afraid,' I say gently. But Kerim is afraid, as are most humans.

'What is it you want?'

I smile, she is brave. 'You seem restless.'

'Yes.' Kerim looks down.

'The silence here is peaceful. It enables you to think.'

'That's right, it does.' She looks into my face, and she sees it is kind. 'The noise up there scares me.'

'You need not fear. The Creator will not forget you. You are His prized people, set apart from all others.'

'But why us? Many have perished while we have survived.'

'We cannot judge what the Creator does. He is the righteous God, slow to anger and abounding in grace. That grace He has given to you.' I carefully draw closer to her, and sit on the floor across from her. 'Know Kerim, that what the Creator has done is right, not a mistake and not rushed into with anger. He has saved you and your new family because He sees in you there is a passion to have relationship with Him. Others who have died, turned from that relationship and rejected that friendship He had offered. None can fathom the depths of God, none will ever understand the mysteries, but you have become a chosen generation among all the earth.'

'But my father was not like the others, yet he would have died today. Where is the mercy for him?'

'Your earthly father died declaring worship to the Creator that saved both you and him. He was not in the earth at the beginning of this day, he had already been taken. He knew you were safe. Do not trouble yourself with things so trivial.' A frown of confusion spreads over my peaceful face. Humans are difficult to understand sometimes.

'Trivial? He was the only one who loved me. I loved him.'

'I spoke in haste. All I mean to convey is that he has been delivered from this world to a place where he can find peace once more. The death of your father is not trivial. But your concerns lay outside of this event. You have a new purpose that you must focus on now.'

Her sadness at her father's death has eased, knowing now that her father had been spared the wrath the Creator had poured out over the earth. The air about her begins to pulse the gentle green that floods these lower decks and pure cyan. Her colour, still tinged with the grey yellow of sorrow now flickers with peace and hope.

'I am grateful that I have been given salvation and I understand that God did not rush into this.' She sounds repentant. 'He knows what He is doing. I must trust Him in whatever comes next.'

'Yes you must!' My glimmering smile returns.

An echoing sound creeps through the floor of the ark and makes Kerim shiver.

'What was that?' she asks.

'The whales.'

'Whales? What are whales?'

'Whales are the creatures of the deep. They are large but peaceful beings. They breathe the same air as you do. They have been joined by other beasts of the sea and are singing their praise to God. They will soon swim in the forests of the land and dive in the valleys where eagles once flew.'

She listens carefully to their praise.

'Your God will not forget you Kerim. His plan for you is perfect, to prosper you.'

Kerim closed her eyes and listened to the whale song. One after another joined in, each repeating and adding to the song.

'What are they singing?' she asked at last as the song faded away, and opened her eyes. But there was no reply. The white robed one was gone. Kerim was alone again, but not afraid. As she clambered up the ramp on the swaying ark and heard the rain hammering on the walls with unfailing power, she felt no fear. She would trust God. He knew what He was doing. Her feeble mind could come up with all sorts of questions and reasonable answers but in this she could do nothing but trust God.

The fire in the living space was now extinguished. She quietly crept over to her room, slipped off Japh's jacket and looked down to the sleeping form of her husband. He was blissfully peaceful, a slight smile playing across his lips.

Kerim quietly lay down next to Japh careful not to let her cool touch disturb him. She put out the lamp and eased the blankets over herself.

17

No Hiding Place

My friend watches as the three of them get thoroughly soaked. The water pouring from the sky is relentless. To add to that, there is a fierce wind that whips at their cloaks and there is a chill to the air that saps their strength as they run from their mountain god.

'I can't go any further,' Jabari complains and sits down on a soaking boulder.

'Get up child!' Urshia orders.

'I can't Mamma. I can't move another step. Surely we are far enough from the mountain now.'

'Keep moving you ungrateful child. I just saved your neck. I won't be killed because of you.'

'Mother I can't move. I'm too hungry and too thirsty. Do you have anything to drink?'

'Does this look like a little outing? Lift up your head and see if you can catch a drink,' Urshia scorns, 'Get up girl!'

'I can't,' Jabari says, 'And I won't.' Her face is set in a stubborn frown.

'Make her move Urshia,' Julio stresses. 'Or may the mountain stop me, I'll hit her.'

Urshia looks up at her father. She sees the anger that she recognises only too well.

'I'm not moving,' Jabari states sulkily.

'Look,' Urshia says squinting further up the unfamiliar mountain behind him. 'Up there! I think there is a cave. Let's rest and shelter for a while.'

Jabari whines as she gets once more to her aching feet.

Inside the cave it is a little drier then the outside; in places the water either drips or streams down the walls. The failing light outside is not strong enough to lighten the interior. None of this matters to Julio or Urshia. They collapse, exhausted, to the hard floor.

'I'm cold. I want a blanket,' Jabari complains. No one hears her, or at least no one answers. Her mother and grandfather are already asleep.

There are other survivors on their way. They head for high ground and the seemingly safety of the caves. My friend still watches, but the vision fades.

18

Ark

Kerim awoke to the gentle sounds of the ark. It creaked and groaned. The rhythm of the rain, now so repetitive on the wooden structure, had not disturbed her. Japh lay with his back turned towards her but she could tell from his steady slow breathing that he was still asleep. Kerim eased out of bed and dressed quietly, leaving their room soon after.

She was fixing her dress when she heard a whisper. 'Good morning dear!'

'Tabitha! Hello.'

'Come now. You can call me Mother like everyone else. You are part of the family now.' As she said this, she peered through the open doorway at the sleeping form of Japh. 'Would you like some breakfast?'

'Erm.' Kerim too looked over at her new husband, and felt a little embarrassed. 'Yes please,' she blushed.

Tabitha urged Kerim to sit in the cushioned area and handed her a flat loaf of bread. 'You know, we should really get some hangings up in this space, it is all so open to everyone. What do you think dear?'

'That would be great!' Kerim took note of the smile of wisdom from her mother in law. If the idea came from Tabitha, she had no reason to worry what the others would think of her. Material would add privacy and deaden sounds throughout the space.

'This place is nothing like home,' Tabitha remarked. 'It is so dull. No colour at all. You can tell it was our men who made it. They made it with practicality in mind, but have seemed to forget that it needs to be a home.' She laughed quietly, looking about her.

'I used to weave when I was at home. The sheep's wool came in handy for that. I would sometimes use the wool as it was and other times I would dye some. I could get some lovely colours from the right plants.'

'Ah. Now you sound like the artistic kind. Maybe we should get the girls together and discuss the decoration of our temporary home.' Tabitha looked over Kerim's shoulder. 'What do you think?'

Kerim turned and saw that Lellia too was creeping away from her sleeping husband. She flicked her dark hair out from the dress she had just put on.

'What's that Mother?'

'It is time to plan a new look for our rather masculine home.'

'Yes, I was thinking the same thing.' Lellia sat next to Kerim. 'Morning!'

'Morning,' Kerim returned passing the bread.

'I think all this open space is a little too open if you catch my meaning.'

'Absolutely,' came the musical voice of Helena from behind. 'Someone was snoring very loudly and it wasn't Shem or me! Anything that shuts out a bit of sound would be wonderful.'

'Kerim was saying she used to weave.'

She half smiled at the attention. 'But I don't have a loom.'

'Well, get Japh onto that. He's the carpenter!'

'We don't really have enough supplies for a whim like that though, do we?'

'I'm sure we can find something! You give up too quickly!' laughed Helena. 'The challenge will make it all the more interesting. Make him work harder!'

By mid-morning, Japh had found plenty of scraps of wood and timber rods. He was relishing the idea of tackling a small project again. The monotony of life on board was already frustrating him. Ham and Shem were the same, yet they were not making themselves busy, except at aggravating their wives and all those around them.

Under his wife's instruction, Japh had trimmed, notched and fixed a frame. She had drawn a diagram of the other working parts on a scrap of wood with charcoal from the burner.

Kerim saw how hard he worked to understand her drawings. He would ask all manner of questions. 'How is that meant to fix to that? Is that meant to move? What is this bit supposed to do?' He found it hard to see what she could see. He needed to lay out the items, to see it in real life. He made her laugh.

He was pleased to be able to do something for her. She had a complex mind that often confused him with all her ideas, yet he would believe that she understood what was planned before raising any doubts. He did seem to be building it correctly as it fixed together. He was all the more pleased when he was able to make her laugh. She was becoming herself again, and he was helping.

While Japh worked, Kerim found herself at a loss of things to do. She watched as the other women prepared food; there seemed no need for help. She finally ended up in her room sorting through the bundles of belongings. Unwrapping the collection of clothes, she folded each item, piling them neatly on the floor. Both Helena and Lellia had given her several skirts, tops and dresses, but her pile of clothes was far smaller than Japh's.

Kerim had packed one bundle from the house near the clearing. She searched it out now. It was small and carefully tied together with twine. Finding it, she placed it onto the bed. She untied the twine and gently spread out the contents over the surface of the bed. Before her were all of Japh's drawings from his old room. Looking at the detail, she now understood why Japh had struggled with her own sketches.

A smaller muslin square held the selection of tacks that had held them in place before. Kerim began to arrange the sketches on the walls, using the same tiny holes made in them before so as not to damage them further. Soon the walls resembled the home she remembered, the place she had felt so welcome in. When she was finished, she was satisfied by what she had done and smiled to herself.

Kerim sought out Japh in the open living space. He sat on the floor, cutting a notch from the end of a long piece of dark wood.

'That seems to be coming together,' she complimented him quietly.

'Hmm. Thanks.' He looked up at her, his smile eager. Reaching up to her waist, he hooked his hand about it and urged her to sit down. She did so with very little resistance. 'What have you been up to?'

'Not much,' she replied catching Lellia watching them as she stirred some herbs into the pot.

'Don't mind them!' Japh whispered leaning closer so that Kerim was the only one to hear as he noticed her reaction.

'Them?'

'I mean Lellia,' Japh corrected himself. 'She likes to see me happy.'

Kerim looked up again. Lellia smiled once more. 'And ...' she began quietly.

'And?' Japh encouraged her to continue.

'Nothing!'

'Please, what did you want to say?'

'It doesn't matter.'

Japh wrapped his arm tighter about her waist. 'It does matter. What did you want to say?'

'Well,' Kerim began, seeing Japh's worry. 'I only wanted to ask if you are happy?'

'My love,' Japh said grinning, 'you have no idea how happy I am.'

'Really?' she questioned. 'Stuck in here, no sky, no fresh air and with little to do but sit and wait.'

'With the risk of sounding a little corny,' he chuckled, 'there is no other place I'd rather be, because you are here.'

That set Kerim blushing more than ever. She turned away from his gaze, and found that Lellia, who was not looking at them, was smiling in satisfaction.

By evening the simple loom was near complete, not particularly graceful, but beautifully made, and most definitely working. Japh had left it unfinished to help his brothers below decks.

Kerim set about spinning some wool from the heavy fleeces that had been stored on board, with a heavy wooden bobbin. The other women, who had rearranged furniture, fixed personal possessions to the walls, and generally tidied the mess from the nights' rolling movement, now joined in with Kerim. Helena sang a simple song as she spun the wool into long threads, the other women catching the tune and words joined in. Kerim had not been happier at any other time.

Tabitha looked her way. 'It is late dear, and time to eat. Would you mind fetching the boys?'

'Not at all ... Mother,'

As she reached the hatch Noah handed her a shawl. 'It is cold down there.'

'Thank you,' she said as she took it from him and wrapped it about her shoulders.

Her slippered feet made very little sound as she pattered down the ramp. It was dark but the light from the upstairs room lit the way sufficiently enough.

Below her she could hear the men having a heated discussion. She stopped to listen as she seemed to be the topic of the argument.

'Spit it out Shem, you've been dropping remarks all afternoon.' The anger in Japh's voice startled her.

'I just don't get her that's all!'

'You're not the only one Shem,' Ham agreed.

'What's your problem?' Japh's voice drifted up to her.

'There's something not right about her.'

'What?'

No one said anything for a moment. 'Well?' Japh asked impatiently.

'I don't know,' Shem said dismissively, and then added. 'It's like she doesn't trust us or something.'

'Yeah. She hardly says a word to anyone except you,' Ham added.

'Does she have a problem with us?' Shem asked, 'because if she does, she will make this so much harder than it is going to be.'

'You just can't see beyond your own world can you?' Japh said now in a much calmer tone.

'What's that supposed to mean?' Ham bellowed.

'She has lost everything.' Japh paused. 'Everything.'

'So have we,' Shem reflected.

'Don't you get it? She's grieving her father's death and her brother's death.' Silence followed. Kerim heard the puffing of one or maybe both of Japh's brothers. There was a pause before Japh continued. 'She is the woman I love,' he declared. 'You need to trust her and me. Give her space to breathe. When she lets you get to know her, you'll understand.'

Kerim heard heavy footsteps coming up the lower ramp. She began to stamp a little as she walked down towards the men, letting them know there was someone there.

'Food is ready,' Kerim said as Ham and Sham strode past her, trying to smile at them.

'Thanks,' replied Ham glancing behind.

'Yeah. Thanks Kerim.'

She continued down the slope a little further where Japh was roughly stacking some wooden buckets into the corner of a stall.

'Food is ready, when you are,' she said gently.

'I'm just coming,' Japh said still busying himself hanging rope to a notch on the wall.

'No you're not!' Kerim approached him and put her arms about him. He turned to face her and his stern face softened. 'Thank you,' she whispered and reached up on tip toes and kissed him tenderly on his mouth. She lingered there for a moment.

'What was that for?' he asked breathlessly, somewhat confused. Kerim had never shown him affection, it had always been him that had initiated it. He almost appeared stunned. Kerim could only smile at his reaction. He leaned a fraction closer to her, and then pulled away suddenly. Was he frightened of being rejected.

'Do I need a reason?' she asked seriously.

'No. You never need a reason.' He winked, 'I never want there to have to be a reason, except that you love me half as much as I love you.' He gulped then continued, 'Did you say food was ready?'

Kerim nodded.

'What are we waiting for then!' He ran up the slope taking her with him.

A loud clap of thunder rent the air outside the ark and vibrated through the boat.

What a development. Human nature is remarkable. I watch Kerim and Japh with keen interest. I see that they are alike in many ways, but they display their true soul by their colours, and those colours intertwine now.

I have work to do.

I watch the thing fall to the ground. It had clung to her for so long. It thought that there was no way it could be banished. It was wrong. She had heard him declare his love, his respect, his trust of her. There was little more it could do. It spat and screamed at her not to listen. It clawed at her hair with its long fingers, desperate for a hold, but she was too slippery all of a sudden. It could not get a grip on her.

'It is only temporary! He will see through you in time! No one will ever understand you let alone let you be you!' it shouts from the floor desperately trying to gain control.

'Enough!' I whisper my command from behind the creature, arrow notched in a raised bow. My whisper is like a thunder clap in its head. 'I have heard enough of all your lies. She no longer wants your presence.'

'But you can't let me go. I need to be with her. I am meant to be with her.'

'You no longer belong here Loneliness.'

'But I can't leave her,' it begs pathetically.

'You will go.' The arrow point now glimmering dangerously close.

'No!' Its sickly breath attempts to mist the surface before it punctures its body.

When Japh and Kerim had sat down and Noah had given thanks, the meal began.

Lellia had created a wonderful stew that filled the room with spicy scents. Kerim had never tasted anything like it before. There were slices of golden peppers, crisp seeds and juicy vegetables. Their goblets were full of creamy milk which complimented the food expertly.

'Lellia, this is delicious!' Kerim leaned closer to her.

'Thank you. It was my mother's recipe.'

'Do you like the spices?' Ham asked cautiously.

'I do ... but it is a bit hot!'

The cook smiled, 'I forgot you haven't tasted my food before. Maybe I should have made it a bit milder.'

Kerim drained her goblet and smiled back.

'Here,' Shem said, kindly offering her the jug of milk. 'Have some more.'

Kerim smiled in thanks and lifted her goblet so that he could fill it.

'Oh no Japh!' Lellia laughed, 'is it too hot for you too?'

Japh just nodded, took off his jacket and fanned his mouth with his hand.

'See, you can't be good at everything!' joked Shem. 'Nice loom by the way.'

'Very elegant,' Ham added looking at the nearly finished article resting against the wall.

'Maybe you could have a think about designing something that gets the air moving in here,' Shem said. 'Helena was saying it can be quite stifling cooking over that fire.'

'And the smells seem to be lingering too,' Helena laughed.

Kerim turned to her husband who was still fanning himself. 'Well I'm sure we could rig up some kind of device. What do you think?'

'Sure!' Japh said taking a gulp out of Kerim's goblet.

'Do you want some more?' she asked as she offered his empty goblet to Shem who readily refilled it whilst laughing at his brother.

The day had revealed far more than Kerim had expected. Night had fallen and bed time approached. Still there was a lack of privacy to their sleeping quarters, but somehow, knowing that she was not the only one faced with this situation, made her feel even more united with her family.

As she lay down, she remembered the words Japh had said. How his brothers had allowed her to join in the conversation rather than have it thrust upon her. It felt good to belong and to have Japh as a partner. He rescued her.

Soon all around, Kerim could hear the slow breathing and snores of those who slept. She knew Japh was still awake. He lay very still next to her. She wondered what he was thinking of. He had seemed so amazed at her all day, and then she had surprised him further when she had relaxed that evening. How could she sleep? She was far too energised to sleep.

The dull light from the central fire filtered in through the empty doorway. Kerim turned to face Japh and looked into his eyes.

'You're still awake then?' she whispered.

'Yes.'

'Sounds like everyone else is sleeping.' Kerim quietly giggled.

'Shem snores very loudly,' Japh said matter of factly. 'Always has!'

'Helena said it wasn't him earlier!'

'Believe me, that's him alright!'

'It's been a good day.'

'Hmm,' Japh considered. It was not a positive tone. Maybe he was thinking over the argument he had with his brothers.

Kerim shifted slightly on the bed so that her body faced his. 'You've not had a good day?' she asked.

'Most of it has been good.' He turned to look into her face, so close to his, and remembered her kiss. 'Some parts were very good.'

Kerim rested her warm face against his shoulder. Japh hesitated a little before he lifted his arm, shifted closer to Kerim and placed his arm around her. She sighed as she rested her head against his chest and her arm over his body.

'Is this alright?' he asked.

'Very nice. I'm enjoying this part of the day.'

'I'm glad,' he murmured turning his head so that his lips brushed the top of her head.

Kerim could hear the strong pounding of his heart. They lay still for a few moments.

'Thank you,' Japh breathed.

'You're welcome.' Kerim smiled. He was very welcome to hold her like this.

'You don't know what I am thanking you for yet.'

'I thought ... what are you thanking me for?' she whispered back.

'For decorating our room so well. It feels like home.'

'I'm glad you like it.'

'I thought all my drawings were lost to the flood.'

'I liked them so much I wanted them here.'

'Thank you!'

Kerim laughed quietly.

A short silence followed, punctuated only by Shem's snore.

'What had you thought I had been thanking you for before?' wondered Japh. Kerim only shrugged, pleased it was dark enough to hide her blush. 'Hmm.'

'The loom is lovely,' Kerim said quickly changing the subject. 'You worked really hard on that,'

'It was good to have something to do.'

'Thank you!'

'Now you're welcome!' Japh said. He wasn't distracted and was still trying to work it out. 'Please Kerim what did you think I was thanking you for?'

She shrugged again, but as it was dark, and her face was hidden, she felt there would be no harm in telling him.

'I thought you were thanking me for this,' she whispered squeezing him lightly.

'Oh!' Japh was taken aback as his heart raced once again. Kerim let out a little sigh. 'I am very thankful for this,' Japh said shakily as he applied a little pressure to her waist. 'You are wonderfully warm.'

'Glad to be of assistance.' Kerim teased.

'That is not what I meant.'

'I know,' she murmured.

Silence returned and neither spoke for a while. Kerim could feel the steady breathing below her head. She feared Japh was drifting off to sleep. This was the only time they had been alone all day and she didn't want to waste it.

'Japh?'

'Hmm.'

'I heard what your brothers were saying today.'

'I thought as much,' he said stroking his lips to her hair once more and breathing in her fragrance deeply. 'I think they might have worked that out, too.'

'Do they all hate me?'

'They don't hate you. You saw what they were like tonight, after my little chat with them. I think they were just curious that's all.'

'Do you think they are all like that?'

'No.'

'Lellia looks at me funny.'

Japh laughed. 'She looks at everyone funny.'

'Please don't laugh at me.'

'I wasn't.' Japh moved his free hand and rubbed her arm that was draped over his body. 'I think she has a look of approval about her. She likes you, I am sure of it.'

'Do you think I am silly?' But before he could answer she added. 'It's just that I am new to your family stuff.'

'I know. I understand.' He tilted her chin up so that he could see her face. Her eyes met his. 'You're good at it. They'll all love you when they get to know you.' Then he whispered, 'But not as much as I do.'

Japh let her look away. She sighed. He resumed stroking her arm.

Kerim said no more. It was blissful to be right there, in his arms. Her breathing deepened and slowed. She relaxed so much that she fell asleep with Japh still touching her tenderly.

He stayed awake for much longer. Having her so close was amazing. Nothing could compare to this. Her fragrance stunned him, her soft skin thrilled him. 'I've never been so happy, my love,' he whispered kissing her hair. Finally he fell asleep.

19

Work

Kerim had never slept so well. The gyrations of the ark didn't seem to bother her. Wrapped loosely against Japh, her sleep had been dream free and she was ever so warm. Even though she was awake, she lingered, enjoying the moment.

Japh shifted a little as he turned towards her, and pulled himself closer. She caught her breath— then relaxed again. She could hear the movement of someone in the living area, and although tempted to stay right where she was, felt slightly embarrassed that she may be found.

She thought about how to move without waking Japh, but it was too late. 'Are you awake?' he mumbled.

'Not yet,' she caressed his arm.

He snuggled towards her.

'I should to get up to help with breakfast.'

'Stay.'

'Japh!' Kerim tried to make it sound playful, but her tone had an air of caution. At the same time a loud cough came from the doorway.

Breakfast was a very quiet event. It seemed that the new movement of the ark, the unexpected rolling, was causing Shem some problems. He hardly said a word to anyone and returned to bed soon after getting up.

Helena ate a little before hurrying to Shem, also feeling a little unwell. Lellia, having eaten and watched Kerim and Japh intently over her meal set to work on the soil troughs. Ham joined her in planting some of the larger specimens they had bought on board.

'Oh no!' Kerim heard Lellia saying to Ham. 'Look, this branch has been snapped off.'

'I think planting them in this will protect them from toppling over again.'

'I don't know how they will survive in this dull light anyway.'

'Maybe,' Kerim began, hoping to help, 'if the rain slows or stops we could open some shutters and get some daylight in here.'

'That would be lovely.' Lellia looked up at the ceiling. 'But I don't think it is going to stop today. It is hammering harder than ever out there.'

'But we're warm and dry inside,' Japh said stroking Kerim's hair down her back.

'Hmm,' Lellia said in a satisfied tone.

'Do you want to help me with the goats?' Kerim said turning away from Lellia's intense look.

'Sure.'

'Japh doesn't do goats,' Shem's voice bounded from his room.

'He does now,' Kerim announced.

There were seven goats, six of which needed milking. Kerim collected a wooden pail from the corner and a short section of tree trunk, used for a stool, and set to work. Japh watched and learned. Kerim sat close to the goat's body, wiped the teats with edge of her apron before gently but firmly squeezing. It took her only a few moments before she had at least a cup full of milk.

'Do you want to have a go?' she asked.

'Er ... I'll just watch for now!'

'You sure?'

'Like Shem said, I don't really do goats.'

'You're not going to let him make fun of you are you?' Kerim teased. 'Well, come on then. It doesn't hurt,' she said as she made way for Japh to take her seat.

'It may not hurt me, but I might hurt them!'

'Just copy what I did.'

It took a little while before Japh had the skill, but before long he was beaming with success.

'There!' Kerim said triumphantly. 'Perhaps Shem would like the first taste!'

'Not sure his stomach would take it!'

Kerim found a second stool and pail, sat at the goat next to Japh and began to milk her.

'So what was your farm like?' Japh asked conversationally turning his head so that his face rested against the body of the goat.

'It was quite big.' Kerim grinned at the mess Japh was making on the floor. 'You might want to watch where you are putting that milk.'

'Ooppps!' Japh scraped some hay towards him to soak up the spillage . 'So it was big ...' he prompted.

'Yes.' She read his silence as interest and carried on. 'We had over two hundred head of sheep at one time. The pasture land was lush and our animals thrived on it. Our sheep would often have twins, the grass was that good.'

'What did you like best about living there?'

'The open space,' she said with a sigh as she looked about her confined room.

The only sounds for a few moments were the hammering rain and the rhythmic squirt of milk in the buckets.

'What about your parents? What were they like?' Japh asked nervously. 'You don't have to say if you don't want to.'

'I'm fine,' she assured him. 'My mother was about my height, her hair was straight like mine but I'm a lot fairer. I have my Dad's colouring. She was quite sensitive but could be very funny when she wasn't in her dark moods. Darius, my dad was a hard worker. I think that is why our farm was so successful. He spent lots of time worrying about my mother towards the end. I think he was one the kindest men I ever knew.'

'Where was your farm?'

'Below a high mountain, outside of the forest, with lots of fresh springs and a beautifully clear river. The mountain began smoking a while ago. That's when things started to really go wrong. The river no longer ran clear and the springs deteriorated soon after that. The water was still alright to drink, but it had a bitter taste. The forest wasn't affected though.'

'I know that mountain,' Japh added. 'I often watched it.'

'Really?'

'Hmm. Did you ever go into the forest?'

'As often as I could.'

Japh stared at his wife who was focused on the task of filling her bucket. 'Does it bother you? Me asking you questions?'

'No,' she smirked. 'The forest was beautiful. But it was the sound there that sent a tingle down my spine.' Kerim smiled at the memory. 'The animals would make such a stir when I went in. I like to think they were telling each other that something new had arrived. After a while, they would settle down. I felt safe there, like it was my own secret spot.

'Did you have a favourite species?'

'The birds.'

He seemed perplexed. 'Really, why?'

Her answer came quickly. 'Because they have such freedom. They can go anywhere,' Kerim stopped milking and moved the goat out of the way. She tethered another in its place and began again. 'There were these birds that had the most amazing tail feathers - they would change colour in the light.'

'I've seen them. We have a few like that.'

'We have more than a few of them,' Kerim chided. 'The funny thing is, the colourful one would do this sort of dance along a branch and then its partner would turn up, only she was dull looking.'

'Not everyone can be beautiful.' Japh exchanged his goat for another one. 'Only in our case it's the other way round!' Crouching next to her, he said, 'You must know that I think you are the most beautiful creature God has ever made.'

'Hmmm.' Kerim looked away from him again and sat quietly milking.

'You are.'

'Thank you,' she said looking up through her long lashes at him.

Japh tipped the pail so that she could see how much milk he had collected. 'So what do you think about my efforts?'

'Well done.' She reached inside the bucket and hooked out a couple of pieces of straw.

Japh lowered his voice and looked around. 'I'll give this lot to Shem and Ham!'

Kerim giggled. 'We better get back to the milking.'

The questions continued. Japh wanted to know all sorts of things about her life. After a while however, there were no more goats to milk and the couple took their pails into the kitchen.

It was nearing lunch time.

Shem had somehow struggled out of bed and joined the rest of the family in the cushioned area. Helena suggested he remain there for the rest of the day. Everyone stay relatively busy, although jobs on the ark were few. Lellia and Ham took care of the plants. Japh and Kerim tended the animals and refreshed their bedding material. Helena and Tabitha took charge of the food and Noah seemed to occupy himself with odd jobs.

Japh spent the afternoon with Kerim, finishing the loom. He made her laugh with his continuing flow of questions, some more serious than others. She returned the questions when given the chance. In doing so she discovered that Japh was similar to her many ways; from trivial things like colour preferences to things that made them laugh, thoughtful or angry. Kerim was amazed at the way they complimented each other, as if they had been designed that way. When he was silent for a long moment and it appeared that he had finally run out of details to pry from her, she began to giggle.

'What?' he asked.

'Are you finally finished?'

'I didn't think it was bothering you.'

'Not bothering me. Just amazed at how much you want to know.'

'There is so much more,' he said leaning back against the wooden wall in the living space and stretching his legs out in front of him.

'There is?' Kerim said astonished.

'Oh yes!' he laughed putting down the bobbin he was fixing together and reaching over to the cup of fresh milk he had beside him, and taking a sip. 'You are fascinating.'

'Japh!' she laughed.

'You are.' He took her hand, which was resting on her lap, in his. Twining his fingers between hers, he lifted it and ran the back of her hand down his cheek. Her skin was like silk on his stubbly face. He hesitated only momentarily than he ran his lips over the smooth surface, lingering there before he kissed it. 'You really are,' he said looking at her earnestly.

Kerim gave no reply. The intensity of his gaze took her breath away and gave her mind no chance to recover an answer. 'Thanks,' was all she could say.

Afternoon ran into evening, and evening into night. Shem and Helena excused themselves early. He was still feeling unwell. Soon afterwards, all the other couples followed and retired as well.

Japh was still in high spirits when he got into bed. He stretched out, arms behind his head and eyes closed until he felt Kerim close to him.

'Thank you for today,' he said naturally wrapping his arm about her.

She shuffled up closer to him, slowly sliding her hand over his torso.

'I'm glad I could be of assistance!' she whispered.

She sighed and relaxed against his body.

Quiet whispering could be heard from the other rooms for a short while before it was replaced with heavy breathing and snores.

Japh breathed steadily, but was not asleep. Kerim stroked her hand over his chest gently.

'Mmm. You have no idea how wonderful that feels.'

They lay silently for a long while, enjoying one another's presence.

'Japh?'

'Mmm.'

She listened to the hammering beat of his heart. 'I love you.'

He kissed the top of her head. 'I am glad to hear you say that.'

She sat up looking at him in the dim light. His eyes seemed gentle and caring.

'Will you come with me?'

'I'd go anywhere with you.'

She knew he would want to be where ever she was. Although it was dark, she knew he could sense her blushing.

Quietly they crept from their bed and gathered blankets over themselves. Kerim took his hand and guided him to the hatch which led below. She couldn't help but giggle a little. Steady snores and breathing soon faded as they headed down the ramp.

Light flashed behind Kerim. She turned to see her husband carrying a lamp.

'I thought it would be a bit dark down here without one,' he said.

'Alright,' she said breathlessly, still leading him downward.

The light gave safety to their feet. Whenever Kerim turned she found Japh gazing at her as if she were the most beautiful woman leading him. Her hair was loose and danced with her movement as she turned her face away from him. The blanket that was wrapped about her slipped to reveal her slender shoulder. Releasing her hand, Japh reached forward to cover her again. His rough fingers made contact with her soft skin as he gently lifted the blanket. She could hardly breathe.

His touch had made her smile.

Soon they were in the very depths of the ark. Kerim made her way over to the pile of hay that she had slept in, briefly, what seemed like a lifetime ago, yet it was only a few days. She laid out her blanket and sat down.

'Will you sit with me?' she asked shyly.

'Of course.'

Kerim shivered, although not from the cold.

'Here.' Japh unfurled the blanket about him and laid it over the both of them. 'We can share this one,' he said bending down to ensure her feet were covered. Kerim cuddled closer. She wanted this moment to last. Each day she had noticed something new about him and each new thing thrilled her.

She looked from his eyes to his lips and back again, and then kissed him. Both their hearts fluttered at the intimacy. He could feel her sweet breath through her parted lips and couldn't help but cup her face in his hands and hold her there. She tentatively draped her arms about his neck and ran her fingers in his hair. He took mere moments to respond. His hands flowed from her face down her body and wrapped around her waist but she did not pull away from him. He pulled her body closer to his.

20

Belonging

It had been very early when Japh had woken Kerim and led her back to their room. She had fallen back to sleep quickly, tucked closely to Japh. When her eyes opened, he was sitting beside her, staring. His expression was one of sheer joy.

Kerim felt the heat rise in her face.

'Good morning my love.'

Kerim pulled the cover up over her head.

'How are you this morning?'

'Good,' she muttered. But even she was surprised that is how she felt. She did feel good, in fact, better than good. There were no regrets. She felt secure and treasured. Japh was wonderful.

She smiled sweetly.

Japh winked. He was more than glad. He was thrilled. 'I love you.'

Kerim rubbed her face against his chest and sighed.

They lay quietly for a while.

'Time for breakfast.'

'Can't we just stay here?'

'Are you not hungry? Are you unwell?' he asked with concern.

Kerim laughed quietly. 'I am fine.'

'Come on then.' Japh tried to get up, but Kerim held onto him tighter.

Japh, willing, stayed where he was. He lifted her chin to tilt her head so that he could see into her face.

'I don't ... want any breakfast,' Kerim said.

'No breakfast?' Japh asked. 'That's not what you were going to say is it?'

'No!' Kerim admitted. Japh waited, trying to be patient. The chatter of his family drifted into their room.

'Please, what is it?' he whispered.

'I don't,' she began again, 'I don't want to go out there.'

'Why not?'

'I feel embarrassed.'

'Embarrassed?' Japh understood. 'Oh! Right!' He laughed.

'See! Even you are laughing at me.' She buried her head into his chest again.

'I'm laughing at myself,' Japh said gently. 'Maybe you are right. I will give it away.'

'What do you mean?'

'I feel so happy this morning. I am sure Lellia will pick up on it!'

'Oh don't!'

'Look, we have to go out there ... some time sooner or later.'

'Later maybe!' Kerim wished.

'The longer we stay the more suspicious they'll get!'

Kerim exhaled. 'I suppose so.'

She let Japh get up this time. They dressed silently, smiling as they caught the others attention. Kerim blushed heavily when she saw Japh's look of pleasure before she smoothed her skirt in place.

'You ready?' he whispered when they were finally done.

'No!'

Japh laughed, grabbed her hand, and strode out into the living space. Everyone was sitting on the cushions, eating breakfast. Kerim distinctly saw Lellia look up, her puzzled face quickly became enlightened with a wide smile. Kerim felt the blood rush to her face and couldn't stop it.

'Morning kids!' Noah said also smiling a little.

They knew, they all knew. Kerim would have run back to her room if Japh hadn't been holding her hand so tightly. He dragged her to the table and pulled her down to sit next to him.

'Morning everybody.'

Lellia passed the basket of bread. Her smile flashed in excitement.

'So, how are you two this morning? Is everyone feeling okay?'

Kerim sighed. Japh shook his head, then turned to Kerim and winked. He seemed to think that would be the worst of it.

'Well I didn't sleep that well last night,' Shem replied. 'I was woken up very early this morning. Someone left the hatch open. It was drafty.'

Helena whipped round to face him.

'That was probably my fault,' Japh admitted.

'Well,' Shem stuffed more bread into his mouth. 'Do you think you could shut it after you, next time? There are other people who live here too?'

Kerim breathed a collective sigh.

'Well,' Helena folded her hands. 'What's on the agenda for today?'

'Much the same as yesterday!' Ham laughed.

Japh interrupted, 'I was thinking...,'

'Sounds dangerous,' Shem added.

Japh continued, 'What if we hinged one or two of the shutters? Then we might be able to let some light in.'

'It would be good to get some fresh air in here,' Tabitha said.

'Good idea!' Noah praised. 'Then we could see if all this geshem is fresh water too. It could keep our stocks up.'

Japh left the table ready to take on the new project. 'There is stock pile of spare wood below, for repairs, maybe we could make up some doors too.'

And so the day began. Each to their own task. Kerim was grateful to be alive.

21

Perish

I watch as my friend stands by. His role is to observe not intervene. Julio, Urshia and Jabari crouch in a small cave on the peak of the mountain. They were tired and hungry. Every shelter on the mountainside is now occupied by the refugees. The peak is cramped with survivors but there is no one to uphold any kind of law. The humans have little regard for one another. Noxious yellow weaves through the air. Even the water doesn't dilute it.

The small family hears stories of massive waves engulfing villages, water spouting from the ground and ripping hillsides apart, there are accounts of stampeding animals destroying everything in sight and then there is the death. The thought of death is never ending, it occupies their every thought. Death fills the landscape. The stench of it blows on the wind and the existence of it floats on the deadly water that now laps high at the mountainside.

There are no escape routes. The only place they could go was up. And up on top of the mountain there is nowhere else to go. They are trapped. The rain continues, like it will never stop. There are no plants in this hostile place and so there is no food.

'Come on child. You must drink,' Urshia says.

'What is the point? We are all going to die,' Jabari murmurs.

'Stop that!'

Jabari has no energy to argue. Her spirit is low.

Julio sits by the entrance to their small cave. His once well kept beard is overgrown and his olive skin is almost pale. He barely says a word these days. He spends his time looking though the sheeting rain at the watery world that surrounds them. His face is grey in the weak light, he looks ill, but he has protected his family fiercely.

A stranger had joined them on the peak the previous day. He had forced a group of adolescent boys from their shelter to make room for himself and his gang. Not all the boys hadn't lasted the night. Three of them had died of exposure while the remaining two look close to death. No one cares for them, no one welcomes them in to whatever space they have, no one wants to become ill from exposure and then die.

'She won't drink father,' Urshia says quietly to Julio.

'Hmm.'

'Is that all you can do? She'll die if she doesn't drink something soon.'

The stranger goes out into the open to see the death he has caused. He stands over one of the corpses and kicks it. He calls a friend over to him and they begin to drag one of the dead boys back to the cave.

'What are they doing? I thought they were dead,' Urshia murmurs.

My friends and I, and Julio watches.

Even Julio can hear the raised voices from the strangers cave.

He continues to watch.

Day after day, death creeps closer. Jabari, who has been convinced to drink is as weak as her mother and they sit huddled together in the cave, drifting in and out of sleep. Julio sits in the entrance, far enough in to not get wet but close enough to keep a watchful eye.

People are too weak to attack and are dying all around. There is one exception.

The strangers group are strong. They may look pale but they have violent moods. Julio heard their fighting from where he sits. Julio has his suspicions. None of them are emaciated and their minds are still sharp. They must have food. But what is their source?

He has been fighting the urge to join them. He fears now that all his fight is gone. He will give in.

He takes his damp cloak, covers his weakened form and leaves the cave. He stumbles over to the stranger's camp. The men at the entrance push him away.

'Please, I want some.' Julio's voice is gruff from not being used.

'What do you want?' Came a strong reply from the darkness.

'Some ... some food,' Julio replies.

The laughing stops.

'Food?'

'I know that you have ... meat. Please, I want some,' Julio says his head bowed in the rain.

'What will you give us in return for such a meal?' the stranger asks drawing closer. He is muscular and well fed, but his face is drawn and his eyes, when Julio meets them, show a slight pang of pity.

'I don't have anything. None of us do.'

'He has women. I've seen them,' says the guard in an excited tone.' One is fair and young.'

179

And so a deal is struck. Julio has his first meal.

Urshia did not hear them advance on her. She is roused from her sleep too slowly to be able to protect herself. Battered and numb from what she was subjected to, she is fully awake, this is no nightmare.

The others draw close to her daughter. The men, strengthened by their food, and energised by evil, throw her aside. Her limp form hits the rock and she crumples to the floor.

The sound of their laughter and Jabari's sobbing fills the dark cave.

After the men had their way of ravaging, the girl is left alone. Out of necessity she creeps from her corner to the sleeping shell of her grandfather. He has something that she needs.

Her hatred is seething from her veins. He snores heavily as she approaches. She gently reaches inside his jacket, cringing away from his body, and pulls out the sharp knife.

She steps out into the rain and staggers a short distance down the mountain to the edge of the rising water. Raising the knife she wades into the water. Her tears mingle with the rain and she raises her head to the blackened sky. With a swift motion she plunges the knife through her stomach. The blood flows swiftly over her hands and into the water.

My friend has been told to show her mercy. As her life ebbs, she feels the drift and drag of the water taking her far away.

The water rises so high that every living soul is forced from their shelters to the peak of the mountain. Julio has lost his mind. He is tormented day and night by what he has done. He has shed innocent blood and from that he cannot escape.

The cold water and exposure take the others quickly but for Julio such mercy is not at hand. He is alone, with the stranger's gang. Together they face a long death. Their energy and strength can endure the chill of the water as it rises about them. They continue to fight for life though survival is not in sight.

Julio wants to die, but he decides this torment is his punishment for bad deeds. How could he commit such evil?

The water is so high now that there is no footing. The currents are strong, but not strong enough to drag him under. He has the muscle to tread water for a while. The time passes, each moment bringing a higher level of agony. Then it happens, a spark of mercy even, his muscles seize up. Julio sinks below the water, but rises again quickly gasping for breath. Water pours into his open mouth. Coughing and spluttering he sinks down again. His body will not show him any kindness. His body fights for life. He lingers above the water for a few moments before he sinks once more, expelling his last breath in a series of bubbles. He gasps and fills his lungs with water. It burns in his lungs and floods his senses. There is no more fighting.

He sinks beneath the waves. The last human without the safety of the ark. Finally the vision is gone. My friend weeps as he speeds to us.

22

Forty Days

The rain and darkness continued. Everything was done in the light of oil lamps and the scarce illumination the slightly open shutters permitted. Day and night were blurred.

The routine of life on board the ark was difficult for Japh. He was desperate for something to do. Kerim had managed to stay distracted enough. She created a covering that would offer she and Japh a little privacy for their room. The colours she chose arrayed the small figures and scenes of her new home. The design was full of hope and seemed to inspire the others. Their spirits were lifted as they sat and watched her weave.

That morning had passed like all the others until a sliver of light broke through the barely open shutters. It cast a golden ray into the ark and creating shapes of warm honey coloured floor. It was a sign.

The family paused, one by one. The drumming had stopped. The ark moved steadily through the waters. geshem was silenced.

'It has stopped,' yelled Shem from the deck below as he ran up the ramp.

'Let's take a look!' laughed Ham.

The family gathered as a group in the centre. Noah, who had been quietly thinking in his chair, sat with a large smile upon his face. 'We should see what the world looks like.'

Each son stood by a shutter, his wife at his side.

'On the count of three!' Noah said. 'One ... two ... three!'

The shutters were unlatched and pulled away. Bright white light streamed in from all sides, filling the room with painful brightness. Dust danced and drifted in the air, caught now in harsh beams of daylight. A cool, refreshing breeze blew across the room, swirling loose debris and hair in circles. It carried with it a strong salty scent, which swept away the sweaty animal smell within a few seconds. The fresh taste was to be savoured.

As Japh's eyes grew used to the light he stared out in amazement. Clambering up on a hay bale, Kerim stuck her head out of the window to take in an uninterrupted view. She squinted. Above her were patches of deep blue, framed by giant masses of white, scuttling across the sky.

The water was everywhere, from one side of the horizon to the other. In the sky to the far end of the ark a painfully bright orb illuminated the expanse. She was aware of the gasps from the others but did not want to be drawn from this magnificent sight.

The light was pure and strong. It glistened off the water and sparkled in her eyes. She had never seen anything so glorious. Their days of gloom were gone as the new light replaced their weary lives with hope. Kerim watched in amazement as the patches of the broken covering she had been used to, floated overhead without care.

The water spread as far as she could see and well beyond that too. The sky domed above hemming them in on every side. Kerim smiled as she looked at Japh. They had been saved. She did not mention that no one could see land. Still, she held it in her heart and offered up a prayer.

'God please remember our boat on this great and vast ocean.'

'Do you see them? They are full of wonder.'

I glance down at the ark. 'It is the sky that captures their attention.'

'They have never seen it before.'

The wonderful light will enhance their world.

'Are we are still to be on guard?'

'Yes. It's only a matter of time before they are discovered.'

'Their race has survived.'

'Yes Trust. And this family will be the new beginning.'

I look on at the awestruck faces of Japh and Kerim, my own face perplexed at the extraordinary purpose and plan of the Creator.

'It is amazing that even now, as they float on this sea of judgement, that they are also surrounded by the totally immeasurable grace that the Lord had bestowed on them.'

I know that below the waves, lay valleys and mountains, deserts and forests. The torrent of mud filled water had carried animals from both land and sea to their deaths. Millions of sea creatures now lay buried under layers of mud all over the world. In other places larger animals were similarly trapped. Some had not even seen it coming; they were in the act of rearing their young, eating or fighting. It had come too suddenly for them.

Many had run, leaving their tracks in the soft ground as the only evidence they had once existed, now also preserved under heavy mud being compressed from above. They had escaped the initial deluge by taking to higher ground, only to be cut off and die by starvation, exposure or eventual drowning. Their bodies consumed by water creatures or left to rot floating on the surface of the waters once they had met their end.

Whole forests standing, halfway up their trunks in mud, canopies covered by deep water, shed seed that now flow on the currents, preserved in cold salty water. Vegetation is trapped between the solid ground in which it grew and silt. It is being squeezed from the pressure of the water above. It is changing in appearance and texture.

The sea animals sense the change in the water. The salt levels are lower and the area in which they roam is vast. Other fish have joined them in their expanded home. There is plenty to eat, and little competition. The fresh water fish adapt to the higher levels of salt, and their bodies cope well. The expanse before them is huge, and the creatures here are far beyond they had experienced. They keep their distance for their own safety, finding food and shelter from objects that float above them, and in the mass of hiding places that had once been above the water.

23

New Horizon

The clouds, ananah (named by Helena) continued to thin throughout the day. The ball of light, the sun, shemesh (named by Noah) had travelled across the sky and was now sinking beyond the sea. As it dipped lower it spread red and gold streaks across the expanse above.

'Where is it going?'

The family on board watched as the day ended. The remaining clouds changed colour before their eyes. 'They are on fire,' Shem shouts.

'No my son. The orb is moving. It is what brings the day.'

He turned and asked, 'How do you know this father?'

Tabitha stepped forward and eased their conscience. 'Your father knows things that you are too young to understand.' She looked at Noah, 'Perhaps it is time to share the knowledge?'

Noah's eyes widened as he contemplated.

Their gentle voices carry over the water and into the night. They have found peace again. How good it is that they have seen this day in its completeness.

I am thrilled that Japh and Kerim have discovered the beauty of this their first unveiled day. They marvel at the sun and the moon, just as I have done for so long. They understand so little of it all, yet have received the sight with enthusiasm.

The oil lamps had been lit, one by one. The women eagerly prepared a celebration for the evening but their energy was too much to constrain them to inside. Together the family climbed out the windows and onto the deck of the roof.

They each gasped as they stood in the night. Their eyes and hearts filled with wonder. They had not realised until this point what it was they had lived through. God had judged the earth.

The whole world was beneath the sea.

Japh stood beside Kerim. 'You are free my love, like the birds in the forest.'

She squeezed his hand. 'There are no words to explain this.'

They were all silent for a moment. Kerim watched the light dance on the gentle waves. The bright yellow orb that had lit the day was now replaced by the cool light from a white disk. It hung in the distant sky, but shadows and variations to its surface could be made out.

The light was clean and gentle, unlike the glare of the day time sun. This was one that could be looked at. Other specks filled the sky, accompanying it. Pinpricks of light dotted the darkness above them; some collected together in a swathe across the expanse.

As the air cooled the family returned inside for the celebration meal. Too enthused to sit down and eat the festivities turned to dancing.

Each family member had taken their turn at entertaining. Kerim had found that Shem was by far the funniest on that night. He had written and performed a song about their journey thus far but contained so much wit that the whole family begged him to perform it again.

Raucous laughter filled the air over the silly words and ridiculous puns he had added. The echo of their laughter could be heard outside the ark. A spark of hope and the smell of life.

They were not alone in the coolness of the night. A scaly creature of darkness hears them. He hovers silently nearby. At once he understands why the Creator has not destroyed the world and removed it from existence. There are still humans here. The Creator has not given up on the human race. There is another chance for them. The demon listens as it glides ever closer to the gentle, uninterrupted chatter.

'You will come no closer!' the voice of my friend booms from above its head. The angel stands above the surface of the water with his blade drawn and shinning. The creature jumps and flees in terror. The spindly creature glances back and sees that there is not just one angel, but a battalion of light.

It is fearful; not wanting to be the bearer of this news.

I stand on the roof, receiving the report.

'The demon approached, but was quickly sent on its way.'

'Thank you.' I turn to Trust. 'We must be vigilant my friend. The news will spread fast to the enemy. We must station ourselves as a barrier surrounding the remnant of the human race and animals.'

'May I suggest that we quickly find this creature to stop the news from reaching the enemy.' My friend is eager to protect.

'I thought that too, but the Creator has said to let the creature do what it feels fit.'

'Even now He shows that He is all powerful to such creatures and their futile ways. He sees beyond it all.' Trust laughs. 'I will set up the guard.'

'Excellent my friend. We are not yet done here.'

24

Trouble

It had seemed such a long time since the night of celebration. Notch after notch was added to the beam counting the days. Several months passed. The water remained and no land could be seen. Japh and Kerim often escaped to the roof once the others had gone to bed. They would lie on their backs and watch the stars, naming the patterns that they made in the ebony sky. They became so familiar with the display that they found some stars didn't move with the constellations, but flowed through them. There were five in all.

Night after night they watched as the ark continued to float in the current. It was up there that they discussed the future. 'What will happen when we get off this boat?' Kerim asked. 'We cannot live here forever.'

Japh put his arm round his young wife. 'The Lord would not save us from the flood to let us die on a boat.'

'But where will all this water go? The land has not floated to the surface with us.'

'Where did it all come from in the first place?' Japh asked.

'It is not for us to know.'

'Well, that is our answer.'

The next morning Kerim awoke with a headache. Japh had snored all night which left her unsettled. Her mind kept turning to different worries; the vast water— where ever would it go. And food, what would they eat as the food supply began to diminish. And the waning moon, was it right to be slowly disappearing? What of the animals below deck, they were starting to stir from their long sleep?

As the day dragged on, so did her mood. Even the goats seemed uncooperative, which made her headache flare more. She made the mistake of getting cross with it. A moment later and the wooden pail lay upturned on the dirty floor, milk spreading though the manure piles.

'That does it!' she screeched stamping her foot. Kerim groaned and hid her head in her hands.

Tabitha called from the family room. 'Where's today's milk? I need it for the midday meal.'

Kerim stomped into the family room empty handed. 'Sorry but you'll have to use Japh's.' He had already finished his chores and had no trouble at all filling his pail.

Japh poked his head around the corner from the cushioned area wiping his mouth. 'Whoops. I sort of doled it out between me and the boys.'

'You drank all the milk?'

'I was sure your pail would have more than mine.'

'Great!' Tabitha turned away annoyed. 'I'll have to come up with something else now.'

'How was I supposed to know?' Japh stated defending himself. 'Everyone had some anyway.'

'I didn't,' Kerim muttered as Japh got to his feet and returned to the goats to clean up the mess.

I lower myself through the roof and watch as agitation and irritation festers amongst the family. This behaviour is unexpected for the Remnant, something is wrong. I listen more intently trying to guess who our evil visitor may be. Rather than assume I call for assistance.

A guard approaches.

'Scan the ark for an intruder. Check the main level and let me know when you find it.'

'Ow!'

'How was I supposed to know you were right behind me?' laughed Shem holding the hatch open again.

'You could have looked,' Ham said nursing the lump on his head.

'Boys! Your father is resting,' Tabitha urged. 'So keep the noise down.'

Ham pushed angrily past Shem, knocking him off his feet. Losing his balance at the same moment that the ark swayed, Shem fell straight into the raised vegetable patch.

'Shem!' Lellia shouted.

'It wasn't my fault,' he said climbing out and brushing off the dirt.

'Look what you've done!' Lellia said and she rushed forward. 'My poor peas. You've squashed them. They'll not grow now!'

'Sorry,' Shem said but turned to Ham. 'It was your fault.'

'Enough!'

Everyone turned to see Noah framed in the doorway to his room.

'Enough fighting. No more, do you hear?' he commanded.

No one spoke.

'Good,' Noah said a little more calmly, although still not himself, and returned to his room.

Kerim had enough. What was going on today? What was with everyone? She thought she had best go and help Japh clean out the goats; she hadn't been very happy herself.

She lingered by the doorway long enough to see that Japh was not really working.

'You alright?' he asked.

'No,' she answered shortly.

I see it, crouched in the centre of the room, waving its arms and causing havoc. The creature has a wide arrogant smile. Its hairy face has parted to reveal a mismatched set of teeth. It seems to take pleasure in the work it is doing. The family are being affected in a way that even they don't seem to understand.

I flare into light. The demon recoils. His smile vanishes when it sees Trust and I.

'Your name is Trouble.'

'Yes,' it replies in a subtle tone, pleased that we know its name. 'I had no idea you were in charge here, I thought the humans had all gone.'

'Leave or you will be banished.'

'I have no intention of causing myself trouble!' It laughs stepping back as it vanishes though the wall.

'He will tell the others?'

'You can be certain,' I reply.

The family worked in silence. Japh had swept up the room before he realised Kerim was crying.

'Alright, I can see you're not okay,' Japh said soothingly as he put his arm about her. 'There's no use crying over spilt milk. There'll be more tomorrow.'

'It isn't just that,' she sobbed wiping the tears from her cheeks.

'What's going on?'

'I didn't sleep well and now my head aches,' Kerim rubbed her temples.

'Do you want to lay down?'

She shook her head. 'No, what I really want to do is get off the ark and run in the meadow.'

'Don't we all,' Japh replied.

'I'm feeling trapped.'

Japh rubbed his hands down her arms.

'Even in the cage I didn't feel this trapped,' It took a moment for Japh to register what Kerim had said. 'At least in the cage I thought it would soon be over.'

25

Forgotten

$\mathbf{D}$ay after day the boat drifted without an island of land to stop its course.

'What of the creature?' I ask.

'It still follows. It remains distant; it has not left the ark these past hundred and forty nine days. It still licks its wounds.'

I look into the murky water and see the little creature sat hunched just under the surface of the water. It spits out swirls of yellow gas as it mutters to itself. I listen carefully to what it says. Its voice is rasping.

'I won't do it. I won't. But I can't hide from the master forever. Forever is such a long time. Let another find them. They should have done it by now if they had looked properly. It is not as if the great big boat is as tiny as a leaf is it now? No. No, they all want to believe that it has been finished; the human race wiped out. What is it with them? Are they blind or something?' It shifts a little and sticks its head out above the water. The ark cuts through the waves some distance from it.

'See! Still no sign of them. What are they all doing? They can't still be that ignorant. I can't and I won't tell him. Let him find out another way. If I tell him now that will be the end of me anyway.' The creature glares at the ark but is not aware that I watch and listen. It follows at what it considers a safe distance away from the guards. Day after day it follows, and no one has come to join it.

'No one else is aware of the massive mistake that the master has made in missing this one!'

I turn away and face my friend once more. 'It lives in fear,' I say, saddened. 'To think, it had once worshipped with us.'

Another angel approaches. 'You asked me to report when the family had sat down to eat. They are just about to.'

'Excellent! Thank you. We will have some action my friends.' I turn to Trust. 'The Lord spoke with me. We are to let the hordes know that we are here.'

'It is done.' Trust disappears in a flash of purest white light.

I allow myself to sink through the roof into the living space of the family.

Kerim was at her loom, concentrating on an intricate weave. Japh, Shem and Ham were playing a game they had devised using different coloured wasted seed heads, every few minutes laughing loudly at each other. Helena and Lellia sat nearby sewing and humming. Tabitha and Noah talked privately in their room but their voices fluttered into the living space.

Lellia smiled as if to say I can hear them too.

'It is my fault we are in this predicament,' Noah muttered.

'It is because of you that we are still alive Noah.'

'You know, that is not what I mean.'

Kerim did not understand why her father was so cross.

'Yes, I know but we can't live on this boat forever.'

'It is an ark, our place of salvation. It is here to save us,' she stated.

'But it is not saving us now. It is killing us slowly.'

'Noah!' Tabitha raised her voice so that the whole room became quiet. 'You have led us here by faith. Don't you go giving up now!'

'Well I want out. I want to be in the fields, working where I can feel the soil under my feet and where a man can come home because he is tired from toiling outside, not because he was indoors and having been lazy.'

'You cannot make those demands and neither can I. You trusted God to build this boat and gave your life for it. You know better than anyone here what it is like to trust. I suggest you remember that.'

All the family started to look to each other. The silence was so thick.

Kerim had felt trapped and frightened. There didn't seem to be any end in sight. She hadn't thought much about the promise, she'd only been bickering with herself. Where had her faith gone? She grasped at the glimmer of hope Tabitha set before them. She should dream of life outside the ark for surely it would come to pass.

'You are right my dear. He will rescue us. I trust Him.'

Noah emerged with his head held high and his shoulders pulled back. He seemed renewed and refreshed, after a little coaching from his wife. Tabitha looped her arm around his, blotting her eyes. She loved him, and everyone knew it.

The family quickly resumed what they were doing as if they each heard nothing.

'Time to eat,' Tabitha said cheerily.

Everyone busied themselves with food preparation and distribution, perhaps a little more enthusiastic than before. The delicious fragrance of fresh bread, still warm, flooded the room and was bought to the eating area by Helena. Lellia picked small, sweet tomatoes from the vines, adding them to the salad on the table next to a large bowl of goat's cheese Japh had made.

The family sat once again to eat together.

The endless season was taking its toll on the family, and spirits were low. But still Noah gave thanks for the food. 'Lord, we are so grateful for your provision, not only the food to eat but for the salvation you continue to bestow on us. Remember us oh Lord. You have saved us; we are trusting You to rescue us and establish us. Draw near to us.'

All the family agreed. 'Amen!'

I hear the prayer. It is loud and clear. It will be heard and answered.

I go straight to the throne room to hear the answer. The beautiful light somehow shines brighter now. The prayer has already been heard. But even before it had fallen from the lips of Noah, the water stopped flowing from the rock bed and a strong wind had begun to blow thousands of miles away. Faith was heard in Noah's heart before it was proclaimed from his mouth. The Creator sees the heart for what it is. He has seen the renewed faith, not only in Noah but in the rest of his family.

The answer is dramatic. The Creator has remembered the small remnant, His people, and is about to redeem them. I rush back to them.

Trust has travelled some distance away and now hovers over the water. He rises slightly and flares himself in light.

A few moments pass before the sea water bubbles and churns as demon troops are sent to the surface. The water steams in the heat of the bodies.

He rises higher into the air, his bow of light already strung with an arrow. Body after body springs from the sea, yet he doesn't flee.

The leader propels itself to the surface with so much force that even his hordes scatter.

'How dare you come here!' it screams. 'This is my planet now! Your creator has been overthrown and has no power.'

'Is that what you think?' Trust replies with little respect. 'How very little you know.'

The creature straightens its death stained body, and rises above the water regally.

'You claim to know something.' It glares, eyes flashing angrily. 'What would a mere angel know? I am the all-powerful one!'

'How little you know!' Trust mocks, as he spins out of the centre of the horde and speeds across the waves.

'Get after that ... thing!' the creature commands.

Trust flies with great speed, but not so great as to lose the great black cloud of bodies that now follows.

The creature reaches out its claws that glint with violence.

Japh was sitting idly at the window twiddling his thumbs. He let out a sigh in frustration. Nothing had changed. He had been discouraged for a few days, feeling boredom, frustration and anger that this was continuing. How much longer? The water stretched from one side of the horizon to the other. It was breath taking as a scene; a few waves here and there, the bright sun glinting off them, the stunning blue of the sky reflecting back at him. It was amazing at how something so beautiful could be so depressing.

'Come and sit with me,' Kerim said quietly.

Japh turned and smiled, but it faded quickly. He clambered down and sat next to Kerim on the floor as she worked with the dyed wool, weaving the intricate pattern.

'Why so low?' she asked at last, as she turned and saw Japh gazing at the material but not really seeing it. 'Is there anything I can do?'

'Not unless you are extremely thirsty,' he sighed.

Japh sat for a moment longer, fiddling with Kerim's hair. She was distracted enough to laugh a little at him.

'Go find something to do,' Kerim suggested.

'There is nothing to do.'

'That's not strictly true.'

'Well, what do you suggest?' Japh ran a finger down her spine.

'Japh!' she sighed. 'How about you reorganise that cupboard you were complaining about the other day.'

'I suppose ... do you want to help?'

'Do you want me to help?'

'It would be more fun with you there!'

Kerim put her work down. 'Come on then.'

They went into their room. It had changed quite a lot since the beginning of their exile. Japh had built shelves on the end wall with a wide lip on the front edge to stop items from falling off with the movement of the ark. The shelves were full of folded clothes and blankets. The end wall was covered in these shelves.

Kerim had made two curtains and tacked them in front of the door frame and shelves. Now their room walls were no longer bare. There were many drawings she salvaged from Japh's old room, but also several new ones. Japh had continued to sketch. Several of his works were studies made of the family or animals on board. There were also some larger, delicate likenesses of Kerim pinned to the walls.

The bed was unmade. Kerim set about straightening the covers.

Japh unhooked the curtain from the door letting it drop and block out the light.

'I can't see what I'm doing now Japh!' Kerim went over and hooked the curtain back again.

'Can't we just sit for a bit,' he said lounging on the bed.

'I thought you wanted something to do.'

'Yeah. I guess.'

'The cupboard?'

'Don't really feel like doing that now.' He turned to look at the wooden cupboard next to the bed. 'It's not that bad really. I can live with it.'

'So what are you going to do?'

'Sit with you for a bit?' Japh said smiling up at her.

'Japh!' Kerim sat down next to him and he wrapped his arms around her.

'You're gorgeous.'

'So you keep telling me!' Kerim sighed stroking the backs of his hands. She rested her head against his shoulder. 'Can you remember what grass smells like?' He didn't answer. 'No, I can't either.'

'What about the sound of the wind in the trees?' Japh asked. 'Do you think we will ever hear the trees or smell dewy grass again?' Kerim only sighed. 'I need to be certain that we will. I can't live like this forever without a little bit of hope.'

'I want to have a farm on a hill with sheep in lush fields, I want to raise children,' Kerim said smiling at her dream. 'I want to enjoy the sun on my face and be free to run where I want.'

Japh kissed her head. 'Farm. Sheep. Children. Place to run.' He sighed. 'Sounds idyllic.'

'It will be reality. We just need to be patient my love,' Kerim murmured.

'I never was good at being patient!'

'The things we aren't good at, we get tested in.'

'I think I've had enough testing!' Japh laughed.

'Obviously not enough yet then!'

'Walking the lower decks is peaceful you know,' she suggested

'It's not the same as the farm, or the forest. It's not the same as home.'

'I know. But maybe it will help to clear your head a little.'

He smiled at her. She was only trying to give him a change of scenery. He rose from the bed, pulled her up to him and into a hug.

He walked slowly from the room and escaped down the ramp.

It was quieter down here. Images of his old home flooded through his mind, and lost in thought he found himself at the very bottom of the ark. The animals still slept. How blissful it would be to just sleep through all this and be woken after it had all happened. To be an animal, without a care in the world.

'Japh!'

'Yes.' He turned but did not see anyone. 'Who's there?'

'Japh!' The voice was soft, almost a whisper. 'I am here.'

'But I ...' Japh span round.

'You need to get the windows shut and your family secure. I am coming, I have remembered you.' Japh felt a pleasant warmth seep through his body filling him with a peace that he had never known before. His mind was now perfectly clear and calm yet eager to fulfil the instructions.

He sprinted up the ramp, realising that as he reached the top just how unfit his confinement had made him, because he puffed and felt heavy legged.

'We need to shutter the windows,' he panted as he bent in double. 'We need to secure everything down.'

'Why so urgent brother?' joked Shem, as he helped Helena grind the corn in the hand mill. She smiled up at her husband, as she gathered the flour in the pottery bowl.

Lellia giggled from the other side of the room. She had been sitting mending Ham's thick jacket that had torn on a pen two days ago.

'Hang on a minute,' Ham said in his low voice as he stood. 'What is it brother? What have you seen?' he asked as he patted Japh's back.

'I haven't seen anything,' Japh began as he picked up the shutter nearest him and clumsily started to fix in back against the opening. 'I heard Him speak to me.' Kerim jumped to her feet to help. The others just looked up from what they were doing. 'Come on! We need to secure ourselves again. He said He was coming.'

The old man, who had sitting quietly, rose from his chair without a word and began to help. The rest of the family quickly followed; if he was helping they should too.

It took a few minutes to fix the shutters back in place, but the bowls and other daily things that were in use were all over the room. They gathered them as quickly as they could.

The swarm moves like a swelling cloud of dirt and grime, somehow attracted to the little dazzling white speck that is my friend, but never quite managing to catch it.

On the horizon, ever coming closer, Trust can see the dark speck that is the ark.

I see him clearly. He turns to observe the mass that follows at such close quarters, their hearts set on power and destruction.

Then I see him, the master of the demonic horde. His body powerful but hideous. His eyes flare with intense anger as he focuses on this fragile human existence. When he again looks towards his prey, there is nothing there. The angel has gone... but not before leading him to the last hiding place.

Trust appears in a flash of light.

'News?' I ask.

'I have led them here Hope!' Trust looks concerned. 'I have only ever once seen him so angry. He does not want to be beaten again.'

'Excellent!' And it is so! This self proclaimed all powerful master must be put in his place. 'Get to your post my friend.'

I stand on the roof of the ark and watch.

The small creature has seen them arrive. It is hard to miss the great, swirling, sinister cloud that is now spreading out to encircle the boat and this precious cargo.

'So they come at last do they!' it whispers, not wanting to be discovered. 'I wonder if I should stay or not. I could leave, but then I would miss out on all the fun. I could quite easily just fit back in to the army; no one would notice me not being there all this time. This insignificant crowd of humans stands no chance against such a force. The nasty little humans would be gone for good. If I flee, and hide, they will find me. I can't spend eternity not knowing.' I see its eyes began to flare again, deep and violent. It is certain that to be part of the winning side, it is best just to slip back in. 'I will not let others gain more glory than me.'

It rasps as it spits out a poisonous cloud of yellow smoke. 'Let me have my glory.'

Self power and glory are like poison; they destroy whatever they touch.

The family sat in silence. Everything had been done in such a hurry that their faces were red and sweaty. Nothing was happening. Everything was extra-ordinarily still.

The angels stand guard within the vessel. Lining the walls. They are still. They are ready.

I step outside and watch.

The swarm of demons forms a smoking ring around the boat. They screech and jeer at the little wooden vessel.

The master of them all, stands at the head of the boat. It stations its most trusted demons at equal intervals in the ring.

'Master! My lord!' A large black toothed demon approaches clutching a squirming ball in its claws. 'We found this one trying to get into the ranks.'

'Into the ranks?' it questions. 'Where was it then?'

'Master have mercy! I was just trying to find a good spot!' The little creature bows low.

'You were not in my ranks earlier.'

'I was my master. I was always here.'

'You were not. And now you call me a fool. I am not a fool. I am all powerful. And do not lie to me. I am the father of all lies so I can always tell.'

'I am sorry my master!' the creature begs as it is released at its feet.

'You have no time to be sorry,' it laughs as reaches out its claws which glint with death.

Its claws dig into the flesh, which sizzles and burns until a moment later, the creature is no more than a swirl of yellow smoke.

'Attack!' it screams.

The hordes hasten to obey its every word and fight their way to attack the ark.

The boat is swallowed by the mass of the army. They engulf it completely.

There is an indistinguishable noise and it is growing louder.

On the horizon I see a cloud being sucked towards the water. It is increasing in size as each moment passes. The progress of the army is swift but this swirling mass is drawing closer and closer.

The noise. It roars as if angry. It is moving this way, directly towards the ark and the motionless army.

'Attack I said!' but its voice is not as strong as the howling now.

The violent wind has gathered strength over thousands of miles. It travels fast and furiously, covering leagues in moments. It churns up the water and lashes at the boat, howling in rage and tossing the water into massive waves. Violent in its intent to destroy, it whips around the cleverly crafted vessel, and bounds off its solid sides, throwing all those around it into disarray.

I see the weaker, smaller demons buffeted and blown away from the vessel, swords flying aimlessly. But the wind still grows in strength. Now even the larger ones are struggling to cling on. They are fighting each other, believing the attack has come from within my own ranks, desperate to save their own necks. Demon against demon. Swirls of insipid gases are dispersed in this infernal wind, as each are destroyed.

'No, this can't be happening.' It screams although I can barely hear its voice. It desperately digs its claws into the bow of the vessel.

Demons flee from the scene, injured and tossed about as if they weigh nothing. They do weigh nothing … in this world. This is no ordinary wind.

The wind is so strong now; it is alone clinging to its prey. Its claws take the strain of holding its serpentine body in place.

The pressure is becoming too much.

It screeches as the claws are pulled from its fingers and its grip is lost. The wind catches, tosses and dispatches it far away.

'Do not rest ... I am not finished,' it screams as it is torn away.

26

Recede

The family sat huddled together while the wind howled. Hour after hour the wind battered and buffeted the vessel. Grateful for the warning, the family had secured themselves, sitting together. Kerim nestled close to Japh as they watched Shem grow increasingly pale with the undulating movements. Helena looked worried as she gently cooled his brow with a cloth dampened with fresh water. He was grateful for the attention.

Waves rise and fall in the onslaught of the wind, smashing into one another, lifting spray high into the air. The mighty crashes are lost in the howling of the wind. Sweeping tiny droplets of water from the sea's surface and carrying them high above, there to join millions of others in the form of clouds. The hot air wafts over the surface of the deep, drinking greedily, evaporating the body of water.

Near to the ark the wind is warm and dry, thousands of miles north, the temperature sinks below which any animal would have survived. Swirls of deadly air stir up the water as it thickens with ice, crushing the crystals together until the water becomes tightly packed and solid. Soon growing bodies of ice float in the slowly freezing sea. At first there are only a few, but before long hundreds cram together, exposed to the chill air. The wind roars over the icy forms, carving elegant hollows and sharp peaks from the slabs.

Deep below the earth's crust begins to move. Large crevices and splits open with incredible force, sucking huge volumes of water and debris into the voids. Underground lakes and seas are being created, but this movement in one place also produces an equal and opposite reaction elsewhere. The huge plates of the earth's crust are being pushed and shoved, little by little, and where there are weak points in the solid rock the forms are changing. The weak points began to fold, rising towards the surface of the water.

'First the water from the sky, the rain, and now this terrible wind. Will it ever stop?' Lellia complained as the whole family sat idle in the living quarters of the ark. That Lellia would make such a remark, in itself was evidence at the uneasiness the family was suffering. Ham reclined next to his wife, even he had run out of patience.

'At least in the rain we were able to do something. Anything would be welcome compared to this.'

'But it must be for the good,' Kerim said quietly to Japh. 'All this must be for our good.'

'Boredom takes its toll on all of us,' Japh replied. 'If the ark would just not roll so much and we could all get on and do something. Time drags while we sit here.'

Noah, who sat in his comfortable chair, was as restless as the rest of them. It seemed from the very beginning of this task, many years ago, he had been working hard, but since entering the ark, there had been very little to do. At first the rest was welcome, but now he was desperate to be out in his fields or at his lathe, anything but sat in this chair.

A few moments into his thoughts and he was jolted back to the stale, dull room. A low sound was rumbling though the floor. Everyone heard it and the irregular chattering stopped instantly.

'What was that?' Shem said reaching out a hand to touch the bare floor.

The room was tense with expectation for several long seconds, before they all seemed to breathe again. Then it came again, only this time the sound lingered a little longer, a rumbling sound added to by a deep toneless note. The vibrations set the crockery rattling and the dust on the floor into smoky ribbons before fading once again.

On the corners of the ark, attached to long thick ropes great levelling stones had been tied. They had steadied the ark in the rolling water. Deep under the surface of the water a levelling stone had brushed against something, it had touched land, the vibrations travelled up the rope and echoed through the hull of the ark. The ark was connecting once again to solid land, be it only for a few seconds before being swept on.

'I think it sounded like something was being crushed or scraped,' Ham said.

They were all quiet once more, sat still and listening.

'I think you are right Ham. I think it may be our levelling stones. They may have hit some land,' Noah smiled, his whiskers twitching.

Japh leapt to his feet and rushed to open the shutter, perhaps expecting to see a mighty landscape before him, but there was nothing but water.

'The stones are dragging on the ground under the water, we must be somewhere where the land is high but still under the sea.'

Again the scraping sound vibrated through the wooden floor and walls, louder than before and not concentrated to the far corner, but spread over three instead. The sound stopped and the ark gave a small jolt, as if snagged on something that gave way quickly under the pressure of the massive vessel. A few moments passed and again the same thing happened, the scraping, grinding sound, the tug on the flow of the boat and then a slight release. Time after time it happened, the noise coming so frequent that the only time when it was absent was when long low creaking moans filled the boat with tension. At one point, as the ark had been held in this tension a large swell of a wave hit the side and a deafening bang echoed through the sea and into the very fibres of the timber that made up the ark. A rope that had held a levelling stone had snapped under the strain and the ark had torn itself free. From then on the ark drifted to one side when the stones caught the earth below the waves.

For half a day this continued, the jolts becoming less vicious and the rolling now a gentle rock but becoming more frequent. Each time, as the ropes strained the family collectively stilled like statues waiting for the movement once more. They thrilled at the turn of events.

Suddenly the whole vessel shook as a deep rumble came up from the very base of the boat. The sound was deafening.

There was no rocking movement at all. The family lay sprawled over the cushions at the abrupt stillness. The ark had been stopped.

The family screamed and shouted in shock.

'What's happening?'

'I'm going to be sick!'

The grinding no longer came from the levelling stones; it was the bottom of the hull that was making contact with a solid surface. It had hit land, or land had hit it. Had the vessel been travelling at the speed of the water current, it would have been fatally damaged, but, as the stones had slowed the motion, the boat came to rest quickly and as gently as possible for such a large structure, on the slowly rising rock bed hidden below the water. The ark now sat trapped in mid sea.

Silence had fallen in the family room. Noah leapt to his feet making the rest of the family jump. 'Boys!' he indicated to the ramp, 'Check the vessel for damage.'

Without a word Ham, Shem and Japh ran from the room each carrying a lamp.

Japh, being slightly leaner than his brothers, reached the lowest deck first. He held up the light to inspect the walls and floor. He could see no damage but wanted to be sure. He unfastened the catch of one of the pens, carefully walked around the sleepy but startled beasts and rubbed his free hand over the surfaces. They were bone dry.

By this time Ham and Shem had joined him.

'Check the walls! Get inside the pens and check the walls,' he said earnestly.

Each brother rushed through the enclosures.

'Nothing!'

'No damage here.'

'All dry.'

'The floor is dry too? That's amazing'

Eventually they returned with no damage to report, everything was safe, everywhere was dry. It was only now that they noticed the sound of the water lapping on the walls of the ark, as the wind tossed the water outside.

The water level dropped day after day, and the ark, even the size that it was, seemed to rise above the surface of the waves as if the great load was slowly being lifted, creaking and moaning under its own weight. Only one shutter had been tentatively opened, but until the wind had stopped howling no one dared open the shutters wide. No land could yet be seen, but the family were certain again that it at least still existed.

Trust and I stand on the roof of the ark.

'It has been a long time for them, Hope, to be inside that ark.'

'Yes.'

'How much longer do they need to wait?'

'Trust, my dear friend,' I laugh a little, 'they need to trust in the Creator.'

'And I suppose, Hope, my dear friend,' his ringing laugh is pure, 'they need to set their hope in the Creator too.'

'Exactly!'

Trust reaches for my back and pulls a long clear arrow from my quiver.

'Then perhaps we should encompass them with this trust and hope.'

I take the arrow from his hand and ready it in my bow. Leaning back, I release the arrow into the sky above me. Trust soars into the air at a speed that exceeds the arrow. I see him grip his sword tightly as he waits a moment. The arrow approaches and he slices the air, splitting the shaft in two. Each section soars away from him, leaving an iridescent lattice work flowing and weaving down over the ark.

What beauty, what wonder! I cannot hold back my joy. I join my friend in the air, both laughing now, both thrilled at the task ahead.

27

Waiting Remnant

The rain had stopped suddenly all those days ago, but the wind seemed to slowly blow itself out. The family had removed the shutters, and had stacked them neatly in the corner. The view had dramatically changed. The water was still abundant, but all around Kerim and her family, mountain peaks pierced the horizon and the ebbing blue sea. The water was in retreat.

Movement on the lower decks had caused the family to throw themselves into override. The smallest animals were waking from their sleep, and they were hungry. The food stores were diminishing quickly and there was no way of replenishing them.

'I am going to find out if there is any land beyond what we can see, maybe there are plants there,' said Noah

'How?' asked Shem.

'I know we cannot leave this ark, but we will very soon run out of food. Only a few animals have stirred, but what will happen when the larger ones wake? They will need food too.' He tugged at his silver whiskers, deep in thought.

'If we cannot leave, how are we going to tell if there is plant life, or soil we can work?'

'I will send a messenger,' he said with a crooked smile. He trotted down the slope to the deck below. The others stood shaking their heads or shrugging their shoulders, none aware of what he was to do.

A few moments passed before he returned. His hands were cupped together; his fingers surrounded a large black bird, its feet kicking at the edge of his palms. He crossed the room, still smiling his crocked smile, stepped up to the open window and set the raven free. The black wings flapped frantically for a few seconds before settling into a steady rhythm as the raven took flight, squawking loudly, glad to be stretching his wings once more, and quickly becoming a dot in the distance.

For many miles the bird has flown. It has found a tall green leafed tree, perfect for roosting, perfect for nesting perfect in fact for just about all a raven could need.

It sits there too, crouched in the branches, peering up into the canopy where the raven perches, smoothing his plumage. It is battered but not beaten.

We won't get there in time. I see it happening, but cannot stop it.

I should have sent a sentry with the bird.

'See how lovely this place is for you. Don't you just love the fresh air and fresh food here?' it whispers to the bird, encouraging it to stay. It chooses its words carefully, so that they are sweet and gentle. The bird listens. If it were to truly see the creature it would find the complete contradiction of those words and sentiments.

The bird will not return.

A few days passed and still the black bird did not return.

Noah stood and waited. Sat and waited. He looked increasingly troubled.

'Still no sign then,' Kerim asked gently.

'No my dear,' Noah sighed. 'No sign.'

'Perhaps it is just enjoying the freedom,' she suggested.

'Or perhaps I have put that species in danger of extinction.'

Kerim wasn't sure what to say. Perhaps the raven was dead and so its species would now die out. She now understood Noah's sad expression. She left him, unable to say anything that would lift his mood and be truthful at the same time. She sought out Japh.

'If you don't mind me saying father,' Japh began an hour or so later, 'Kerim has a few ideas.'

'I'll be glad to hear them.'

Japh beckoned to Kerim to come forward.

'Do you have something insightful to say my dear?' the older man asked, kindly.

'It is about the bird,' she began, looking shyly at Japh. He put his arm about her.

'I had a feeling it would be.'

'You sent it to find dry land didn't you?'

'That I did. Only now, as I said before, I feel I have put that species in danger of extinction.'

'I think it may have been the wrong bird to send,' she said. And then quickly added. 'I don't mean to be disrespectful.'

'You are not.'

'It is just that the raven, as a bird prefers the tall trees. It is quite happy to perch there and find scraps of food there.'

'Yes my dear, you are right,' the old man frowned, intrigued by what she was saying.

'It probably found a perch.' Japh smiled at his father. 'It would have the whole earth at its feet.'

'I feel that a ground loving bird, one that would travel fair distances, but one that would be happy to return to a warm bed, would be a good choice to send.'

'Yes! I see what you mean! And which would you suggest my dear Kerim?'

'Have you considered the dove?'

'I had not.' He smiled and winked at her. 'But I will now.'

He walked briskly to the cote, and took a dove gently in his hands. The dove bobbed his head as Noah reached the unshuttered window and felt the pressure of Noah's hands slowly release his body. He flapped his wings and took to the air. Up he rose above the ark and the water. He circled once then went on his way, quickly and quietly.

Kerim's role is vital. She sees herself as unimportant, but she has been chosen.

Nightfall had come. The family sat together to share a meal of rye bread and vegetable broth. The shutters lay piled against the walls of the ark, and the sky was open to be viewed. The incredible blackness, deep and dark, yet not empty with the stars bright and the moon in half light.

The calm chatter of the family was disturbed by a soft cooing from the open window. The dove had returned tired and weary. It had found no ground.

Noah was patient. He watched for the dove to regain his strength. Each day he checked, and each day the others would ask.

'Is it time to send the dove again?'

'Not yet.'

Seven days passed before the dove was once again sent into the watery wilderness.

It circled the ark, and then flew east.

For hours the dove flew, sometimes flapping energetically, sometimes gliding on a thermal. The horizon, to the human eye, the same blue line, but to the dove something quite else. He was mapping this blue world in the way his instincts had always allowed him. He saw things that a human eye could not see. Mountains were nearby; he knew it because the impulses of the earth told him so. He would not rest, could not rest until he reached them.

Far below, the dove is being followed, but I follow too.

The family sat down to eat. They were quieter than usual. Noah, who was distracted by his thoughts, barely ate a thing.

'What is it dear?' asked Tabitha after a while. Then taking in the glance Noah made to the window she understood. 'There is still time for it to return.'

'I fear I have destroyed another species for the sake of my impatience,' he said looking sadly at his hands as he rubbed them slowly on his tunic.

'Father! You are the least impatient person I have ever known!' Shem laughed.

'If my Shem had been in charge,' Helena joked, 'there would be no birds left!'

'They would have been sent out months ago!' Shem agreed laughing with his wife.

The mood lifted a little as the family finished off their meal.

Night was closing in. The dove, exhausted from a day of flight, was further from the ark than it had ever been. He had not changed his course to return to his roost, but was driven by what he could see on the horizon.

The dove flew as fast as his tired wings could carry him towards the silhouettes of trees, each beat taking him closer. Even in this bird, there was a sense of excitement. He had found trees! Crashing clumsily into the canopy, the dove found a tight clump of branches and breathed deep. Collapsing out of exhaustion, he fell asleep.

The creature watches with eager eyes.

Morning dawned, gloriously. The dove woke and cooed gently. There was no reply. The canopy above was rich with colour, and there below was ground. Firm, gritty and covered with shoots of new growth. Jumping from branch to branch the dove found a space to launch then to glide to the ground.

Seeds and berries grow everywhere. A table fit for a king. The dove is hungry, and here, before him, are all manner of sweet pickings.

This place is eerily quiet. The rustling in a branch catches my attention.

'Eat up my sweet pet.' The deathly creature coos.

The dove, startled by its voice, flies to a nearby branch.

Silence falls again and the dove returns to his feast.

'Fill yourself with these delights! They are all yours!' it whispers again, from the shadows.

The dove, not disturbed this time, continues to eat.

'All earth is yours, yours to own.' Its voice rises high and shrill.

Launching himself into the air with a clatter of wings, the dove speeds past the creatures head and lands just out of reach. The bird looks down at me, and I look up at him.

'You are mine now!' it hisses though its stained teeth.

The dove does not flinch. He bows his head, in what could be an act of submission. The creature leaps.

The dove however, lifting his head, had broken off a small sprig of the tree in which it had sat. Energised by the sweet food, it departed from the scene noiselessly, rising into the air, unnoticed by the dancing creature below.

It flew, twig in beak, the long journey home. The sun above him, warmed his back and a wonderful sea breeze made each wing beat twice as effective.

Flying in tight circles, I create a swirling wind within the grove which makes the creature dance. It is tossed and blown about ... again ...

'Where's the bird?' it shouts with a mouthful only of dust.

The food was laid out. Everyone was seated.

'We thank you Lord for this food which you have supplied for us. Your mercy and grace we gratefully receive,' Noah prayed.

A small tapping sound followed. Noah lifted his eyes to the window, out of habit, as he had done so often in the day. The white head and body of the dove appeared, greeted by the friendly coo from his mate.

It gently fluttered over to its mate who sat perched on a shelf in a cosy corner. It offered the green leafy olive twig which was swiftly taken by the other dove and carefully woven into her nest.

The human inhabitants watched in silence as this simple exchange took place. The silver haired man sat back in his chair and wiped away the tear that had rolled down his cheek.

'It seems that it is nearly time.'

'You mean, we will soon be out of here?' Ham said in his gruff voice.

'Indeed!' Noah chuckled.

The meal commenced in loud chatter and laughter.

'Did you see what plant the dove bought back?' Lellia asked Ham.

'It looked like an olive sprig to me,' Ham replied.

'I'd like to grow an olive grove when we get out of here,' she said to Ham who nodded and smiled.

'What about you Helena?' Lellia asked.

'Well, Shem and I have said we would like to have a vineyard, and fields of barley.' Helena smiled. 'Although anything that grows in the ground sounds novel at the moment!'

'Kerim and I are going to raise sheep and goats,' Japh stated turning to his bride.

The family talked for long about their plans for homes and farms. It was late before they settled down for the night.

Kerim snuggled close to Japh. 'Thank you!' She pulled his arm around her.

'For what?' he said, ruffling his hair with his free hand.

'For letting me continue the legacy that my father left. To raise a flock the way he taught me. I am so grateful.'

'Well, I don't suppose my trade will be much use anyway.'

'What do you mean?' she asked gazing up at him.

'A boat building business may not be required. I have a feeling we might just want to keep our feet firmly on solid ground for a while!'

'Oh Japh!' she said turning and putting out the light.

'I can't believe this is nearly finished,' Japh whispered.

'Or just beginning!' Kerim teased as she leaned over and gave him a lingering kiss.

Each day over the next week seemed longer than the one before. Eventually Noah reached for the white dove and took him from his nest. Briefly a clutch of white eggs were revealed in the divot that was adorned with a single green leaved twig. The mother dove took his place. Noah released the dove early in the morning on the seventh day and then they all stood back and waited.

The dove did not return that night, or the night after. It never came back to the ark.

But still the remnant waited.

28

Rescued Remnant

Each day Japh and Kerim climbed up to the window to marvel at the changing view. The ark sat lodged firmly on ground, yet the ground was not yet revealed. Distant peaks in the north began to emerge, then others in the east. Mountain tops, rough and jagged. Smashed together in the violent water surges in the days now far behind.

The water was slowly draining away before their eyes. It lapped lazily at the hull. It was clear and deep. Dark shadows in the depths below them became recognisable as rocks as the days passed.

Then it happened. The first breach of land appeared beneath the ark. Rocky, just like the peaks far away. The prospect both cheered and frustrated those on board.

'The land below us is not suitable for farming,' Shem said frustratingly as he too looked out at the ground.

'We will have to wait for the water to recede further in the hope that there is a deep enough valley,' Ham supposed.

'God has brought us this far,' Japh whispered in Kerim's ear, 'I don't think He would forget us now.' She nodded. Her husband had more faith than his brothers.

She tried to see the landscape with the same optimism that Japh showed. With her back resting against the edge of the weathered window frame, he told her of the months and years he spent building the ark. There were days when he would gladly haul, cut and mitre the timber. The work was joyful and fulfilling, however, there were also depressing times, when the mocking words of strangers would come and starve his motivation.

Kerim wondered which type of day they would have now? Would they allow what they saw with their eyes dictate how they should feel? She had to look beyond her present circumstances. Japh was right. For years he had toiled alongside his family, and they had been rescued from the fate of human kind, she should expect mercy even now.

'We have come to rest on high ground,' Japh finally said to Kerim. 'The water is still disappearing,' he smiled and nodded at her. She was glad that he sounded confident. 'There are bound to be some amazing valleys with rich soil under this lot.'

'All we need to do is wait a little longer.' Kerim leaned back and closed her eyes. The warmth of the sun was so peaceful.

The next morning Kerim lay quietly on her pallet while Japh slept peacefully beside her. She smiled at the familiar creaks and clicks as the ark warmed up in the heat of the rising sun. The hour was early and no one had woken as of yet.

She rolled on her side staring at her latest weave hanging in the door. The design was of a herd and the land they grazed upon. How she wished she was there now, under the open sky.

As her mind began to dream, the sound of muffled footsteps drifted across the deck. 'I am here Lord.'

Noah had risen.

Kerim toyed with the idea of crawling out of bed to watch him speak when a pure white and dazzling light slid under the door hanging. She sat wide eyed and terrified.

This was not the yellow glow of the rising sun. It was both harsh and gentle. It had strength and piercing intensity that pulsed with energy.

As the light poured around and underneath Kerim's woven screen it began to reveal details she had never seen before in her own handiwork. The light seemed to emphasise the beauty of the woven fabric, bringing to life the characters within. It played on the wood grain, showing texture and colour she had not noticed even in the long time she had spent confined. The light banished the darkness, pushing it far away, finding nowhere to hide.

'Yes Lord. I will do as you have said.' Kerim heard Noah's voice drift into her room, yet even that seemed consumed by the light.

Several things happened within moments of each other. Firstly, the light vanished and with it all the revealed beauty. Then, large grumbling movements, groans and squawks vibrated through the ark. Then Noah called out to his family.

'Wake up!' he laughed. 'The time is now. We are leaving this instant.'

No one really knew what it would be like to set foot on dry ground again. As the family excitedly dressed then scurried through the ark, to the lower deck and to the sealed opening, they each responded in different ways. Lellia could not help but dance, whilst Helena walked silently with tears flowing down her cheeks. The men were excited, they bustled and jostled each other, laughing and slapping one another on their backs. Kerim walked behind nervously. The ark had been her safe haven, her saving grace, the one place she had felt real happiness and peace and she was not keen to enter the outside world again for fear of it.

Noah and Tabitha stood at the sealed door and surveyed their family. When the others noticed, they became still and silent. If it had not been for the raucous animals, birds and insects, it would have been a solemn occasion.

The men nudged at the beam securing the inside of the doors. Eventually it shifted, and was lifted out of place.

Smiling, Noah reached out a hand and touched the door. Immediately, the sealed boards were freed and the doors burst open. The room was drenched in the blinding, brilliant, sun light. The cloud of dust and straw twisted and spun in the air until a gentle gust of wind carried it away to reveal dry land. Fresh green, new and succulent vegetation filled the scene before them. The sun, still fairly low in the sky, shed it's light over the breeze rippled grass, and glinted off a shallow brook near the base of the ark.

'Unlock the pens!' Noah commanded. 'Let's let the animals taste what this beautiful land offers!'

Each member of the Remnant went to a pen and set the animals free. A few of the creatures moved slowly and sleepily, blinking at the bright sunlight. Some ran for the open air, while others seemed to pause, lost in the moment, before grabbing at the freedom of open space. Soon the land surrounding the ark was covered in the multitude of assorted creatures grazing and drinking in fresh water. Many resorted to rolling in the fresh grass, savouring the sweet scent, while others played chase. It was pure joy.

The time is here. They are to walk on solid ground again.

'Are you ready with the door?' Trust asks me.

I ready my bow with an arrow and aim.

I hear the animals inside but the reverent silence of the Remnant is louder in my ears.

'Now!' Trust shouts the readying signal.

My arrow embeds in the doors which shatters the seal. They burst open in a blast of brightest indigo and sunflower yellow.

A shout of praise rises in the host.

'Glory to God in the highest!'

The fresh green of the landscape speaks of newness. There is joy in the host, unspeakable, unexplainable, unhindered joy!

I see their rushing to bring freedom to the animals.

'Ensure the creatures remain peaceful, we don't want any extinctions now!'

The angels move among the carnivores, bringing to them the joy of freedom and restraining their hunger for now.

'What's he up to Mother?' Shem questioned as they watched his father.

'He's doing what he knows best to do,' she answered.

The others had gathered at the entrance to the ark, the stalls now empty of animals, and the ark deserted. Their attention, at first was given to the animals, but slowly they became distracted as they each watched Noah.

His silver hair was tossed by the exhilarating wind, and his robes flapped about his legs. He was gathering rocks, large flat rocks and laying them one on another. He worked hard, his muscles wasted from what they had been before entering the ark, sweat streaming down his face and back. But he did not stop, it was essential that this was built. Finally, when the mound was waist height he stopped, turned and began to walk purposefully back towards the ark where the family were still gathered inside.

At that moment, the sun went behind a large cloud and cast a large dark shadow over them. Kerim was pale and shaking from head to foot. How could it be that she had been safe all this time only to meet her end at the hands of her own family?

'Please ... don't let him take me,' she begged as she fell at Japh's feet, sobbing.

He bent down to console her and she grabbed his tunic, kissing his hem. She looked up and saw her father-in-law drawing close. 'Please!' she begged more earnestly, 'Please!' Releasing Japh, she knelt at the feet of Tabitha.

'Have I not been a daughter to you?' she wept. 'Have I not been of help, made my contribution? Did you not save me and promise me new life?'

Tabitha turned to her son. 'You are my daughter Kerim.'

Japh bent down and lifted her chin so he could see her face. Relentless tears streamed down her cheeks. Her green eyes, usually so full of the light of life, were dark. She was terrified of something. 'Kerim what is it?'

Noah climbed up the ramp and walked over to her. 'What is happening?'

'Please!' Kerim whimpered prostrating herself on the ground before Noah. 'Have I not been a good daughter to you? Why would you do this?'

Noah looked up into the faces of his family, searching for an explanation. None was given.

Kerim pointed to the stone altar that had been made. Her face was contorted with dread. He suddenly realised what she had been thinking and gently touched her head, 'My dear, that is not for you.'

He looked at the piled stones. 'Be at peace. Your blood will not be spilled.'

Japh, now understanding the horror that had shaken his wife, fell to the ground beside her and lifted her into his arms. He held her close.

'My love,' he soothed, 'Have no fear. You are part of us. We will protect you,' he whispered. Her sobbing slowed and her body relaxed.

'But I thought ...' she stammered into his neck.

'I should have understood.' Japh held her tighter.

Moments passed before the old man came down the ramp carrying a bundle of wood and a perfect sheep. 'Fetch one of every clean animal and bring it to the altar.'

The sons hurried to their task.

Noah went up to the altar and arranged the large pile of dried wood he had collected from inside the ark. Shem carried a sheep, Ham a large basket of the finest corn and barley they had and Japh led a goat up to his father. He examined them.

'They are perfect?'

'Yes Father, completely unblemished. The best we have.'

A strong blaze was set on the altar. The dry wood roared to life as tall orange flames flickered in the breeze. Noah knelt and his sons, daughters and wife followed his lead.

'Most glorious God. You have set your grace upon us, saved us from the flood and set our feet on firm ground. To you we bring our sacrifice. May it be pleasing in your sight.'

Noah, Shem and Japh each took an animal and slit its throat. They piled their sacrifice onto the altar which blazed vigorously. Ham and Lellia took the corn and barley and threw it into the blaze. The flames licked at the sacrifice and burnt up the offering. The plume of smoke and aroma lifted into the air. They stood nearby and offered thanks for their salvation before returning to the entrance of the ark.

29

Promise

I stand next to the altar. Noah worked hard to raise it. I saw him strain and exert himself, I saw the effort he put to the task. His heart has remained faithful to his God.

I gaze at the extravagant offering that has been made. I am not alone in the viewing of this spectacle as the multitude are nearby, focussed both on the sacrifice and the Remnant. The angels marvel at the humans, and I have to agree, they are fascinating beings.

Trust draws his sword and begins a salute to the Creator.

'Glory to God in the Highest!'

'Glory to God in the Highest!' I shout, echoing the excellent praise of my friend.

'Glory to God in the Highest!' The multitude joins in as they draw swords pointing skyward to the heavens and fire arrows towards the horizon as a salute.

Suddenly, there stands with us another being.

We fall to our knees and bow down low.

I hear the distant shriek of the enemy. This is no place for them.

This being is the one that shines brightly with pure light, brighter than the sun in the sky, a beautiful light that seems to flow in His veins. The light is so bright that no one can make out His face. There is no shadow, no darkness in His presence.

He is like no other and no other will ever be like Him. Then He speaks. His voice rings out with authority, clarity and gentleness. It has the power of the rushing waters of the flood.

I worship as do all the multitude. How we love Him!

'Be fruitful and multiply, and fill the earth.'

What a blessing to bestow upon this remnant of the human race! How could they not fulfil such a thing? It is as much a command as a blessing as a promise.

'The fear of you and the terror of you will be on every beast of the earth and on every bird of the sky; with everything that creeps on the ground, and the fish of the sea, into your hand are given.' A burst of indigo flooding from the Creator saturates the area then is gone as soon as it came. There is sudden change in the atmosphere around us, in the green pastures and around the ark. The animals become nervous and jittery, many jumping as it seems they notice the Remnant for what seems the first time. All of them moving away from the humans gathered there, running, leaping, crawling or flapping, instinct to flee, spreading through them like a ripple on a pool.

'Every moving thing that is alive shall be food for you; I give it all to you, as I gave the green plant. As for you, be fruitful and multiply; populate the earth abundantly and multiply in it,' resounds His voice.

Again the command, blessing and promise come. They must know now that they will be fruitful.

'I establish My covenant, My eternal promise with you and your descendants and with every living creature that moves on the earth, sea and air. I will never again destroy the earth by flood.' As He emphasises the promise, violet ribbons flow from His mouth and wrap about each member of the family, encircling and covering them completely.

Suddenly the air is filled with a fine spray of water, flowing from the clouds above. It is raining once again, the first time since the forty day period. Had it not been for the certainty that fills their hearts that what their God said is true, the Remnant would have feared. But I see no fear in their colours. The spray is cool, sweet and refreshing, soaking their skin, hair and clothes. The Creator knows that in whatever circumstance the Remnant find themselves, it is His water, His Spirit that no longer brings judgement but life. He may come as if in the gentle patter of rain or the gushing of a turbulent storm, but in Him all hope and life is found.

From behind the cloud, the sun in its amazing yet weak glory appears. It is weak in comparison to His. Beams of bright light warm the backs of the family.

I see something unseen before. Something truly beautiful. The rain is being transformed. The sunlight pierces each droplet, is refracted inside it then reflected out. Flowing through each droplet the sunlight is split and separated into differing colours. I see the separated light from the millions of droplets. Before my eyes there is a staggering display of rich coloured light draped across the sky forming an arc from one side of the horizon to the other. As each droplet falls, I see only one of the colours reflected back at me, but because they are many raindrops falling, seven colours appear in the sky. I hear my friend Trust, gasp at the sight. It is magnificent.

It is a reflection, as if seen through weak eyes, of the colours that surround the throne, and dance in the throne room.

The bands of unhindered, pure spectral colours, overlap in strong glowing bands. It is awesome.

The coloured display accentuates the character and desires of the Creator. The crimson of love and forgiveness, followed by orange of compassion. Then sunshine yellow that tells of happiness and joy. The message of peace and hope come after in the vibrant green and blue. Holy fear, untarnished is represented by the indigo band and finally, violet protection. Each colour overlapping the next. Each colour with a message of its own. Each colour working in harmony with the whole. What a story! What a sign! His promise will never be broken.

I see other colours displayed here. The human eye will not detect them, although maybe now they see the full glory of the sight. Above the red of love and forgiveness, there is an intense colour. There is a little more of this band than all of the visible colours put together. The importance of it therefore is to be taken note of. It tells me of an amazing forgiveness and love that is yet to be seen. A gift that is yet to be given and yet to be received but still promised. Truly beyond all our dreams.

Another colour, much smaller in quantity, but very fierce in energy sits below the violet that signifies protection. I consider this for a moment. This colour symbolises fierce protection, a strong safeguard for His people. He desires a people that belong to Him.

I turn to the family. Each one has a differing intensity of peaceful green about them. I see they are amazed at what has been revealed. Kerim, in particular looks confused. I smile at her. How blessed are they above all living creatures both natural and supernatural, to be chosen by the Creator.

'This is the sign of the covenant which I am making between Me and you and every living creature that is with you, for all successive generations; I set My bow in the cloud, and it shall be a sign of a covenant between Me and the earth.

'It will be there when I set the clouds over the earth, and it will be a reminder of the covenant between Me and you. Never again will the water become a flood to destroy all flesh.'

Every one of the angels stands in the spray, gazing at the rainbow set in the sky. This is an amazing visual promise, a covenant that will not be broken. Silence falls over the land and we are left alone once again.

Kerim's legs felt weak below her but she refused to let that overcome her. The fear that had been so real and so near, so paralysing, now felt foolish. How could she fear that her loving family would consider such a horrendous monstrous act of barbarism? They never would. Japh had shown nothing but concern and love for her, he had not mocked her irrational actions. Perhaps he had not considered them irrational at all. And now, there he stood at the summit, offering a sacrifice in her place.

Kerim watched the smoke twist and turn in the ever increasing breeze on the brow of the hill. The dark plume rose high above the altar before it could not be made out against the dark sky. She saw her husband, his brothers and her father-in-law raise their arms in worship and prayer. The women joined them.

Their attitude seemed subdued and almost solemn as they approached the entrance to the ark once more. Japh took Kerim in his arms.

'Good now?' he asked quietly.

'Good now,' she whispered back.

'What an offering!' exclaimed Noah, causing his family to observe the smoke on the hill once more. They were silent for a moment then suddenly a voice rang out across the land.

'Be fruitful and multiply, and fill the earth,' it said or blessed or commanded, Kerim wasn't sure which.

The voice was powerful. It filled the air, yet felt as if it were coming from a friend standing next to them. Everything was still before it. Everything, even the animals, were listening to it. It was familiar and pleasant yet contained such authority.

'The fear of you and the terror of you will be on every beast of the earth and on every bird of the sky; with everything that creeps on the ground, and the fish of the sea, into your hand are given,' the voice announced.

It was as if Kerim truly saw for the first time. Everything was clear and crisp, beautiful and detailed. She heard Japh gasp beside her and he gripped her hand tightly.

'Do you see it?' he whispered.

'Uh huh!' was all that she could reply.

The sky was filled with white robed beings, bowed down low in worship to the one at the centre. Light pulsated from Him. And although Kerim could see everything else clearly, this one stood shrouded and hidden with light. It is His light that brought clarity.

A sudden and pure burst of indigo light saturated the area. It was so quick Kerim was not sure she had seen it at all.

A ripple of movement ran through the animals. The family were acutely aware that the atmosphere of peace had changed. As the family watched, they saw the animals look at them with fear in their eyes before running, bounding, flying, creeping and crawling away. For a few moments varied animal cries filled the air, before fading away.

'Every moving thing that is alive shall be food for you; I give it all to you, as I gave the green plant. As for you, be fruitful and multiply; populate the earth abundantly and multiply in it.'

The family listened. The animals had fled; they had obeyed the warning in the voice. Kerim gripped Japh's hand tightly as she again heard the blessing with the command and promise attached. Populate the earth! It felt as if there would be no possibility that it could not and would not be done.

'I establish My covenant, My eternal promise with you and your descendants and with every living creature that moves on the earth, sea and air. I will never again destroy the earth by flood.'

As he spoke, violet ribbons flowed out from the light and floated in the air. The family watched as the ribbons moved steadily closer to them. Kerim stretched out her free hand as did Lellia. She heard other family members gasp or exclaim their wonder.

One of the ribbons reached Noah first. Kerim watched as it began to wrap around him. His face was one of pure joy. The other ribbons wrapped about each member of the family, encircling and covering them completely.

Kerim was shocked at the intensity of emotion that her ribbon carried. Although it was made of light and had no weight, it felt as if it had substance. It draped gently over her body, enveloping her with love, but a love so intense she felt overwhelmed with it. As it covered her mind, she knew for certain that His promise would never be broken. As it entered her soul, there was no doubt that she was complete.

And as the voice rang out and through each of them, the promise felt as if it lived and breathed, as if it had been sealed inside each of them.

The promise so fresh was tested straight away. From the heavy clouds, droplets of rain began to fall, soaking the family head to foot. None of them flinched or panicked, there was no cause to worry. This rain, the first since the forty days, would not flood the earth.

Then, from behind the cloud, the sun in its amazing glory appeared. Beams of bright light streamed across the pasture, warming the backs of the family.

The rain was suddenly transformed, a staggering display of rich coloured light draped across the sky forming an arc from one side of the horizon to the other. The family group collectively gasped at the bowed stripes of pure, unhindered colour, overlapped in strong, glowing bands. It was awesome.

Kerim gazed at the sight and wandered at the significance of its multi hued beauty. Her attention was distracted when she heard those wearing white robes gasp in amazement. How can they be amazed at this? Surely they are forever in the presence of the one made of light, the Creator of all things. She watched the white robed beings revel in the sight before them. One, who she felt seemed oddly familiar to her, turned and smiled at her. Then she suddenly understood the beings' amazement. It was the fact that the promise, blessing and glory of the most high was being shown to them, to humans.

'This is the sign of the covenant which I am making between Me and you and every living creature that is with you, for all successive generations; I set My bow in the cloud, and it shall be a sign of a covenant between Me and the earth.

'It will be there when I set the clouds over the earth, and it will be a reminder of the covenant between Me and you. Never again will the water become a flood to destroy all flesh.'

Everyone stood in the spray, gazing at the rainbow set in the sky. Silence fell over the land.

The detail and clarity faded. They were alone once again.

Noah stood eyes full of tears and a smile hidden beneath his whiskers. He knew that he had fulfilled what God had asked of him. All he felt now was an overwhelming love for his Master, his God. The love was not one sided. God's love was at the beginning of it all and now was burning fiercer than ever, in Noah's heart.

'Did you see all those angels?' Helena asked, her face beaming.

'Certainly did! But that voice ...' Shem said.

'It kind of shook me from the inside. Amazing!' Lellia added, almost dreamily.

'We are safe.' Tabitha laughed, and began hugging her boys and their wives. 'My family is safe.'

'That promise will never fail,' Noah said nodding. 'Our God is one that keeps His promises.' He wiped a tear from his face and kissed Tabitha on the cheek.

'What a beautiful promise.' Kerim said quietly to herself not only referring to the colours that stretched across the sky. 'Japh, we have been promised that we will be fruitful.'

'And multiply!' Japh smiled.

'Actually, I have something I need to tell you.' Kerim said shyly patting her slightly swollen belly.

The dark creature looks on, trembling at the voice. It cowers in the shadows. It is battered and cannot put up a fight, at least not yet.

'I will not let them win,' It says darkly, no doubt planning another attack. 'That blessing I will turn into a curse.'

'You will lose this battle and you know it,' Trust says as he swings his sword above his head and brings it crashing down where the demon had been sitting. A sickly scent is all that is left as the demon vanishes before our eyes.

I turn to Trust as he sheaths his sword.

'These humans. What do you make of them?' he asks me.

'Well. The Creator has a marvellous plan for them. He has singled them out as special and unique.' I think for a while before I continue. 'I can only wonder at what it is He has planned for them.'

'Our work is still not complete Hope.'

'I know!' I reply.

'They will stumble and fall again. They cannot be perfect.'

'I know! Which makes it all the more marvellous, don't you think, Trust?'

'How do you mean?'

'Well, we know the enemy will do his best to destroy and damage the human race.'

'That he will.' Trust nods.

'Yet even when they falter, the Creator will remain faithful to his promise. Next time, it will not be a boat that saves them. There will come a time when He will save them completely; He will give them His perfection.'

With thanks to ...

Special thanks needs to be given to the legend that is Andy Back. You gave me such encouragement and made my sides ache with laughter with your extensive notes. May your life be well rounded!

Without my parents, Rick and Carol, I would never have had the time. Thank you for teaching my children how to cook and giving them the opportunity to have such amazing relationships with their grandparents.

For Benjamin, Asher and Elouise, thanks for the delicious dinners, puddings and cakes!

Thanks also to my husband, Bob, who listened when I needed to talk plot, even when I wouldn't let on to the whole story. He left me to my imagination on my day off, not expecting me to catch up on housework. That is a gift of love.

Thanks also for those that read the first edition with its mistakes and problems, for being patient and still receiving the story into your hearts. for your encouragement and stories of realising the closeness of the Creator when you read.

Last, but definitely not least, thanks to my best friend JC for extraordinary inspiration, gentle guidance and steadfastly loving me through it all.

Watch out for new titles by Katy Hollway
www.katyhollway.com

Other books by the author in this series

Read on for a taster of the Days of Eliora
Book II in the Remnant Chronicles

1

New

Eliora was alone. She thought that this was surely the most beautiful place there ever was. How could she possibly consider working here to be as awful as the pits? True, she did feel a little uncomfortable. It felt dark and oppressive inside the thick walls of the palace despite the early morning sunlight but she put it down to her feeling apprehension about how she would be received.

'Keep up!' her mother had warned. 'We can't be late.'

Eliora scurried after.

She had risen early and had got dressed in her new cotton tunic. Her mother had applied the irritating eye makeup to herself before turning to Eliora. It felt stiff against her young skin but she was happy about the distinction it gave her.

Everything about this morning was new. The time, her appearance and her mother's demeanour. She had seemed agitated and nervous somehow. What there was for her to be nervous about, Eliora had no idea. She was the one who was going to meet the most powerful woman in the known world for the first time.

Eliora's new simple sandals cut into her feet as she sped from the hot little house towards the cool palace.

The heat of the morning was creeping over the sands and into the shallow river valley, but all of that was left behind as they entered through the statued gateway. The smooth stone floor left a chill in the early morning. The silence was punctuated by the lonely, echoing tapping of their sandaled feet. Eliora gazed at the scale of the corridors and the clean crispness of the architecture they passed by. Huge columns in the shape of elegant palms held the roof high above. Guards stood alert at either end of the hall.

They hurried through a series of doors, each one with a guard stationed outside.

The last room was beautiful yet terrible. The walls were decorated with colourful paintings depicting people walking and sitting. The images were mesmerising but made Eliora feel uncomfortable. She felt a shiver go down her spine as she saw half human half beast depictions.

There was very little furniture to be seen. A couple of shining gilded stools sat to the side of a large opening that welcomed in the sound of rustling rushes of the river. The scented breeze wafted the light cotton curtains.

'Wait here!' Eliora's mother cautioned. 'Don't touch anything,' she added before quietly rushing through the ornate door opposite the window.

And so Eliora was alone.

The polished floor gleamed as beams of shimmering morning light bounced from the surface and highlighted a section of the wall painting. It depicted a man kneeling with his arms outstretched and flowing from those arms were green and red feathers, as if he had wings. It was unnerving and exotic. Eliora focused instead on the regular patterns of triangles and circles that bordered the image.

Suddenly three other women rushed into the room through the door Eliora had come from. They wore pristine white tunics, tied at the waist with a gold and green braid. Their faces, although quite different, all bore the same almond emphasised eyes and rouge lips and cheeks. They each raised their chins and glanced down at Eliora as they passed her, entering the same door that her mother had.

Eliora felt, maybe for the first time, small and insignificant.

Gentle and hushed voices could be heard from the neighbouring room. Eliora could now hear her mother's voice singing a slow but elegant tune and the slightly shriller voices of the other women giving instructions.

Eliora waited. She rubbed her sleepy eyes and yawned.

Another voice, more commanding and authoritative spoke, although the wooden door muffled what was said.

Eliora fidgeted a little. She leaned over and peered out of the window. It was already a hot morning and the breeze that drifted in was full of promise that it would get hotter still. She welcomed the clean light in this unfamiliar place. She wandered over to the curtain and drew it back. The rushes nearly came up to the window ledge. A ramp, that appeared to be suspended in the air, gradually led down to the water's edge. This was not part of the river, but a hand dug pool that branched off from the water source in the distance. This pool was secluded and private. This is where it all began.

I stand on the ramp. She remembers as a story told, I recall it perfectly, as I was here.

Eliora jumped as the door behind her opened. She spun around and saw the most elegant looking woman framed in the doorway. The woman was tall, slender and pale skinned. Eliora could not help but look into the beautiful face, even though her mother had warned her not to. She looked as perfect as the images painted around her. There appeared to be no imperfection. There was something about her dark eyes that was frightening. Eliora quickly diverted her gaze to the floor and gave an involuntary shudder of fear.

'Who is this child?' Eliora glanced up. The woman's voice was richly toned and strong. She had a long neck where she wore multiple gold necklaces, and a chiselled face. Her dark eyes were enriched by her carefully painted makeup. Her long, thick, dark hair hung completely straight, and woven into her crown was a bright circlet of jewel encrusted gold.

'She is my daughter your Majesty,' Eliora's mother said, standing behind the queen, her head bowed. 'You commanded me to bring her before you when she reached her age.'

'Will you work hard in my household?'

'Yes,' Eliora stuttered, how could she refuse to do so? 'Your Majesty.' She remembered.

'You shall be called Ebonee.'

Eliora heard the stifled giggles of the three other women and looked up. Her mother looked on Eliora with concern.

Her own mother had been named by the queen when she was Eliora's age but she never used it outside the palace.

'If you are like your mother, you will be good at singing. Is that correct?'

'Yes, your Majesty.' Eliora struggled not to look into the queen's face. It felt rude not to make eye contact, although she had no desire to feel that fear again.

'Then you will be assigned to the care of my cats. Sing to them.'

'Thank you your Majesty,' Eliora said aware of her mother's relieved sigh.

'Simra, show her the way.'

Eliora's mother bowed low and escorted her daughter from the room.

'Simra. What does that mean?' Eliora asked, barely out of the room. 'What does Ebonee mean?'

'Oh Elli!' Her mother sighed. 'Simra means song. That is my name here. And you are to be called Ebonee. That means black.'

'Black?' Eliora looked at her mother confused.

'Yes black.' She pulled a small square of muslin from her braided belt. 'You will need this.' Eliora took the square. 'Look at your reflection in the disk here.' She led her daughter to the mural, and the gilded disk held by the horns of the painted symbol.

'Oh no!' Eliora said mortified.

As she looked into the disk, her reflection stared back, only it was not the pristine and beautifully made up face of this morning, but a kohl smudged, black eyed child who looked back at her. She had rubbed her tired eyes and smeared the makeup right up into her eyebrows and also halfway down her cheeks.

Eliora began to scrub away at her face. 'What is wrong with my own name? It seems unfair that I have to have her choice.'

'Here, let me.' Her mother took the muslin and carefully rubbed away the traces of unconscious sabotage. 'You could have waited until she had named you before you did this!' she laughed. 'Now you are stuck with that name!'

'How come you ended up with a nice name like song?' Eliora pouted.

'It was grandmother's voice that she heard first. She was singing to your uncle. I inherited her name.'

'Do you think she will change my name?'

Simra laughed.

'I'll take that as a no then.'

'It isn't all that bad. At least you are not a number like the others.'

Eliora frowned.

'You have been given a great honour, to take care of her cats. To you that is nothing, but to these people, that is a big deal.' Simra stood back from Eliora and nodded. 'You'll do.' And led the way down the corridor.

Eliora checked her reflection. The result was not as neat as this morning, but she was looking Egyptian again.

'Ebonee!' her mother called. 'Eliora, come on!'

'You never told me she was so frightening.'

'You think so?' Simra hesitated a moment. 'Yes, I suppose I had thought that to begin with.'

'You aren't scared of her now?'

'No. She says she needs me.'

'But her eyes.' Eliora shuddered again.

'I told you not to look into her face.'

'How can you not do that? I mean, haven't you looked into her eyes?'

'Not for a long time,' Simra said quietly.

'I don't know how you go to her every day and not die each time.'

'Elli, don't be so dramatic.'

'Why does she need you? Those other women didn't want you there.'

'No one wants us here.' She sighed. 'The queen says that my singing calms her soul.'

'And her soul definitely needs calming. You should have seen her eyes.'

The two of them strolled through a series of empty rooms before they came to a blue painted door surrounded by carvings of cats. The guard at this door was muscular and severe looking. He took no notice of the newcomers and allowed them entry without question.

Inside was a bright sunlit room with many cushioned seats and the sound of a gentle purr. Many cats lounged on the soft chairs and at the tall windows. The floor was littered with excrement. The stench made Eliora retch.

'Keep this place clean, and for your own sake, keep these cats happy.' Simra marched over to the ornate cupboard in the corner, opened it and pulled out a broom and a pan. 'Waste must be taken to the pile, outside the kitchen, and food can be found with the cooks. You should have no trouble.' She held out the broom to her daughter. 'Ask the guards for directions. They are allowed to speak to you as you wear the royal servant colours in your belt.' Simra pointed to the embroidered stitches that adorned Eliora's belt and kissed her on the cheek. 'Work here until your replacement comes.' She looked anxiously at her daughter.

'I'll be fine. How difficult can this be?'

'Alright. I'll see you at home,' Simra said and she closed the door behind her.

It was difficult work. Eliora had been fooled by the cats' graceful movement and soft purring. The cats had wills of their own. They were quick to pounce on the broom and quite happy to attack with their claws out. She had finally collected all their mess and left the room having sustained two angry looking scratches to her forearm.

The bald headed guard was far too frightening to ask for directions, so, Eliora, left to her own devices, searched for the kitchen herself. Every corridor looked the same, every doorway led to similar rooms, every wall decorated in the typical Egyptian manner. In the end it was the smell of cooking that led the way. But of course, Eliora had not paid attention, and was uncertain of the way back.

I walk with her. I stand guard over her. She is lost and is panicking.

I quickly transform.

Eliora was lost. She took the next turning on the right and nearly bumped into an elderly man, sweeping the floor.

'I'm sorry,' she apologized. The guard standing a short distance away flicked his gaze towards her. He looked confused as to whom she is talking.

'Easily done, my dear.' The old man was kind to her. She was relieved, at last, to find a kind soul.

'Excuse me sir, I am looking for the queen's cat room. I don't suppose you know ...'

The old man gave her directions, telling her to take note of visual aids to guide her. She would not get lost again.

As Eliora walked past the guard, she glanced up into his face. He pulled away as if he considered her crazy.

Eventually, and reluctantly, she returned to the cat room.

It was lonely work. The cats were very poor company and vicious with her. She felt very sorry for herself as she cautiously sat on the cold stone floor. As the day had progressed, it was her own soul that could do with calming. The images painted everywhere disturbed her, the long echoing corridors and unfriendly faces disheartened her and her unappreciated job depressed her. This was the place she was destined to be. Why did her family have to be picked for this? What had her friends been doing today down in the pits? It would have been hot, but at least they would have had someone to talk to.

She feels lonely. Turquoise shimmers and pulses from her. But she will not be alone. I cut through the musky scent of cats with calming aloe.

What if compassion was not an emotion that evoked a response, but was a prize to be won?

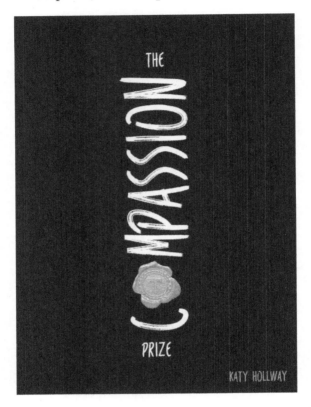

57124 has only ever known the reality of Outside, the place where he has to glean a lonely existence from the discarded rubbish of Tropolis.

Everything changes when he receives the crimson Post. It invites him to the competition that is the Compassion Prize offering wealth, happiness and a place in Tropolis if he succeeds.

How could he refuse to enter?